A Light In The Dark

Love United #5

A Light In The Dark
By
Melyssa Winchester

For information related to the cover please visit Evgenyatamanenko at Dreamstime.

The love story within these pages is dedicated to the two people that took a chance on an unknown author when she barely even knew what she was doing herself. Jennifer Weiser and Ryan Ringbloom, thank you for all that you do and even more than that, for reminding me that there are real angels among us. I'm privileged enough to know two of the very best. Ladies, this one's for you.

Prologue

Three Months Prior

Graham

This is the worst movie ever.

It's not a movie of course. What I'm sitting here witnessing, it's very real and as much as I hate it, I can't get up and walk away. I'm frozen in place and there's nothing I can do about it.

The girl standing at the front of the room is mine. She's been mine since the day she moved in across the street when we were sixteen. It's supposed to be me up there with her right now, not him. She should be pledging her undying love for me, but that's not what's happening.

If this were a movie, that would be the ideal ending. I would wrap my arms around that angel, bring her as close to me as possible and worship her for the rest of our lives. With the way everything in my life goes though, that won't ever happen.

She's not meant to be mine, despite the bond we share between us. She belongs to the man standing across from her and while I want to be the one that cherishes her for the rest of her life, he's going to do it. He's going to be the one to make her smile, wipe her tears and give her the happy life she deserves.

Him—not me.

Serenity Richards has been the keeper of my heart since the day she moved in across the street. There was something about her, even then. It's only in the last two years that I've learned what we share between us, but it doesn't change the fact that back then, I knew she was the one for me.

She's my soul mate. I don't know everything there is to know about it, but what I do know makes sense. We are halves of the same whole. There is a connection between us that runs deep and it's all based around the heart. She's everything to me because whether we're on the same page or not, she is me.

Despite the bond we share, her heart belongs to someone else. By the time I realized what this connection was between us, she had already moved on. I could have fought and probably won her away from him, but I went about everything the wrong way.

For all the goodness Gabriel told me I have inside, I still managed to screw everything up. Even owning it all doesn't change it. I'm not sure everything I did can ever be fixed. There's one thing I know though, beyond a shadow of a doubt.

She's better off where she is even though no one can ever love her as much as I do.

Being here, watching her marry the man that at one point had been sent to destroy everything that is truly right about her, makes this unbearable. I can't stand watching her do this even knowing he's not the same guy he was then.

Ryan McGregor will always do right by Serenity. He's been doing it from the start. There's no other person besides me that can love her the way he does. I know I should be happy about that, but I'm not.

It should be me up there, even if she deserves better than what I can give her.

I just want to get the hell out of here. Not only do I have to sit and watch the woman I love marry someone else, but the very thing that turned me into the monster I am now, is the one walking her down the aisle. I know she only did what she was meant to do, bringing her father and Lucifer together, but it doesn't make it any less wrong.

How can she agree to help redeem the person that broke me?

He tortured me, ripped me apart at the seams, possessing me when it was done and now he gets to walk her down the aisle? It's not often I go against what Serenity chooses to do, because I trust her judgment, but this time she's wrong.

Redemption is the last thing Lucifer deserves, even if he has to work at it. He should be rotting in hell the way Ryan intended that day in Green Haven. Not standing in a church, possessing another man, wearing a smile and watching Serenity and Ryan get married.

I hate him and I hate being here. I just want to go back to my room and finish off what's left of the whiskey I didn't drain last night. It's where I'm happiest. Sitting here, Emma beside me, watching this, it's not my thing. I don't even care how it makes me look. I just want to get up and walk out.

Shit. She's squeezing my hand now. She can tell I hate this and she's doing everything in her power to help me through it. I wish she'd stop. Emma needs to understand that I don't need or deserve her sympathy or pity, whatever this is. She's better off putting her attention on someone that will actually respond back.

Not wasting her time on someone that can never be what she needs them to be.

That's what it all comes back to. I'm not good enough for anyone anymore. Lucifer broke me apart and I let him. Where I could've gone to Michael or even Ryan and asked for help when I noticed the change, I kept it a secret and made it all worse. Now I'm so destroyed there's no way I can ever come back from it.

I'm as good as dead and there's nothing anyone in this room will do to change it.

Emma

This is possibly the best day ever, at least for Serenity, and instead of being happy for her the way I want to be, I'm depressed.

It's not because I don't think this is right. I mean she's marrying the man of her dreams. She's getting to walk down the aisle, even though they've done it before, pledging her life to the one person that will love her unconditionally. She even gets to have her father walk her, which is a big thing. I'm beyond happy for her. Everything is finally working out and I'm so glad I get to be a part of it.

I'm depressed because I see how hard this is on Graham.

He's doing his best to appear as if none of this bothers him, but it's so freaking obvious that it does. You wouldn't know it to look at him though. He looks the same as always, even if the smile pasted on his face is fake. He wants to be happy for Serenity and he's trying, but he forgets that I know him.

I know he wants to be the one up there with her, completing what started the day they met. I also know that because he's not up there, it's ripping him apart. He loves her, they're bonded. They'll be bonded forever. If it didn't bother him, I'd be even more worried.

It can't help that he's here. Lucifer is a part of this and Serenity is completely okay with it. I'm not sure I agree with that decision, but considering he hasn't done one thing so far to ruin this day for my best friend, I'm handling it. He's joined with Gregory Richards and is on his best behavior. If I didn't know this was real life, I would swear I was in some fantasy book. The devil himself being on the same side as the angels is unheard of.

Lucifer did horrible things to Graham, some of them I was even a part of, so I know this can't be easy for him. Sitting on the other side of the church from the devil himself, knowing he's accepted has to be turning him inside out.

That's what the whole hand squeeze was about. I want him to know that I see what he's going through and he's not alone.

He won't acknowledge it, he never does, but I think he needs to know that despite the way everyone else seems to accept Lucifer with open arms, I don't.

Graham needs to know someone cares about him right now. I just wish he could see it for what it is and not believe everything I've been doing has to do with pity. I don't pity him. I care about him. There's a difference.

I wish I could talk to Serenity about this, but I can't. There's still a bond between them and telling my best friend how I feel about her soul-mate probably isn't the best move. It's awkward. She might be marrying Ryan, making Graham available, but somehow I doubt Graham Hudson will ever be available where Serenity is concerned. She's always going to love him, despite not being with him.

See? It's awkward to the extreme.

I've liked Graham for years. The way he was with Serenity only made me feel for him more. He's such a good guy. He would have died for her, for any of us really, and I honestly had no idea they really made guys that inherently good. He seems almost flawless; at least he did until a year ago.

Everything changed for him then and despite my attempts at reaching out to him, I can't seem to break through. He's shut off from me, from all of us and I want nothing more than to change that.

Graham Hudson is still that amazing guy underneath, no matter what he's gone through or what he did to me so long ago. Despite believing he deserves to suffer and end up alone, I know better. He deserves to be happy and I swear when we can finally get out of here, away from this wedding and all the hurt it's bringing up in him, I'm determined to show him exactly that.

I don't care if it's the last thing he wants. It's too damn bad. I'm going to do whatever it takes to bring the real Graham back.

He deserves nothing less.

Chapter One

Present Time

Emma

"Did you hear she slept with Roger at the rave?"
"No wonder Cody dumped her, she's easy."
"She spreads easier than peanut butter."
"That girl is the kind of dirty that can't be washed off."
Emma Daniels, resident whore. That's me.

I've been hearing things like this since I started here. It's nothing new. The only difference is, before, I had Serenity with me and I could ignore the comments. With her off living with her husband now, there's no one here to block it and it floods me constantly.

Contrary to what these girls think, I don't put out. I've never put out. That's my dirty little secret, I guess. I might like to go to parties and have a good time, but I don't sleep with anyone. With the amount of guys I turn down, I'm surprised I haven't heard about how frigid I am.

This has been happening since middle school. It's actually one of the reasons my mom had me locked away in the center. As much as I hate admitting it because I loathe the place, the center wasn't all bad. If I hadn't gone there, I wouldn't have met Serenity and honestly, my life would pretty much suck without her. It's also the place that helped me manage my issues.

I'm a severe manic depressive and if that wasn't enough they tacked on suicidal as part of it. One time, I take a bunch of sleeping pills because I'm sad and just want to pass out for awhile and suddenly, I'm the poster child for suicide. It's not like I wanted to die because I didn't, but I needed relief and the pills brought me that.

I've been depressed since I found out my dad was screwing around on my mom. My life before that seemed pretty close to perfect. Walking into his office that day and seeing his pants around his ankles, with some naked ladies legs wrapped around his back, well that turned my perfect little life to shit pretty damn quick. That alone didn't turn me into the mess I am now though. It's telling my mom that did it.

I lived with it for two years and for a little kid, that's brutal. I tried to talk myself out of what I saw, pretending it was just a scene from a movie I stayed up late watching the night before. That seemed to work for a while too; I mean, I started thinking I imagined the whole thing. At least, that's how it was before the nightmares started.

Closing my eyes every night and seeing my dad moaning his climax inside the woman I know now was his secretary, is a nightmare I didn't want to see. I couldn't deny the reality after that and it just made everything that much harder when I saw the way him and my mom were together. It was the worst when I caught them making out on the sofa.

How could he go from making out with my mom, to screwing his secretary? If she made him so happy, why bother looking elsewhere?

I ended up coming clean after about two weeks of sleepless nights. I couldn't take the nightmares and my mom finally started to notice. It tore my family apart and it wasn't long after that when my dad moved out. Enter the depression and my need to close myself off from the world around me.

It started small. I would cry a lot, listen to sad music and wish death on myself for tearing my family apart. I guess that's not really small, but it's whatever now. I internalized everything. It was my fault, not my fathers, and somehow I became the sole reason the entire world had issues.

I was a completely different person at school. I appeared to be an outgoing, fun party girl. The boys loved being around me and the girls loved to hate me. They were jealous that what took hours or days of effort, I seemed to be able to do effortlessly. I had my first boyfriend by the time I was 11 and he happened to be the most popular boy in our school, let alone the class. That made the girls start the name calling and even with all the time that passed, they've never stopped.

After the pill incident, it's like my mom woke up to what was going on because she wasted no time finding a place for me. Normal therapy didn't work for her. No, she had to go straight for the worst case scenario. She threw me in the center without a second thought and until Serenity; I thought I was destined to spend the rest of my life alone.

It totally blows, but I faked it in the center too. At least I did until Serenity caught me in my lies. Somehow she knew that everyone there had something off about them and she couldn't figure out what it was about me, so she went looking. She found what she was looking for and even though I expected her to run in the other direction once my secrets were revealed, she did the complete opposite. She stayed and we've been best friends ever since.

It's why right now, hearing these girls whisper about me, I miss her.

I miss my best friend.

Spending years focusing on her ability to hear voices took the attention off my own. I could easily remain that fake, happy girl I was at school when I didn't have to think about myself. I need that now. I need to focus on her issues so I can make it around this campus and not think about mine.

Well, think about them anymore then I already have been.

Cody was my first boyfriend when I got here. He cheated on me because I wouldn't put out, but as you can see, the story got turned around so I'm the whore. The thing is, I'm okay with that. I don't give a crap what people think about me. I just wish that if they're gonna spread something, it would at least have some factual information in it. I'm the one better off being apart from Cody, not the other way around and Roger only wishes I'd spread my legs for him.

I think I'm starting to see why Graham hides. If I could use that as an option, I might do it too. It beats walking around campus and hearing lie after lie spread about me or even having people say my name at all. I want to go unnoticed just one time in my life, but it seems that just like when I was a kid, I'm not that lucky.

It's been weeks since he's been to class and here I am again, gathering up all his work and bringing it to him, hoping that in doing so, this will be the time he lets me past his front door.

He's gotten worse since the wedding, pulling away even more. I want to bring it up to Serenity so between the two of us we can come up with a way to fix it or even have Michael do it. I know the angel wants to help, but just like he's shutting me out, he's doing the same to the angels too. I can't bring this to Ser though because she's finally got the chance to live happily for the first time in years and the last thing I want to do is take it from her. She saved the entire world. She deserves that and so much more.

I'm going to have to handle Graham on my own. It's the only way. I've got to put those stupid girls and their comments, along with my walk down memory lane out of my head and remain focused.

Graham deserves it.

Graham

Jesus Christ; I knew moving here was a mistake.
Someone has been banging on my door for at least ten minutes and despite proper etiquette saying you shouldn't knock more than twice, they just keep at it. It's driving me insane. Apparently the big stay out sign I posted on the door

isn't having the desired effect, which means I'm gonna have to either block this out or get up and deal with it.

When I moved all my stuff here, determined to take the courses I needed for my art degree, I had a roommate. That didn't last very long once he saw the way I am. He booked it faster than the road runner and I can't blame him. I'm such a mess, I want to run away from myself. I can only imagine the way it appears to other people.

I'm pretty sure the kicker was waking up to find me covered in my own blood. I gotta figure that's a definite turn off for a roommate. The thing no one gets is, it's all because of the nightmares.

They always start the same. I'm back in the church and I'm tied to the chair and he's leveling me with memories of my life, moments I want so badly to do over. He's beating my body, burning it and flashing his twisted grin at me while he laughs at my pain. It's so bad, especially when the memories are of my mom, that I've been scratching myself up pretty bad while I'm sleeping, which is what my roommate Kyle woke up to.

He was so freaked he went to the Dean about it and I was told I needed to start a treatment program. The man thinks that because of my mom's passing, I'm dealing in unhealthy ways. He has no idea what the hell I'm dealing with, but because I didn't want to get kicked out, I agreed. It's too bad I haven't gone to see the school shrink once since that meeting.

They can save the head shrinking for someone who actually gives a shit.

Hearing the banging on the door again, I sit up and turn toward it. I smell the familiar scent of rust almost immediately. I've cut myself open again. By now it shouldn't surprise me, but I swear every single time it happens, I'm even more surprised than the times before. Am I ever going to stop doing this to myself? Is there ever going to be a time where the shit I went through won't get to me?

You could ask for help.

I've had four people wanting to help me for months. Every time one of them comes to me, I turn them away. I'm Graham Hudson for fuck sakes. If I can't handle my own shit then there's no way I'm letting someone else do it for me, even if all they want to do is rid me of it. I've been through hell and back, and even though it's that hell that brought all of this on, I want to be able to deal with this the way I did with all that.

I just don't have it in me to be that Graham anymore. I'm losing more of myself with each passing day, but the stubbornness remains, so I won't ask for help. Even if I can't handle this on my own, I won't wuss out and beg for relief either.

"I know you're in there, Graham! Answer the door!"

Emma Daniels.

The most annoying person on the planet, of that I'm sure. She's been doing this every two days like clockwork. Coming to my door, under the premise of having work for me from the classes I'm skipping and wanting to be sure I don't get behind. The funny thing is, I've been taking the work and completing it and she's been picking it up and taking it back. I can't seem to deal with my life, but I can do my homework. How screwed up is that?

Her real reason for stopping by has nothing to do with the coursework. She's coming by to check on me. She pities me, the same way she did at Serenity's wedding, holding my hand the way she did. I call her on it and she says it has nothing to do with pity and everything to do with being a friend. That's bullshit. She pities me and she's doing what Serenity and Ryan want her to. I have no doubt they're the reason she's coming over here so much. There's no other reason for her to be this nice.

Too bad for her that I see through it and want no part of it. She can keep bringing the work over all she wants, but she won't get anything else from me. I'm too done for that.

I know I said I wanted to make things right for the way I treated her during Lucifer's time riding around in my skin, but

I don't have the strength. It takes too much energy and honestly, if I knew she was going to be coming around this much, I never would have said that to begin with. She's got to realize how much better off she is being as far away from me as she can get.

"Go away!"

She bangs again and I look around for something to whip at the door. I just want this girl to screw off already. When nothing appears, I drag myself off the bed and to the door. If the girl wants face time, she's gonna get it, even if it's the last thing I want to put myself through. So far, she hasn't seen what happens to me when I'm sleeping; I'd really like to continue sparing her the horror.

Throwing on a sweatshirt and wiping down my hair, hopefully getting rid of the extreme level of bed head I've been living with, I swing the door open and come to face to face with the blonde on the other side.

You can never really prepare yourself for Emma. It doesn't matter if I'm completely lucid or blasted off my ass, she still hits me the same way. Despite knowing what I'm going through, she's always right there on the other side with a smile on her face, and deep down, it gets to me, which I suppose is the reason she does it at all. There's a small part of me that softens seeing that smile and it makes me wish for easier times.

Times I won't ever have.

"This isn't high school, Emma. You can stop bringing my assignments so I don't flunk."

"I'm well aware. You gonna let me in this time or treat me like one of your conquests?"

I don't want that to sting, but it does. She's right though. If I'm not drinking to erase the headaches and the visions, I'm out picking up random women and bringing them back here, ditching them easily and without feeling in the morning. Emma is definitely not one of those girls and I hate that she even puts herself in the same breath with them.

"That really what you think?"

"You mean that's not how you feel?"

"No, Emma, that's not how I feel. You know why I don't let you in."

Well, I hope she knows. I don't want her to see the way I live. I don't want the bottles strewn all over the room or the mound of unwashed clothes piling high in the corner to gross her out. That's only for me.

"No, Graham, I don't know."

Shit. Now I'm gonna have to explain or talk myself around it. The sooner I get her out of here, the better. Any extra time and I might use her as a lifeline, and I just can't bring her into this. I need to deal with it myself.

"Look Emma, it's real nice of you to bring my work to me, but you need to stop. Just go back to your perfect life, with your perfect friends and leave me the fuck alone."

Her face sinks and I know I've hit my mark. The problem is, I'm not sure how great I feel about it even though I got what I wanted. I've known Emma for awhile now and she's never been anything other than super happy, at least that I've seen. Seeing her eyes lower and her face sink in, there's something off about it.

"You don't mean that."

"I mean every word. I don't want you here, so run back to Ryan and Serenity and tell them you failed."

Her head rises and as she levels her eyes on me, I realize she's confused. I thought I was pretty clear with what I said, but with the look on her face, it seems it was only clear to me.

"You think Ser and Ryan sent me?"

"Are you gonna tell me they didn't?"

"Yeah, I am. I haven't spoken to either one of them in a week. So if you want to tell them they failed, call them up and do it yourself."

She throws the paperwork at me and turns her back and I swear something dies in me watching her. As much as I want her to walk away from me and never come back, I can't let her do it.

Reaching out at the last second, I wrap my hand around her wrist and spin her back around so she's facing me. It's only when she looks at me, this time her expression as close to angry as I've ever seen her; that I'm at a loss for what to do next.

"Let me go, Graham."

"No."

"I'll scream."

"I don't care. Scream. It's not like it's the first time the guys around here have heard a chick lose it."

"What do you want from me, huh? You told me to leave you alone; well I'm trying to do that. Just let me go."

"I can't."

"Why not?"

I don't have an answer for her. I have no idea why I can't let her go; I just know that if I do, it's going to break me. I can't tell her that though, she'll think I'm even crazier than I am.

"I just can't. Okay?"

She sighs and the small release of breath bothers me. This girl needs to be off doing things that make her happy. Not standing here with me, confused and torn. It's just further proof that I'm no good to be around. I'm turning one of the happiest people I know into something she was never meant to be.

I'm turning her into me.

Releasing the hold, I motion to the hall. She needs to get the hell out of here and whatever the hell that just was, me trying to keep her with me, needs to screw off. It was a response born out of some kind of weakness and that's the last thing I want to be.

I'm a lot of things, but weak is definitely not one of them.

"Graham..."

"Go, Emma."

"I'm not going anywhere."

Chapter Two

Emma

Graham thinks I'm an idiot.

I've been in a center where people act the way he is and I see through it. Granted, he doesn't know anything about my time there, other then what Serenity shared with him, so he has no idea how much I know about what he's going through or even the real reason I'm here at all.

Helping him heal has always been my prime motivation, but when he told me to screw off, there was a second where I almost gave him what he wanted. It hurts, hearing him speak to me this way. It's not the first time he's been abrupt, but it doesn't mean I'm unaffected. His words still cut deep.

Despite what he believes, I'm not doing any of this for Serenity or Ryan. I'm here on my own. I told him the truth when I said I hadn't spoken to them because I haven't. I'm choosing to handle Graham and his mood swings on my own. He's not broken or defective like he thinks. He's just trapped under the pain.

I've only known about everything for a few months. The angels made a decision two years ago, one that I don't agree with. They wanted me kept out of the loop, which meant I didn't know anything and even worse, my best friend had to lie to me. I hate them for that, but I hate them even more for what happened to Graham.

Angels are powerful beings. What he's suffering from should be a pretty easy fix, yet here he is, still being driven under by it. If they are as good as people say, why hasn't Graham been healed? Is redeeming Lucifer more important than saving the very person that fought with you in order to take him down?

I can't think about this stuff. It's only going to give me a headache. I'll never understand angels, demons or even Heaven and Hell the way the rest of them do. I don't think I'm supposed to. All I know is that I won't walk away from him when he's like this, even though I can tell it's exactly what he wants.

He won't let me into his room because he doesn't want me to see the way he's been living. He's so dense. I've dropped his class work to him for the past couple of months and the times when we have come face to face, he looks like he got run over by a truck. One has to figure his room looks even worse. I'd just tell him that and push my way into the room, but the idea is to make him comfortable and safe, not alienate him.

He doesn't realize it, but Kyle came to me about him. He did the right thing taking this to the Dean. After my time in the center, I'm not a fan of any kind of doctor, but Graham needs help. If he's got to be forced to get it, so be it. Kyle let me know what he saw when he was staying here and it's pretty scary. The doctors in the center used to be scared of what I would do; I can only imagine what they would think of the trauma Graham is suffering through.

He's hurting himself, but has no knowledge of how he's doing it. He's bled on his sheets more times than even Kyle could count and he's keeping it all to himself. It's another thing I want to call him on, but won't because I need to keep him close. For whatever reason, keeping him as close as possible is the way I can help him. Doing anything else is unacceptable.

"I'm not letting you in."

"Did I say I wanted to come in?"

"Actually, yeah, you kind of did."

It's true, I did ask him if he was going to let me in or treat me like a conquest, but I didn't mean it that way. I don't care if he lets me in or not, as long as he doesn't push me away entirely.

When he grabbed my wrist, I thought this would be the moment everything changed. I saw the look in his eye when he turned me around to face him. There was a silent plea hidden there. He's dying for a lifeline, but won't allow himself to have it because he's a pigheaded guy. Just as quickly as I saw the plea, it vanished and now I'm left with the cold Graham again.

"Can you do something for me?" I ask, not sure where I'm going with it, but knowing there's no turning back. "I need your help."

"Of course you do. Ya know, you and Serenity aren't so different after all."

"Excuse me?"

"You heard me. She always needed my help, stringing me along as she asked and now you do. Is that what you're about to do, Emma? Are you going to string me along like Serenity?"

If I didn't like the guy so much, I'd give serious thought to kicking him in his balls for that comment.

"You don't seem like the type to be strung along, so no."

"What do you want then?"

I'm pretty sure I'm going to earn a big fat no for this request, but it's all I've got. It's not exactly what I was thinking when I opened my mouth, but it's a way to break the cycle and right now, he needs that.

"There's a party tonight and considering what happened at the last one, I don't wanna show up alone."

"You want me to take you to a party?" he laughs, but he may as well have cleared his throat with how forced it sounds. "You're kidding right?"

"Yeah, you know me. I'm a jokester."

"You can't be serious."

"I'm dead serious. You have no idea what happened at the last party. If you came with me, it might make it tolerable and let's face it, you need to get out of your room. I can smell it from here."

I wasn't going to mention of the state of his room, but it slipped out. It's not like I'm lying. I mean, it really does smell like dirty wet socks. If it wasn't Graham I was dealing with, it would actually be pretty gross.

"Going to a party is what you think I need to do?"

"Well, when you put it like that, no. You need to get out and what better way to get out than with someone you know?"

"I don't want to go anywhere with you."

Okay, so that hurt, but he doesn't mean it. At least the Graham that I knew before didn't mean it. This new version though, I'm not sure what he means and what he doesn't. All I do know is that a lot of what comes out of his mouth stings.

"So, you'd rather mope instead?"

"I'm not moping. Emma, shit. You know what's going on. I'm not explaining it."

He's right. I do know what's going on, but I'm not giving up. It's that simple. He might want everyone to turn their back on him and some of them might be listening, but I'm not. Not now and not ever. I don't give up on people I care about.

"You either take me to the party or I spend the night. It's your choice, Graham, because I'm not letting you spend another night alone."

It's a ballsy move and I'm aware it's probably one that's gonna cost me, but it's a risk I've got to take. I don't really need to go to the party. I planned on staying in, opting to study for a change, but now that I've put the idea out there, I'm sticking with it, no matter what he decides to do.

I mean it. He's stuck with me.

"So, what time's the party?"

Michael

I have to hand it to the Daniels girl.

As timid as she had been in approaching him minutes earlier, she seems to have completely switched gears now. Her idea of getting Graham out of his room and among the land of the living again might not be one I would have chosen, but it seems to have worked.

It has only been a couple of months since I last appeared before the boy, but it appears as though he has only gotten worse during that time. It has gotten to the point now where I want to forsake everything I have been taught and put the boy out of his misery. If I had been able to work magic on the lingering darkness that resided in Ryan McGregor, I could surely do the same with this human.

Graham Hudson is in desperate need of help, but due to his stubborn nature he refuses to reach out and ask for it. It displeases me. I could heal this, just as I have in times past if only he would open himself up to the prospect. Sadly, it is just another way I am different. I do not understand the human condition. Stubbornness can only get you so far. There has to come a point where you give yourself up to the horror you are experiencing. Graham is no exception.

When I agreed to watch over the boy, doing what Gabriel started years before, I expected that at some point I would be called upon. As it appears, that is not going to be the case. He wants nothing more than to tackle his demons alone. I am thankful Emma will not let him. She is turning out to be so much more than I imagined in the beginning.

Ryan has filled me in on the feelings that exist between them, but even if he had not done that, there can be no mistaking it. Emma seems to care a great deal for the Hudson boy, though I am sure if asked, she will not be the most forthcoming admitting it. Those feelings are going to determine what takes place moving forward. They will determine everything.

I cannot believe I am even thinking this, but for the first time, I believe human emotion may be what saves the boy in the end. The very thing I told my brother I did not understand, I am going to end up using in an effort to ensure the peace Serenity set in motion.

In my time watching over him, I have seen what before Ryan had only been able to explain to me. Graham is pulling himself apart, one seam at a time and if he continues down the path he is on, there is no doubt in my mind that he will crumble and be lost to us forever. As my brothers continue to eradicate what remains of the hell Lucifer created, I now have to do the same here.

This should really be up to him to rectify. It is what he put in motion possessing the boy to begin with. I am not fond of cleaning up another's mess, but in this regard, I realize that if Graham wants no help from me, it is a given that he will not want Lucifer anywhere near him. The boy that Gabriel spent years watching over and grooming in order to be his vessel was on a road that my younger brother would be made sick by.

Gabriel would want me to be the one to do this and I want to do whatever it takes to honor my brother's memory to the best of my ability. I will do whatever needs to be done, but not before trying one more time to get through to him.

Chapter Three

Graham

I don't know what the hell I'm doing.

Agreeing to go to a party might be the stupidest thing I've ever done. I'm not a party guy, never have been. Seeing a bunch of my buddies getting so drunk they're retching in the bushes after was enough motivation to keep me out of that scene. If my other choice is Emma staying over though, a party seems like the lesser of two evils.

My agreement had the desired effect. She's gone now. I'm on my own again. I'm just not sure how I feel about it.

Reaching out to her had been such a stupid move, but I did it and I know the reason why. I might think I can handle all this shit on my own, but I don't want to, at least not anymore. I'm not stupid enough to bring it to the angels or even to Ryan and Serenity, but Emma; I can bring it to her. She won't try to 'fix' me or change me back to what I was before. She just wants to help me feel okay again.

So I'll do what she wants. Get through this damn party with another fake smile plastered on my face and use her for what I need until she finally gets a clue and screws off for good.

You don't want her screwing off.

Everyone has that nagging inner voice, the problem with mine is, it sounds a hell of a lot like Gabriel. The angel's dead yet the lessons he tried to make me see still haunt me. My inner voice has become an angel. Of course it has. My life isn't screwed up enough already, obviously.

It's right though, no matter who it comes out sounding like. I don't want her screwing off. I still want to do what I told her months ago. I want to make the things I did while Lucifer rode around in my skin, better. I don't want her to fear me the way she did then. I'd done it all despite what was happening at the time and it's up to me to make it right.

Admitting that I find the girl attractive, it feels like a betrayal. Even with her married and happy, I'm still completely owned by Serenity. Having any kind of feeling as it pertains to her best friend is wrong on every level imaginable. It shouldn't be happening. Hell, I've gotten into it with guys for going after their exes best friends before. With as many girls as there are in the world, you really have to go for the one that's closest to what you gave away or lost?

I can't deny it. I'm attracted to Emma. More than that, I genuinely like her. As much as Serenity cares, she hasn't been here for any of this. She's been detached. Sure, I made it that way, keeping her at arm's length so she couldn't see the real trauma I've been experiencing, but it doesn't change the fact that she hasn't seen me at my worst.

Emma has. She's seen it all. Well, other than the state of my room and what I've been doing to myself when I'm sleeping. She's seen the after effects. She knows I'm drowning in the alcohol and that I'm bringing random women back to my room a few times a week. She knows all that and still tries.

I hate that she tries but I can't help admiring it. Women have walked away for less. She really is amazing. It's no surprise that they're best friends. They're a lot alike that way. They don't give up, even when that's exactly what they should be doing.

The party tonight, I said yes to get her off my back, but there's also a selfish reason attached that I won't admit openly. I want to be around her. I want her to have the light around her again. With as much time as she's spent coming here over the last few weeks and making herself a part of whatever I'm going through, she deserves to have a good time. I can't drag her down with me. So I agreed so that at least for one night, I can see Emma happy again.

"You humans never learn do you?"

Well, I know who the annoying voice was earlier. I think to myself, turning around and coming face to face with the only angel besides Gabriel that I will let within ten feet of me.

"I can say the same thing about angels. What do you want Mike?"

"As it pertains to the angels, you are bias. You have no idea what we learn."

"Yeah, you're right. I don't know, but you forget that I don't care. So again, what do you want?"

"I have been tasked with looking over you, but just as in times before, I feel that I need to inform you of it and appeal to the part of you that remains untainted by the darkness."

"Appeal to me about what?"

"Even the strongest warrior cannot deal with what you are going through on their own. I want to appeal to the part of you that Gabriel believes is made of the brightest light so that I may get your acceptance for help."

"I don't want your help. That hasn't changed, man."

"I figured as much. You are unwilling to accept the olive branch from me, yet have no problem taking it when it is given to you in human form. Why is that?"

I have no idea what he's talking about. Angels talking in riddles has been going on for centuries, but the last two years of it has driven me crazy. It would be so much easier if they just said what they wanted or felt without all of the other useless words attached.

"Just spit it out."

"Emma. The Daniels girl has somehow weaseled her way past your defenses and is able to get through to you in a way that until now I have been unable to. Even your soul-mate has been unable to penetrate it. Why is that?"

"Well, that's easy. I don't need to have Emma crawling around in my skin in order to help me. She can just be with me and the other reason, well; I thought that one was pretty damn obvious."

"You consider us to be clueless as it pertains to you, so please, enlighten me to what this other reason is."

"Lucifer."

"What about him? I am aware that all of this is happening to you because of him, I do not deny that, but I get the feeling you mean something more."

"Your father is letting him earn his redemption. If you're all willing to do that, then I want nothing to do with any of you. That bastard is the last person that should be earning his spot back. In fact, I don't want to go to Heaven at all if he's going to be there when I die."

"Graham, with the road you are currently on, spending time with Lucifer when you die is the last thing you need to concern yourself with."

"What's that supposed to mean?"

"Even if no longer exists, you will find yourself in Purgatory based on your current attitude and actions. You are not fit for entrance to the light. That is why I am here. I want to bring you back to the place you once were. The place at which Gabriel always knew you should be."

"Leave Gabe out of this."

"Gabriel may have passed, Graham, but he is still a part of this and he will remain that way. You were his choice."

"How does it feel, Mike? Going home every day and knowing that your younger brother won't ever come back? Has the hole in your heart healed already?"

The angel falls silent and I know I've made my point. Michael and Gabriel for all of their differences loved one another like no other brothers before them, and I know the pain of losing him is still there. If I want all talk of Gabriel to stop, I need to hit where it hurts.

"The loss of Gabriel will never heal, but I do see your point. All talk of my brother will cease. It is not why I am here anyway."

"Yeah, you want to save me."

"I want to heal you, there is a difference."

"I don't want it."

"That is obvious, but I am not against taking you by force."

I can't help it. Threatening me with the force of Heaven is the funniest thing I've heard all day and that's after being asked to a party by Emma. I laugh and for the first time in months, it's a real laugh and I can't stop it.

"I find nothing funny about what I just said."

"If you were going to fix me using force, you would have already done it, Michael. The threat is bullshit and you know it."

"Fine, let us go on the assumption that it is false and I won't do things that way. It does not change the fact that things have gotten worse since the wedding and you are in desperate need of healing. I want to be the person to help you, Graham. Despite what you believe as it pertains to my fallen brother."

"Why do you want to heal me so bad? I get that Gabriel saw something in me. I saw something in me during our time in Hell, but why bother? You know the things I've done. Do you really think I deserve to be saved?"

I can tell as his head shifts that he's confused by something I've said. I'm not sure what part of it he doesn't get, but I'm having a hard time caring. I've only got a couple of hours until I'm supposed to pick Emma up for this stupid party and I don't want to waste it explaining things to an angel.

The world is at peace since Serenity did what she was made to do. He shouldn't even be here anymore. His job is done.

"My job is never done. Just because Lucifer may have changed his position, it does not stop the work I still must do."

"Reading my mind Mike? Really?"

"It is required at present because you think far more than you actually say."

"So, you looked confused before," I start, changing the subject and hopefully keeping him out of my mind for the foreseeable future. "What caused that?"

"The things you say you have done. I am unaware of anything that you have done that would disallow you entrance to the light when it is your time. There is nothing that would prevent you from receiving help from me or even one of my other brothers."

For an angel that's supposed to know everything, he doesn't know shit. This is just another time where I miss Gabriel. He's the one that told me about the things I'd done in past lives. He knew what I am. I don't want to have to explain all of that again.

"This is about your past lives? What you did then has no bearing on the life you are living now. You are not even the same person."

"I'm exactly the same person! Don't you get it? Lucifer was right. I did those things back then and I didn't feel an ounce of remorse."

"Maybe you didn't feel it in that lifetime, but you have felt it in every one since. You cannot continue living that way."

"That's easy for you to say, Mike. You didn't kill someone."

"I beg to differ. I have killed quite a few someone's as you say. Far more than you realize. I have stripped people of their light, soul and everything in between. I have gone to war more times than I can count and have had others blood on my hands for centuries because of it. Do not tell me that I have not felt death."

For the first time in the conversation, I feel lost. He's right. I made assumptions based on my own pain and of course I was wrong. Michael is an archangel; he's seen more death than all the humans combined. Of course he understood what I'm going through.

"It doesn't change the fact that I did it. I killed two people. Yeah, they might have been possessed at the time, but it doesn't change that two innocent humans died by my hand."

"My dear boy, you are so misguided. The human's that were possessed by Ryan's father Daemon were far from innocent the way you believe them to be."

Daemon. That's the first time I've heard the demon's name and it just makes everything I'm going through that much worse. I don't want to know names, places and faces. It's going to make me connect with it and I can't afford that. I'm too damn close to it all as it is.

"I still killed them, Mike. It doesn't matter who they were before it all went down. I did it."

"Graham, I know that none of what I say will get through to you when you are in this state, but I want you to really hear what I am about to tell you."

"Why even waste the words if you know nothing is getting through?"

"I see better for you that is why. Now listen to me. Heaven in no way blames you for what happened during that period of your life. Not when it happened and you were sent back home to be prepared for your next lifetime and not now. What you did happened because it was what needed to be done. I am sure that it did not take place the way Father imagined it, at least not entirely, but make no mistake. It was what needed to be done."

He's right again. I don't want to hear this. An angel standing here, bathed in light, telling me that what I did was a good thing. There is something so wrong about that. It's something I would expect Lucifer to say, not Michael.

"Furthermore, I do believe you need to continue on the path you are on currently. If you will not let me help you in the way that will fix what has been torn down inside you, then you must let Emma do it. She, like me and the others, want nothing more than for you to be back on the right path again."

"You want me to let Emma in?"

"Yes. What you were thinking about before I arrived, as wrong as you believe it to be, is the path you need to follow. I have no doubt it will be the one that brings you back where you need to be. What Gabriel saw in you so many years ago, is still there, Graham. It is just buried under the weight of what you experienced. Do what Serenity wanted you to do months ago."

"What would that be?"

"Fight and for heaven's sakes, let Emma help you."

Chapter Four

Michael

There are many of the belief that even with the eradication of Hell and all that it contains, darkness will never truly die. It will continue to rise, even with Lucifer no longer controlling it and we will never be at peace. There will always be wars that must be waged and innocents that we must save from it clutches.

Much work must still be done, even with the events Serenity put in motion months before, but I have already seen the changes. In places that had once been riddled with death and disease, there seems to be none. The humans seem to be going through the motions of their daily lives in a more peaceful state.

Is there still darkness? Yes, but that does not mean much at this stage. It will take years to rectify everything Lucifer put into motion and no being of Heaven is blind to that. We do not believe that just because a plan has been put into motion that it will change everything in the moment. It takes time for change. For all of us, not just the humans.

I do believe we will reach a level of peace that was previously unknown. I also believe that the darkness most believe will always remain can be erased. When the world and even Heaven is again at peace, I will enjoy the satisfaction I will experience at proving all the naysayers wrong. Every being in existence is in dire need of this change and I will do whatever it takes to see it come to pass.

It starts with Graham Hudson; at least as far as I am concerned. Lucifer had done a lot of despicable things, but that boy may be the worst. Twisting a being with so much potential and turning him against it, is beyond evil and definitely needs to be rectified.

My fallen brother confessed that he wanted to do the right thing by not only me, but every person he had affected during his reign in an effort to honor Gabriel. I do believe that Graham Hudson is his one and only chance to do the right thing by our brother. Gabriel cared a great deal for the human, in more than just a vessel capacity and any harm that comes to him now, he would be destroyed by.

As much as I want to be the one to bring Graham back to what Gabriel always believed him to be, I do not think I can. It is apparent just in my talk with him that he is not willing to listen to me. I cannot break through. It is not that I think Lucifer will have better luck, because I am not that delusional. I just believe he is our last best hope.

He will be the one to bring Graham Hudson back to the light. My conversation with Father after what happened in the boy's dorm room solidifies that.

As always, I have concerns that Father is again keeping things from me, but this time I do not feel it is anything negative. In fact, I believe it's the complete opposite. During his time with me, he wore a smile I have not witnessed since the day Serenity reached her true destiny. There is something much deeper going on that I am not privy to, but it's obvious that whatever it is, Lucifer is attached to it in some way.

*****

"It would appear as though Graham is still unwilling to accept heavenly intervention."

"That is an understatement, Father. He is unwilling to accept help of any kind. There is hope on the horizon as it pertains to the Daniels girl though."

"Yes, I have seen that. It seems that we did the right thing informing her of everything. She will be the very thing to bring Graham back to where he belongs."

"You seem so sure of that."

"My son, you forget I have seen the way everything will play out. There are things that slip by me, by all of us, but thus far, the overall ending has not changed. Graham was never supposed to feel this darkness and for that I am saddened, but it does not change his end."

"Are you saying what I think you are?"

"Yes, Michael. The events leading up are different, but as long as no one steps in to change it, his goal will be reached the way it was meant to."

"How is Emma supposed to fix the damage Lucifer inflicted? She may be able to help in the most basic of human capacities, but not in the overall way he needs."

"Your fallen brother plays a part in this as well, Michael. I cannot tell you more, but know that I am aware of everything that needs to happen and it will take place as it is supposed to."

"Are you planning something?"

He smiles and it is as bright as it was the day the undertaking was put into place so long ago. Father at his finest is truly a sight to behold, even when I do not trust his motivations.

"It would appear that you are not the only angel that is concerned about what happens with Graham Hudson in the future, Michael. So you tell me, am I planning something?"

"Will the day ever come when you share your secrets with the rest of us?"

"All will be revealed in time, my son. Until then, just trust that this is most unlike times past. This ending will be a happy one, of that I can assure you."

*****

It should be easy to determine who is helping Father with Graham, but considering there are three other angels invested in the boy, it's impossible to nail down just who it could be. I cannot say it does not bother me, but I will do whatever Father asks of me because this time I do not believe I have anything to fear.

It is that belief that brings me where I am now or rather who I am here to see.

It is no secret that over the last few months, we have been in each other's company. That has everything to do with Serenity and never giving up on a project she believes has the potential to be righted and nothing at all to do with my actual feelings on the matter.

Despite having the chance to live a long, happy existence with the pure angel, she reached out to both of us and attempted to garner a sense of peace and love between us again. I have not hidden my true feelings as it pertains to my fallen brother, but she refuses to let that stop her. So we have been meeting and slowly working through our issues.

I will never understand Lucifer, but I am willing to see another side to things. In the end, if I want the peace that I speak so openly about, than the first step has to happen with me. Taking a step such as this though, one where I am doing it without the aid of Serenity, it is new ground and I can only hope it works in my favor. I do not want to ruin what the ball of light has worked so hard for.

"This is a surprise, brother."

"Are you telling me you never expected this visit?"

"I've come to learn over time that nothing is expected with you Michael."

"We need to speak." I answer, getting right to my reason for being here. "Have you gone to Father regarding the Hudson boy?"

"No. I want to rectify that situation, but Father has done his best to keep me out of it."

"How much have you been made aware of?"

"The boy is a mere breath away from death if he continues down the road he is on."

This is an area I did not want to broach, but there is truth in his words. It is something I would not make Graham aware of because I do not want to make the situation worse, but there is no denying how close to the end he is.

"We cannot let that happen."

"Well, we are in agreement on that, but with Father shutting me out, what do you suggest I do?"

"Make yourself available when I call. I am determined to save that boy, even if I have to go around him to do it."

"I never expected to hear those words cross your lips. You would really go against everything you have been taught, in order to save Graham Hudson?"

"When it is the right thing to do, absolutely."

"Well, it appears as though we are not so different after all."

"I am nothing like you. This is your chance with me Lucifer. You want to prove that you are willing to do whatever it takes to earn your place at home, here is your shot. Be prepared to right your wrong."

"He will not let me anywhere near him, you must be aware of this."

"Yes, but leave all of that to me. This is not about you and me anymore. It is about doing what Gabriel would want. He would not want that boy suffering one second longer and I am going to make sure, as only I can, that he never suffers again."

"Where do we start?"

"Emma Daniels."

I am aware of the history between my brother and the human, so the smile he wears now does not come as a surprise. Graham may believe he had been the one controlling their time together, but I know better. Lucifer had his mark all over it and it has never been more obvious than right here in this moment.

"When do we begin?"

Emma

This is the stupidest idea ever.

I've been standing here, staring at the inside of my closet for at least an hour and I still can't decide what the hell to wear. This is a problem I've never faced. I own more than enough clothes, choosing something should be easy. It's always been easy every other time I've done it. This time isn't like those other times though, because this time I'm actually bringing someone with me and not doing it alone.

Parties aren't his scene. He agreed to this because I didn't give him any other option. This is a pity date at its finest, yet here I am, freaking out over what to wear, how to look and act almost as if it's a real date.

Like a guy like Graham would ever go on a date with someone like you.

This has been happening since he agreed. The angry voice in my head telling me what I already know to be the truth. Graham is too good for me. He deserves so much better and is only doing this because I'm forcing his hand. It's getting harder to ignore it the more it happens. I try to combat it with other thoughts, but it always comes back to the truth.

He wouldn't be interested in me.

Sure, he liked Serenity and she spoke to not only the dead, but angels too, so there's no reason for him not to like me, but I'm not Serenity. I'm not even close. She was always the stronger of the two of us and that's only proven by the fact that she's an angel now. She saved the world and became what she was always meant to be, yet I'm still the same old useless Emma.

I'm so freaked out over this pseudo-date that I'm starting to lose it. Closing my eyes and inhaling a breath, I try my best to get my breathing in order. It's a coping mechanism the doctors at the center gave me years ago and it's one that actually works. If I want to make it through this night, then I need to get my head screwed on straight. I can't let him see me break, not when the point is to help him.

Episodes like this, where I feel like crawling in bed and never coming out, have been few and far between. Even with the girls talking shit behind my back and the guys thinking I'm an easy lay, I still manage to keep getting up and going forward. I'm having a hard time doing that now because this isn't some shallow college girl or immature guy. This is Graham. The one guy I've met that seems so inherently good underneath it all. He's the guy that doesn't see me as some dumb blonde with big tits that if he plies with enough alcohol, will end up flat on her back underneath him. He just sees me.

Him being that kind of person is what makes all of this so freaking different from any other situation I've been in. I may have been able to fake interest with the other guys I've surrounded myself with, but I can't do that with Graham because I actually like him. I want him to see the real me, even if all I am is a big jumbled mess.

I could really use Serenity right now. I might not be able to tell her exactly what guy it is I'm freaking out over, but I could tell her why I'm acting this way and she'd be there for me. She would give me advice even though until Ryan, she didn't even date and I could get through this night with some semblance of my sanity still intact.

She's not here though and she's never going to be here again, at least not in the way she used to be. That means, I need to pick myself up, shake off this fear I have and get on with it. I need to be the Emma Daniels the rest of the world sees, not the one that's standing here falling apart.

Why do I have to be so messed up? Why can't I just be the girl everyone thinks I am? The strong, powerful, take no bullshit girl? I want to be her so bad I can taste it, but as great as I am at faking it, I don't think I can be her. She's just a persona. The real Emma is one gigantic mess that not even the sweetest person in the world wants to get within ten feet of.

Emma, you must cease all talk of yourself in this manner. It is most unbecoming, not to mention wrong.

Now I know that's not my inner voice. For one, it's male. I don't have a male voice and definitely not one that speaks like that. I mean seriously? Most unbecoming?

"Show yourself. I'm not dealing with your Jedi mind tricks."

I don't expect anything to happen, but the minute I say the words, the light above me starts to shake and the room completely glows. The first time this happened to me, it almost knocked me on my ass. In fact, I think it might have, but this time, it has no effect. Well, other than the gigantic blonde angel standing stiff as always in front of me.

"What is this Jedi you speak of?"

"Not a George Lucas fan, I take it?"

"George Lucas? Is that supposed to mean something to me?"

"No, I guess not. It's a movie thing. I forgot angels don't watch movies."

"You are wrong. I happen to enjoy the movies you humans create."

"Really?"

"Oh yes, though the way I have been depicted in some of them leaves something to be desired. Those need to be recreated."

Am I really having a conversation about movies with an angel? What the hell happened to my life?

"You befriended a certain ball of light. You brought it on yourself."

"Of course I did. What can I do for you?"

"I am displeased with the way that you speak of yourself. You are so much more than just the girl that struggles with depression and sadness."

"What do you know about what I'm struggling with? You've known me, what? Like five minutes?"

"I have known you since the day you were created, human. My brother is the very reason you are even here now and have the knowledge you do as it pertains to Serenity and the rest of us."

"Which brother would that be? The sadistic son of a bitch that controlled Graham or the one that screwed with my memories?"

"The latter and he had his reasons for altering your time, Emma."

"You always have your reasons. It doesn't make any of them right."

"You would be correct. We are not unlike you in that regard. Sometimes we do things we think are right for the wrong reasons. We all have failings."

"Wow."

"What?"

"That's the first thing you've said that I agree with. We're all screwed up."

"I would like nothing more than to agree with you, but I do not see failings as screw-ups the way you do. They are merely what their name implies. We are all imperfect, but that is the beauty in being who we are."

"Yeah, okay, whatever you say. Did you really come all this way to give me a pep talk?"

"In part, yes. There is more to it, but it would appear as though you need the pep talk more."

"Fabulous. Message received, you can leave now."

"What you are doing with Graham, you must continue doing it. I know that it is hard to get through to him and that at some point you feel that it would be easier to give up. Please do not do that. If I am to bring him back to the way he is meant to be, I need you."

Unbelievable. An angel, especially one as strong as the guy standing in front of me now, needs my help? Since when? What am I able to do that someone like him can't? I'm just a normal girl.

"You are more than a normal girl. You are the only one aside from Serenity herself that can break the hold that lingers over the boy."

"If she can do it, why are you talking to me? She's an angel now right? Let her fix it."

"She is not the one meant to fix it, Emma. I cannot go into much detail with you because I do not have all of the information myself, but it has to be you."

"Let's say I buy what you're selling. How am I supposed to fix Graham? You've seen me, know all about me. How is someone like me supposed to fix a guy like him when I can't even fix myself?"

"I was unaware that you were broken and I am not a shopkeeper. I am not selling you anything."

"Michael, it was a figure of speech."

"My apologies."

"You're getting off topic. Why can't you help him? Why is it me?"

"I am sure you recall your time with him only a few short hours ago. He reached out to you, the way that I have wanted him to do for some time now. I would have preferred it be me that he called to, but the fact that he did it is what matters. He did that with you, so it stands to reason that you must be the one to help him."

"How?"

By doing what you have been."

"So bothering the hell out of him?"

"If he was truly bothered by what you were doing, do you think he would respond to you in the manner he does?"

This angel speak is getting harder to understand. Serenity deals with this, not me. I'm trying to understand the old school speech, but all it does is give me a headache I don't need. Isn't there an angel somewhere upstairs that can speak like a human?

"There was, but he passed."

Gabriel. I didn't need him to say the name to know that's who he's talking about. He's the angel that spent the most time down here with us. Of course he would be the only one that I would be able to understand. I didn't know him before he passed, but I can't help but miss him just for what he could mean right now.

"He was a most extraordinary being. It is a travesty that you will not get to know him as I do."

"Yeah, I'm seeing that. Look, I'm not familiar with all of this stuff, so can you at least try and make a bit of sense for me?"

"If Graham Hudson was bothered by what you have been doing so far, he would not respond to you in any way. You would be as cut off as the rest of us seem to be. That is not the case, so you must see that you can reach him where we cannot."

"That's better thanks."

"You are most welcome. Emma. You were chosen to know everything because while you are human, you are made of nothing but goodness. That goodness in you is the light. It will be what guides you to Heaven when your time here is done. So, you are more than just a human. With Graham in the state he is in, it is because of that goodness and your human temperament that you are the only one that can do this."

"So, because I'm human and good, I'll do what you can't?"

"Precisely. Graham needs you Emma, but more than that, I need you as well."

Well crap. No pressure there at all.

"I know it seems daunting, but I have to ask. Do you believe you can handle this?"

The funny thing about my answer is, I think being there for Graham is easier then picking out an outfit for the party I'm taking him to. I might have my own doubts about myself, but when it comes to doing the right thing by him, I know I can do it easily.

"Yeah, I can do it."

"You must remember one thing as you move forward."

"What's that?"

"It will get worse before it gets better."

Fantastic.

If everything has been put back the way it's supposed to be, why do things have to get worse?

"Because anything worth doing, human or celestial in nature, has to ride through the darkness before it can be brought into the light."

Chapter Five

Graham

I have no idea why I was so against this.

When I picked her up an hour ago, I dreaded it. I didn't want to be around other people, much less a bunch of them that were drunk off their asses. If I want to get drunk and these days, I seem to want to do it a lot, I could easily do it in the comfort of my own room. It made me want to split so bad before I even knocked on her door. I was actually about to until it opened and I came face to face with her.

I've seen Emma in a whole lot of different ways over the last couple years, but the way she was when that door opened, fuck, she was hot. I might be screwed up in the head, but it doesn't seem to be affecting any other part of me. The minute I took in every inch of her, especially the red heels, I wanted nothing more than to push her back into the room and take her right there.

I'm burning up inside and she's not even near me.

The minute we got here, she took that tight halter top, black mini skirt wearing body and went in search of someone to dance with. The uncomfortable pull in my groin at watching her leave didn't go unnoticed. It took a tremendous amount of restraint not to keep her body glued to me the entire night.

No other guy needs to be touching her. I'm pretty damn sure there's been a ton of guys before me that have, but now that I'm here, I want to be the only one with my hands anywhere near her. I want my skin pressed to hers, the sweat that she's experiencing as she's dancing with some random college asshole to be the sweat that's dripping on my body as she's tucked underneath me.

The playful grin she wears when she's teasing someone, I want her to wear it as I'm teasing her. Fuck, the burn is so bad inside of me; it's making me want to take her right where she is now, in the middle of a crowded room, her arms around another guy.

Lucky bastard. Getting to feel that beautiful bird's body as it's attached to his.

Shit. I need to lay off the beer. With all the liquor I downed before even leaving to pick her up, it's not mixing well. I'm not sick, but I'll be damned if it's not messing with my mind, making me think things I should never think.

I've thought this way one time before and it almost ended in disaster. I can't afford to do it again, despite the way my dick twitches every time I see her body move.

The way she's shaking her ass on that dude right now is driving me insane. I want her doing it to me. The fabric of that skirt, blending with the movement of that sexy dance she's doing as she's rubbing up against me.

Shit, the burning is now a hard throb. I need to do something about this before I lose my mind.

I start to take steps toward her, but before I can make it even halfway to her, she's in front of me, sweat running a line down from her forehead, one droplet at a time until they fall from her chin and drop down into her partially exposed chest. It just makes the throbbing both in my head and my pants that much harder to ignore.

She's flashing that smile at me, the one I've seen countless times before, but none more important than the day she caught me and Serenity together. The same smirk she wore before she smacked me on my ass. Oh yes, I definitely need to have my hands on this girl right now. I might've been against coming to this thing before, but I'm not anymore.

Dipping my head as I watch another two droplets of sweat make their way down onto her breasts, I pull her into me and do what I've been thinking of doing since I saw the first beads of sweat appear minutes before. I run my tongue across her chin, and down her neck, breathing in her scent as I do; intoxicated more by it than the liquor I've been consuming all night.

She tastes even better then I imagined.

"Gra—Graham, what are you—doing?" she chokes out as she shivers under the feel of my tongue on her bare skin.

What am I doing? This is Serenity's best friend, the last person I should be doing this with, but I'm powerless to stop it. One taste isn't enough, I need more.

Bringing my mouth up to her ear, so she can hear what I'm about to say, I answer her and watch as her body shivers again in response before she leans even more into my body.

"What I should have done months ago."

"Graham..." she says, the words a breathless whisper.

"Emma, I need you—now."

Responding, she laces her fingers through mine and I feel my body being pulled, as we weave our way through and around the hoards of people that now seem to be gathered around us. It's only when we hit the stairs that there's a moment of hesitation.

With as blitzed as I am right now, can I go through with this? Despite what my body obviously wants and what the intense throbbing in my head means, can I really do this, with Emma of all people?

The short answer is, yes I can and I damn well will. I've never wanted another woman so bad in my life and that included Serenity.

We reach the top of the stairs and she takes a step back, a look now present in her eyes that I haven't seen before. She's having doubts. The girl that I've heard puts out for the entire damn campus is actually having doubts about what she's about to do with me. If it didn't bother me so much, it would be laughable.

Emma was made to do this and just like before, I can tell she needs the release as badly as I do. I'm going to enjoy giving it to her, as many times as she'll let me.

Finding a room that is thankfully unoccupied, I pull her into it quickly and kick the door shut with my foot, effectively blocking out the rest of the world. I definitely don't need an audience for what I'm about to share with this girl, something I've been craving so insanely that I'm afraid I'll shatter if it doesn't happen.

Turning on her quickly, I pick her up, throwing her legs around my waist and slam her up against the door, wasting no time as my lips crash down onto hers, hungry for the teasing taste of her I experienced minutes before. As she parts her lips and responds to the kiss, with just as much eagerness and desire as I am, I feel her fingers graze my skin as she wraps them around my neck pulling her body even tighter into mine.

Damn, even that insignificant of a move is driving the heat up in my body. The throbbing ache in my pants is now beyond ready to escape, burying itself in her, experiencing the movements her body is sure to make the minute we connect.

Calling on every bit of my upper body strength, I pull her away from the door, our lips still connected, the both of us devouring each other, making my way over to the bed. Laying her down as gently as I can, given the growing need inside of me to rip her completely apart, I climb on top of her and place my lips to her shoulder, sucking on every bit of her exposed flesh until I again reach her lips and pull them back into mine.

Her hands are on my back now, rubbing slowly, as if she's taking in every bit of me as my shirt starts sliding up. Pulling back, I lift it the rest of the way and bring it over my head, throwing it to the ground before returning to her body again.

It's only when I hear the small whimper escape her lips that I freeze in place. As turned on as she's made me, there's something in the sound that brings the reality of the situation crashing down around us.

"Ems—are you okay?" I manage to somehow choke out, even though the pounding in my head is at an all time high.

"Mhmm." She murmurs, giving me everything I need. This is finally going to happen. I'm going to have Emma Daniels naked underneath me. I'm going to be buried completely inside her, just the way I've been craving since the day in her dorm room.

I feel her hands, making quick work of the button and zipper on my jeans, my dick pulsating at an even quicker pace with as close as she's coming to freeing it. Sliding my hands under her shirt, I pull it off and over her head and as I do, I catch her eyes.

With the sound of the murmur a few seconds ago, this is not a look I'd been expecting to catch. Even covered in the sweat from the lights earlier, mixed with the desire that's paramount in her eyes, it's still there. Uncertainty. Doubt. Fear.

And it's turning me the fuck on.

Sliding my hands down into the top of her skirt, I start yanking hard, wanting nothing more than to get it off her body and on the floor with the rest of our discarded clothes. Driven by the blood rushing to my head, I rip at it until I hear it tear in my hands. Laughing softly, I pull the ruined material from around her and toss it to the floor.

"Fuck, Emma, I need you so god damned bad."

Letting my words fall, not waiting for a response, I rip at her panties with my fingers, sliding them down her legs, slightly more careful then I had been with her skirt. It's only when I'm about to bring them over her shoes that I feel her body tense.

Looking up, I'm met again with the same look of fear from before. When we were downstairs she wanted me, I could see it, and even a couple of minutes ago she wanted it, her body telling me with the way she made quick work of undoing my pants. So what changed?

"Graham, stop. "

"What?"

"Not like this, Graham, please."

She's teasing me. That's all this is. She's playing hard to get. She wants our first time to be a game. Well, if that's what the lady wants, it's what she's gonna get.

Pulling the lace bra up, releasing her breasts, I bend down and begin sucking on them, starting with the left, running my tongue over her now pert and exposed nipples, before moving on to the next one and repeating it, throwing my body into overdrive in the process.

"Graham—please—stop!" She cries out, louder this time, her voice no longer husky with the desire of before, only fear.

I'm not sure if it's the wounded way she sounds or the actual pitch, but whatever haze I had been in that got me to this point seems to lift the second I hear it.

"Son of a bitch!" I say, the reality of the situation hitting me.

Pulling myself off her, backing off the bed entirely, not stopping until I'm standing by the door that only seconds ago I'd had her slammed up against, I really look at her. Her torn skirt is on the floor in a heap with my shirt and hers. Her panties are still hanging loosely around her ankles and there are now tears falling from her eyes that hadn't been there before.

I did it again. What the hell is wrong with me? I took the only girl that's ever wanted to do right by me and I broke her apart again.

I did this, all of it.

Not even Lucifer can be blamed for this. I acted all on my own.

I'm even worse than the devil himself.

Emma

This is why everyone talks so much shit about me. What happened in this room a few minutes ago is the reason for all of it.

I knew Graham was drinking before he picked me up. I could smell it on him the minute I opened the door and in my brilliance, I brought him to a party where even more of it is given out freely. He went straight for it the minute we got here and I let him because I thought it was the right thing to do.

Getting him out of his room and back around a bunch of people his own age, ones that didn't have the weight of the world on their shoulders is supposed to be the right thing to do. Except it's anything but the right thing and now I'm paying for it.

I have no idea where he is; he took off the minute my eyes locked on his when he backed away. I know I can't stay here. I need to get up and go, before someone catches me half naked and finishes what Graham started, but I can't will my body to move from its spot.

When he told me he wanted me, something happened. I responded to it because I wanted him too. I've wanted him for months. I like him and for some stupid reason, I thought being with him this way would be right. Michael said I'm the one that can save him. If that's true than it means us being together, even with him half drunk and me, well, being me, was a step in the right direction.

Wrong. It's all wrong.

I did what I always do, except this time it was with Graham and not some random guy I would be too drunk to remember the name of in the morning. I let Graham touch me in ways that I've never experienced before and I liked every second of it. Michael may believe me to be something better than I am, but it doesn't make it true. I'm exactly what they all believe me to be.

I'm a whore and I just used Graham to drive the point home.

Staring at the crumpled mess of clothes on the floor, it hits me that he left without his shirt. That in his hurry to get the hell away from me and the horrible situation I put us in, he's going to risk his own health running out in the middle of the night with next to nothing on. Of all the stupid things I've done over the years, this one definitely wins. I made one of the nicest guys in the world so sick, he left without clothes to escape me.

Score one for the useless waste of space.

I need to get out of here and now that my legs are going to cooperate, I want nothing more than to do it, but I can't. The perfect mini-skirt I spent half the night debating over, is a destroyed piece of fabric on the floor. I've got nothing else to wear to get out of here that won't earn me the walk of shame.

I'm stuck.

Sliding my way over to the end of the bed, I stand, sliding my panties back up and sitting back down, making quick work of getting the heels I had been so excited to wear earlier, off my now aching feet. It's only when I make my way to the door and flip the lock, guaranteeing no one is going to walk in and see me this way that I see it. On the night stand, clear as day is a phone.

I've never been so happy to see electronics in my life.

With my cell in my purse downstairs and no real way to get out of here without being noticed or called out, I do the only thing left that I can and pray that he's home and can help.

I call Ryan.

Chapter Six

Michael

What good is heavenly intervention when you cannot do it at a time when it is most needed?

There have been times lately where I have questioned exactly what our purpose is and this case is no exception. What just took place between Graham and Emma should never have happened. I am aware that I told her that things would get worse before they got better, but I did not mean that she had to go through what she just experienced. What they both went through is wrong and I foresee it having long lasting implications.

Implications that even if I am allowed to intervene, I may not be able to fix without completely altering their memories and time.

I happen to like Emma, far more than I ever thought I would. She may appear to be a certain way because of the issues she faces, but she is so much more than what the humans that call themselves doctors have surmised. She is more than her sadness, but with everything that has happened now, I am unsure I can get her to the point where she will believe it.

Going to a college party might not have been the best idea for Graham considering the self medicating he has been doing, but I believed just as Emma did that getting out and among other people like him, that he would walk away better because of it. It should never have taken such a dark turn. It is just further proof that even with my fallen brother well on the road to redemption, there is still one avenue he needs to atone for.

Graham's behavior is reminiscent of what he did when under Lucifer's control. It may be a different location, but what had been put into motion that day, has finally taken place in the bedroom that I see Ryan arriving at. I am thankful it ended before it went further because not being allowed to intervene was threatening to break me. Standing idly by and watching as a man, fueled by whatever dark force has a hold on him, takes advantage of a girl that deep down I know he cares deeply for makes me sick.

This is not what I signed up for and I have seen darker instances then this since my creation. Ryan spoke previously of Lucifer being the king of rape and pillage and he was not mistaken. My brother lived for it during that period of his life. Seeing Graham reacting in much the same way, upsets me. It appears as though he is becoming more like the man that possessed him then he was ever meant to.

The boy needs to be healed. We cannot let him continue going down this path. Not only is the self medication a serious problem, but if he is indeed becoming like Lucifer, than the need to put an end to it is even more urgent. Graham is not meant for a life such as the one he is living. It may go against Father and his wishes not to have anything upset the natural order of things, but I no longer care.

It has to be done and if it cannot be done by me than it has to be done by Lucifer.

The time for following the rules is over.

Graham

"You were different. You've always been different."
These random memory flashes make me sick. It's bad enough waking up and finding a mark that wasn't there the night before, but to relive moments like that one with Serenity while I'm awake on top of it? Is it really necessary to drive the knife in any deeper than it already is?

When she called me different that day, she meant it in the sweetest way possible. She has been treated differently her entire life and I was one of two people that made it their life's mission to show her a different way. Emma started it when she became friends with our lost girl and I picked it up and finished it.

I have no doubt that if she knew what happened last night; I wouldn't be sitting here right now. There's something about the idea of her killing me that soothes me. If Serenity got mad enough and just did away with me than none of this would be happening right now. I wish she'd pop by and visit just so I could make it happen.

Man, I really have changed. The differences Serenity saw in me are dead and gone. I'm not the same guy anymore and even if Heaven did heal me the way they want to, I don't think they can ever bring back the person I used to be. I think I'm stuck this way forever.

Leaving Emma at the party last night might be worse then what we did before I walked away, if that's possible. I tore the girl's skirt, knowing it's the only clothes she had. Instead of staying behind and doing the right thing to get her out safely, I left her to rot alone. I've always been the king of bonehead moves, but this latest one might earn me the crown once and for all. Even worse, I came home, passed out and didn't give her a second thought until now.

I've been spending so much time hating on the things Lucifer did, but really, everything I'm doing lately is earning me a spot right there with him.

The worst part about this is, I actually like the girl. I didn't want to go to that room with her just to get laid. I wanted to get laid with her. God, it even sounds stupid to me and I'm the one thinking it. She's more than just a lay and somehow, I treat her no better than I have the other chicks I bring back here all the time. If it's possible, I treated her worse.

I only hope that with what happened, she'll finally get a clue that she's better off and leave me alone. I warned her that she didn't want to be around me and well, I think I've gotten the message across loud and clear.

"You know, the day you found us in your bed, I always wished it was you with me instead of her. I think the two of us would have a lot of fun together."

"You sick bast—"

"No need for name calling, sweetheart. I'm just stating facts. I distinctly remember you slapping my ass, so I bet you've given it some thought too."

Not again.

As much as I hate the memories, this one is right. I was a bastard to her that day, fueled by a hunger I've never known and I'd taken it out on her. She was right to call me a bastard even if I cut her off before she did. The thing is, I'm still that same guy, except I had to kick it up a notch and take things to a level that I don't think she can ever forgive me for.

The banging on the door stops my thoughts and instead of ignoring it, this time I'm on my feet and making my way over before I can even process who might be on the other side. Every time there's been a knock over the last few weeks, at least since Kyle moved out, it's been Emma. Part of me wants it to be her now.

I'm not sure what I'll do if she's on the other side of the door, but now that I'm at least partially in my right mind, it can't be worse than last night. Maybe I can actually get her to believe that I really am sorry this time.

It's not Emma though.

"You and I need to have words. Now!" he snaps, pushing his way past me and completely into the room, not evening waiting around for a response. What I've got to talk to him about, I don't know, but judging by the tone and the look on his face, I'm pretty sure I'm not gonna like it.

I wonder what Serenity got herself into this time.

"Nice try, jackass. This isn't about Serenity."

Jackass. That's a new one.

"What do you want?"

"I've tried, ya know. I really have. No one knows better than me what spending time with Lucifer is like, and I sympathized so hard with you man, I did, but I can't do it anymore."

"What the hell are you talking about?"

"Emma goes out of her way, despite me telling her otherwise, to try and help you and how do you repay her? You attack her?"

I don't know why I didn't think about it sooner. If he isn't here about something related to Serenity, of course it would be about her. There's no one else in the world he gives a shit about, but the two of them.

"You're an asshole, you know that?"

"Excuse me?"

"I worked with Michael to try and fix you. I did everything possible to make things right. You're the one that turned us down. So don't stand here and say that I don't give a shit about anyone but my wife and her friend."

"Can you stop reading my mind, it's fucked up."

"No, the only thing that's fucked up here is you."

Well I can't argue with that. It's exactly what I've been telling everyone for months.

"Did Emma tell you she was the one leading me up the stairs?"

Ryan rubs his temples, sighing and I'm struck with how much of an asshole I am, putting what happened on her. It's no wonder he's annoyed with me. I'm starting to get annoyed with myself.

"Do I really need to spell this shit out for you, Graham?"

"Spell what out?"

"I can't believe I'm actually gonna do this." He says, before picking up where he left off. "She went upstairs with you because despite you being a complete idiot, she likes you and what do you do with her once you've got her that way? You attempt to get laid, fail and then ditch her. Smooth move, might I add."

The way he seems to know so much about it makes me wonder how long he's been aware of her feelings for me. Did he know before we went to Hell? Is that why he asked me about her back then or is it just something he learned over the last few hours?

"Holy shit, the guy has a brain after all! I've known since before Hell, Graham. I know how you both feel and it didn't come from her."

"What do you mean 'how we both feel'?"

"Contrary to popular belief, you're not as closed off as you think. Lucifer might have been the cause of it in the beginning, but it's been all you two ever since."

"She likes me..."

"Yeah, man, she does and it should have been you bringing her home last night, not me."

"Does Serenity know?"

"No. Emma is scared shitless to bring this up despite her being married to me. She's afraid the bond will change everything and make things worse. So she's holding on to it pretty tight."

"Why haven't you told her?"

"Because I don't need to."

"What does that mean?"

"It means exactly what I said. I don't need to tell her."

"Shit! I really fucked everything up this time, didn't I?"

"Yeah you did. I came here to pound your face in, but seeing as you really are as clueless as you appear, I figure you'll do that enough yourself when I leave."

"What the hell am I supposed to do now?"

"Fix your shit. We told the angels to do it before. Now it's your turn."

If only it was as easy as he makes it sound. If I could just blink and rid myself of everything I've been going through, I would have done it already. It's not something that can be wished away. Whatever is going on is long lasting and I don't think it can be fixed.

"Everything can be fixed if you want it bad enough."

"Where, oh wise one, do you suggest I start?"

"Start at the beginning."

"Green Haven?"

"Lucifer."

Chapter Seven

Emma

I can't believe I'm standing here about to do this.

What's even worse is that no one knows about it. If something happens and it all goes bad, there isn't one person that can come to my rescue. I made the decision to do this, keeping everyone out of the loop and I just hope I don't live to regret it.

When Ryan picked me up at the Pi Sig house last night, he gave me the idea and as much as I appreciated it at the time, I blew it off, which is another reason standing here right now is strange. I know I should just go to the door and get on with it, but I can't will my legs to move. This might be the only way to fix things, but I still don't feel right about it.

Graham wouldn't want this. He hates anything related to the person I'm about to beg for help. If he knew I was standing here, about to take this step for him, I'm pretty sure I'd lose whatever's left of our friendship. With the way we left things though, maybe there's not much left to lose.

Admitting everything to Ryan was hard. I didn't even want to call the guy, but since the only other option was Serenity, I had no choice. Whether he wanted to be involved in this or not, I knew he would help me out once he heard what was going on and I wasn't disappointed.

*****

"Thank you for coming." I say, after changing into the clothes he brought me. "I didn't know who else to call…"

"I'm just glad I was home. Work's been a bitch lately. I don't think I've slept in days."

"Not the way you pictured it huh?"

He laughs, but it's awkward. He's not sure how to respond to me and I don't blame him. I didn't tell him anything on the phone, except that I got myself in a jam at a party and needed his help. It's actually a blessing he showed up at all. It's not exactly a secret that I'm the queen of these parties. This is the first time I've ever had to reach out.

"So you wanna tell me how you ended up locked in here alone? Maybe you can start with whose face I need to beat in."

He thinks it's some random guy that left me here like this and he's doing what he's always done. He wants to defend me. It's no wonder why Serenity fell for him. He's the only other guy I've met besides Graham that might be completely decent, even if he wasn't always that way.

Half demon or not, he's definitely my savior right now.

"Emma, you're thinking too much. Can you stop and just tell me who did this to you?"

I forgot he can read minds now. Shit. I'm only glad I didn't say who did it. I don't think he'd take it too well.

"If you don't tell me who it is, I'm going to go down there and go through every guy until I figure out who. Spare me the concern and spit it out."

"Is it really that easy for you to read me?"

"It's easy to read everyone lately. I do my best to block it out, but sometimes, like right now, it's damn near impossible. I'm really starting to hate it, so do me a favor and just tell me."

"Graham."

"Excuse me?"

"Graham was here with me. I had this bright idea to get him out of his room, ya know. Get him out with people like him and it backfired. I think I made it worse. He's the guy that was here with me and he's the one that left."

"He the one that tore up your skirt too?"

"Yeah."

"Emma, fuck." He says sharply exhaling. "What did I tell you about him?"

"That he was going through some pretty heavy stuff and needed to be left alone for awhile."

"Nice to see you listened to it."

"Walking away from him isn't the answer, Ryan. I know you think he needs time, but we've given him time and nothing's changed. I wanted to try a different approach."

"How far did it go?" he asks as he rubs his temples. I can tell he doesn't want to ask it, that it's too much information.

"Pretty damn far."

"Jesus, Emma!"

"It was a mistake, okay? I know that now. I never should have brought him here tonight. I just didn't know what else to do. When Michael said I was doing the right thing, that I was the one that could help him, I guess I lost my head."

"Michael told you that?"

"Yeah. Ryan, it's not exactly a secret how I feel about him. I want to help him. I just didn't realize it was going to lead to this."

"Did you want to sleep with him?

I blush before burying my face in my hands. That is definitely too personal for me. Ryan knows how I feel, I told him months ago. I asked him to keep it a secret from my best friend, but it didn't mean I had to sit here and admit just how much I did want to sleep with Graham.

"Okay I got it. Stop thinking about it."

"Sorry..."

"Sleeping with Graham isn't going to help him. You've seen what he's been doing since he moved back. You don't need to become one of his girls. You're better than that."

That's something we don't agree on, but with the help he's giving me, getting me out of here, the last thing I'm going to do is argue it with him. I don't think I deserve much of anything anymore, especially after tonight.

"It doesn't matter now. It's done. He's gone. I just want to go home and forget it ever happened."

"Are you ready to listen to reason now?"

"What do you mean?"

"Stay away from Graham. I know you want to help and I know it's made worse when you've got an angel telling you that you're supposed to be the one that does help him, but you need to listen to reason. Stay away."

"I can't do that."

Again his face scrunches and his fingers rub across his temples.

"I figured as much. If you want to do the right thing by him and nothing I say will talk you out of it, then there's only one thing you can do, but it's something I don't think you're gonna wanna hear."

"Just spit it out."

"You need to talk to Lucifer. I know Michael's been tasked with taking care of Graham, but if you really want to fix him, than he's the one you need to see. He's the only person that can fix this."

"And if I don't want to go to him?"

"Then you're gonna have to walk away. Lucifer did this to him, Emma. He's the only one that can fix it and deep down, I think you know it."

*****

That conversation brings me to where I am now. I'm about to come face to face with the devil. Well, if the devil looked like Serenity's father anyway. He might be hidden underneath a human disguise, but it didn't make the fear easier to handle. I can't imagine there's a single person in the world that wants to have a conversation with Lucifer, especially about fixing something he broke. I want to be anywhere but here right now.

I know everyone thinks he's changed and he's trying to live his existence on the straight and narrow path, but I'm not sure I buy it. He could hear what I've got to say and turn me down. He could want to wash his hands completely of the things he did and there's not much I can do to stop it. I'm only human after all.

There's also the very real fact that despite his so called changes, he's still the devil underneath and if I say the wrong thing, I'm pretty sure it would easy as hell to get rid of me and no one would be the wiser.

Yeah, I definitely don't want to be here.

"I was wondering when you would show up."

The voice, I've heard it before because I spent time with Serenity's father at the wedding, but I know now that even though it's his baritone speaking the words, it's most definitely not him. Turning back is definitely off the table now.

"It should be never."

"Emma, you wound me."

"If only that were true."

"I suppose it's customary in times such as this to ask which one of us you are here to see, but I am sure I already know the answer."

"I need to speak with you."

"As I suspected. This is regarding the Hudson boy is it not?"

With Ryan able to read my mind, I have to wonder if it worked the same with Lucifer. Is he able to see inside and know that Graham is the reason I'm here, and if so, why is he wasting precious time with useless conversation?

"Yeah, it's about Graham."

"Well, standing out here will solve nothing other than giving you a sickness I do not believe I am at liberty to heal. Why don't you come inside?"

I really don't want to go anywhere with this man. Sure, Gregory is there, but the grin on his face, I don't trust it.

"I assure you; no harm will come to you at my hand. Despite what I have subjected you to in the past, I am here to listen and help. That is all."

Not entirely sure I can believe him, but agreeing that standing out here might not be the smartest thing, I follow him as he turns until we've made our way completely into the house. It's only when he motions to the chair that the fear builds again. Maybe I should have brought Ryan along after all.

"Michael and I have spoken at length about Graham, so it is no surprise to me that you are here now. I am also aware of your feelings for the boy. I cannot say that comes as a surprise."

"You have no idea what I feel about him, or anyone for that matter."

"That is where you are wrong, young lady. It is my understanding that the boy wants to take the blame for what happened between the two of you so long ago, but the truth is; I exploited what was there between you both. I am as much to blame for what transpired as he believes he is."

Nothing he says comes as a surprise. Graham did take the blame for what happened, he's said as much on more than one occasion, but I always knew Lucifer was the real mastermind of it, even if I didn't know everything about him at the time.

"I don't believe you've changed the way Serenity does."

"I am aware of that. You have every right to doubt my sincerity. I would expect nothing less from you or Graham. What I put the both of you through cannot be explained away with a simple apology."

I always thought that when I came face to face with Lucifer, I would want to wrap my hands around his neck and choke him for everything he had done to not only me, but everyone I care about, but listening to him, it's the last thing I want. I want to believe in what he's saying because he sounds so damn sincere.

"I need your help."

"Tell me what it is that you wish me to do and you have my full cooperation."

"You're not even going to ask what I want."

"No. I may have been against earning my entrance to Heaven again when it was presented to me originally, but I have since seen the error of my ways. I know that there is much work that needs to be done to rectify all that I have broken and I am determined to do that. Regardless of the request."

"Can you heal Graham?"

"Yes, but I have to ask you something."

What could he possibly have to ask me that he doesn't already know?

"Michael has the ability and the power to heal him easily and it would happen with much less pomp and circumstance. So why are you bringing it to me and not him?"

That's a question I don't have an answer for. Ryan warned me that Michael could do it; in fact it would go easier if it came from the other, more righteous angel, yet I'm sitting here across a table from Lucifer and asking him for help instead. Could it be that I want him to earn his way home the same way Serenity does so I'm giving him a chance?

"I don't know why I'm here, honestly. I just think that since you're the reason any of this is happening, you should be the one that fixes it. You claim you want to rectify everything you've done; well this is a chance to do that."

"It will not be easy. Graham Hudson is most unwilling where I am concerned."

"I know, which is why I've come up with a way around that."

"Well, do not keep me in suspense. How pre tell do you propose I heal your friend without his knowledge?"

This is the part that's easy for me. I've given this a whole lot of thought. With the way Graham drinks in order to dull the pain and the nightmares, the best time for this to happen is during one of those episodes. If Lucifer can heal him while he's passed out, then we can do it and there won't have to be a fight. I'm not ready to tell him all of this though. I still have trust issues, which means I need to take this one step at a time and pray that in the end it's the right thing.

"Can you come when I call you?"

"Yes."

"Then for now, that's all you need to know. Let me deal with the rest."

Chapter Eight

Graham

"That strong façade you put forth will only last you for so long. The only question now is, just how much pain can you take before you break?"

"I can take whatever you've got. Bring it on, asshole!"

The fire grows in his hands and I swallow the lump building in my throat. With all his talk of pain, I know what comes next, it's happened before. He's going to burn me with it, until all I can smell is the scent of my charred flesh.

I lied. I can't take whatever he's got. He's dangerously close to breaking me as it is, but I can't let him figure it out. I can't give in no matter how bad it gets. I have to take it with a smile on my face so he thinks he'll never break me.

As the heat connects with my chest, I scream in agony before struggling with the restraints around my wrists, yanking at them as hard as I can, praying that they're close to breaking. I need to get free. Once that happens I can show him what I'm really made of and make him pay.

"You are remarkably strong, Graham. It pains me to do this to you knowing that the strength within you will serve me well with what is to happen next."

"Just wait until I'm free. I'll show you how strong I am!" I scream at him, the fire now burning through the exposed skin and the smell slowly making its way up until I'm bathed in it.

He pulls the ball of fire away, placing it on another exposed part of my chest and I see the bright red and brown burn now scarring my skin. If I didn't need to stay strong, I'd be losing what was left of my lunch. Not only did it hurt like a bitch, but the skin peeling back, is enough to turn my stomach inside out.

"Just give in to it. The pain stops the minute you break."

"I will—never—break." I choke out, resisting the urge to scream as the smell of charred flesh rises up from my chest, the urge to expel my insides even stronger than before.

"You all break. I just need to find the right part of anatomy and you'll bend to my every whim."

Knowing what his words mean, I feel like crying. He will burn every part of my body that's exposed to him until he gets his way and there is no way out of it. I'm stuck here, the metal bindings digging so deeply into my wrists that they're bleeding, the blood sliding down and over until it drips onto the floor below me.

It doesn't stop my struggle. I continue to fight against the binds, crying out in pain as he pushes the fire even deeper into my chest. I can't take the agony anymore, but I can't give him what he wants. I can end up dead for all I care, but he will not get his way.

I will not become his vessel.

*****

I jump up in bed and shaking off the effects of the nightmare, I take a look around the darkened room. I don't remember even going to bed, but I can tell as I take it all in that I did a whole lot more than sleep.

There are eyes on me now, ones I don't recognize, but ones filled with the same fear I had seen in not only Kyle the first time he caught me after a nightmare, but the same damn look that had been on Emma's face only a couple of nights before at the party.

How this girl ended up in my bed, I don't know, but there's no doubt now that she needs to get the hell out of it.

"You're—bleeding." She cries, pointing down at my exposed wrist and my stomach ties in knots.

Of course I'm bleeding. I had the nightmare again. The one where he burns me and I struggle so hard against the binds he put me in that I break my skin wide open. The rusty smell of the blood rising up so strong that it erases the burn smell that had been there only seconds before.

"You need to get out of here." I answer in response, not giving her any indication I heard what she said about the blood. It's easier that way.

"I can't leave you like this. You're hurt. Do you want me to call an ambulance?"

When will these girls learn? I don't give a fuck about them past having them underneath me. The minute they start caring, it makes me physically want to throw them out of the room altogether. The last thing I want from any of these whores is sympathy.

"It's just a scratch."

"Pretty big scratch."

"Thanks for the diagnosis, doc. You mind getting the fuck out of here now?"

"You're an asshole, ya know that?"

"My life's mission has been accomplished. A girl thinks I'm an asshole. Guess what, sweetheart? I don't give a shit what you think. I just want you out of my bed."

I'm rewarded as she slides from the bed, my dick responding immediately as her naked form makes its way across the room to where we dropped our clothes hours ago. It takes all my restraint not to reach back out to her and throw her underneath me again. She entertained me well hours ago. I have no doubt, even with my dickhead comments she'd do it again.

They always do. Whores.

I don't reach out to her though because the minute she levels me with her look of hatred, all I can see is Emma and Serenity in her eyes. The fear I put in Emma and the disappointment Serenity would have if she knew about it. I can see both women clearly, which means she's definitely overstayed her welcome.

"Do me a favor would ya Graham?"

"What's that?"

"Don't call me."

"Wasn't planning on it."

She stalks from the room and I can't help laughing. I never keep my intentions a secret. The girls I'm with know what they are when I take them to bed. This girl was no different. She was just a means to an end. A distraction, one that for a few hours did what I needed so that I could forget.

That's what it's all about. Forgetting. I want to forget not only the nightmares, the agony and pain of everything I've been through but I want to forget what Emma looked like the night I walked out on her. Drowning in the whiskey and the women worked out well. For a short time Emma was the last thing on my mind.

Now she's back and I get the idea that no matter how much I drink, she's never going to be gone completely. She'll always come back.

"She went upstairs with you because despite being a complete idiot, she likes you."

Now is not the time for Ryan's words to haunt me. I've been haunted enough. The girl wasn't wrong. I am bleeding again, this time on my wrists. The very place that Lucifer placed the wire bindings, knowing that any struggle I made would cost me. I need to get up and take care of it, but I can't do it. His words keep playing over in a loop and despite my best attempts at ignoring them, they won't go away.

Emma likes me.

She doesn't just like the guy that she knows because of Serenity. She even likes the person I've turned into. It's the reason she keeps trying so hard. I had a feeling there was more to her coming here, part of me even knowing that she liked me, but I didn't want to believe it. There is no way a girl like Emma could like a guy like me, or at least the version of me I am now. What girl in their right mind would like the broken mess I've become?

Emma does.

Shit. I screwed everything even more bringing that girl back to my room. I've known the truth for months and even though I blew it all to shit the night of the party, it didn't change the facts. I screwed up bringing another chick back to my room because she's not alone.

I like her too.

It's half the reason that things went down the way they did that day in her room. I've been attracted to her from day one, but my love for Serenity overrode all of it. It still overrides it. I will always love Serenity Richards and it's unfair to any other girl I come into contact with. It's why sleeping with these random girls is so fun. There's not connection. There's only sex and they're gone. I never have to worry about feelings building and becoming a boyfriend. I just need to screw and run.

Emma deserves better than that, no matter how much I like her.

She's got issues. I know this. Serenity didn't exactly tell me everything about it, but she told me enough for me to understand that the last thing Emma Daniels needs in her life is someone that will only cut her deeper than her past ever could. She might appear to be as strong as her best friend, but there's softness to Emma under the surface that no one else sees and it's because of that softness that I'm no good for her.

I can never be good for her.

If you did what Ryan told you to, you could be good enough for her.

Definitely don't want to think about that. I don't care how bad this gets; the last thing in the world I'm going to do is go to Lucifer for help. I'm not even sure what Ryan was smoking when he suggested it. He has to see how crazy of an idea that really is. The only time I want to stand before that son of a bitch again is when I kill him.

The very thing Ryan supposedly did in Green Haven. The fallen angel deserves to die and despite what my soul mate believes, no amount of good deeds in the world can redeem him. The last person I would ever reach out to is Lucifer.

Ryan could take his bright idea and shove it. If I'm turning down Michael, you can be damn sure I'm turning him down too.

With as adamant as I am about not doing what Ryan suggested, it doesn't stop it from making itself at home in my head. If there's another person alive that hates Lucifer as much as I do, it's him. I have no doubt it was hard for him to bring it up, especially since he knows better than anyone what I'm going through. He just wanted to give me a choice. A way to end the torture I've been going through so that I can get back to being me.

He might be doing it for Serenity, but it didn't make it any less true. I could get rid of this, if I could just get over the stubbornness of wanting to handle it myself and ask for help.

Being this stubborn, there are times where I feel I'm letting more than my friends down. I think about my mother and what she would think about all of this if she was here now. She wouldn't want me suffering like this. She would understand my reservations at wanting to ask the angels, both fallen and otherwise, but she would push me to do it because she always wanted the best for me.

I'm definitely letting her down right now, turning myself into the jerk the way I am. This is not the boy she raised and if it's possible for someone to roll over in their grave in disappointment, I'm pretty sure my Mom is doing that right now.

Lucifer is the reason she's not here.

That's another reason I can't swallow my pride and ask for help. The fallen angel that is on his way to redemption is the one that caused everything wrong with my world. He not only tried to kill the very person that decided to redeem him, but in an effort to break me, he killed my mother in the most heinous way possible. They might be able to forgive him for what happened to Serenity, but I could never forget or forgive what happened to my mom.

I'd rather live in this darkness forever then do something that would taint the beautiful memory of the woman that gave up everything in order to give me life.

My decisions been made and not even Emma can change it.

Chapter Nine

Lucifer

I knew it would only be a matter of time before the Daniels girl came to see me. I had been hoping that I would have the chance to come face to face with Graham the way that I did with Emma, but I will take it in whatever form it comes in.

Graham Hudson and my treatment of him is the one aspect of being topside that bothers me to no end. He is my greatest failure and not because he did not serve his purpose. It is not a dark reason at all. He is my greatest failure because I should never have used him in that way to begin with.

The day I captured him in Green Haven and found out who he was and what he would mean to not only Serenity, but the world overall, it seemed like I had been blessed. I once believed Ryan to be the perfect specimen, but nothing compared to that of Graham. He was everything that Ryan was not. Where he had been made of the darkness or at least I believed him to be at the time, Graham was made of the light.

He was made of the very light that I have been craving for as long as I can remember.

If only I had done what Gabriel wanted of me years before during our private moments together, that boy never would have walked through the darkness I put him through and he would most definitely not be walking the fine line of evil and pain he is now. What is happening to him, I am completely responsible for and I want nothing more than to fix it.

It has nothing to do with returning to my rightful place at home. I want to do this for the man and those that care about him. I admit that I can bring the selfishness into the equation easily, but I am doing what I can to resist it. That is the way I would have acted during my centuries long temper tantrum. Not the way I am now.

Emma does not believe me changed and as I told her during our visit together, I do not blame her for it. I admire her for taking the chance in coming to me when I am sure she wanted to do anything but. I could have easily read her during her time here, but that is another aspect of my old life that I want to let go of. I cannot resort to reading people and twisting their thoughts for my own selfish purposes. If I had done that with Emma, I have no doubt I would have reverted back to the Lucifer of old and twisted her.

I will do as she needs and help her heal Graham Hudson. I will become one with the boy when she calls for me and do as I should have done months ago. Putting him back together, turning him back into the very strong pillar of light that Gabriel knew him to be when he took him on as a vessel.

Doing it will endear me even more to Serenity, proving to her that her risk months ago was worth it, but again I cannot think of it that way. I want to of course; it is what is engrained in me, but for this to happen the way that it needs to, it needs to be done for the pure reasons and not the selfish ones.

Michael coming to me was a warning. I knew in the end that he would never do as he said and turn against the light he is guided by. He was warning me of Emma's arrival. She will be the one to work with me to bring the man she cares about back to his true form.

My only concern moving forward is that none of this has come from Father. I have no doubt that he wants Graham healed as badly as Michael and Emma do, but it is unlike him not to inform us of his thoughts. Have things changed that much in Heaven since my time there that now he does not let his feelings be known?

I want to reach out to him, but I do not believe I have earned that quite yet. I know that he agreed with Serenity and even admitted that things were always meant to end this way.

He admitted how he felt about me despite the things that I have done during my time apart from him, which should make going to him now easy, but it makes it that much harder.

Father may love me, as I do him, and it may be one of the most powerful experiences in the world, but it did not change the horrors I have created and what my brothers and Father himself have to clean up now that everything has been set right. Going to him is premature. I still need to earn any face time I get with him and I do not believe I have done that quite yet.

Maybe when Graham Hudson is healed and brought back where he belongs that will change.

It is my greatest hope.

Emma

I will not let this get to me.

It's easier said than done, because this time it's not some random girl. I know the girl making her way out of Graham's room and down the hall toward me. She's in our English class and she's actually one of the nice ones.

I don't mean that the ones he normally picks are horrible or anything, but by now, they should all know what he's about. What he wants from them. It's not exactly like he's hiding it. The sad thing is, I'm one of those girls. I used to do the exact same things. A guy at a party would show me a little bit of attention and I would jump at it, like it was fresh water and we were in the desert or something. I was pretty bad.

If you ask my mom, it's another one of my issues. I have this whole attachment issue. I want to be loved so badly that I'll pretty much get it from anywhere, even if it's not realistic. For instance, when I was dating Cody, I knew something was going on long before I actually learned the truth, but because he was Cody and I thought I loved him, it didn't matter. I ignored it until I couldn't anymore. It's sad. I know I deserve better, yet that doesn't stop me. I want love so badly that I'll keep looking until it knocks me on my ass.

I want what Serenity and Ryan have. Neither one of them will admit to it, but I knew they would end up together that very first day. I picked him up in the Dean's office and I just knew he would be the one for her. I had no interest in him whatsoever and for me, that's saying something.

Ryan McGregor if you look at him a certain way could be a dead ringer for Jared Leto. I did a whole double take and everything when I was asked to bring him to psych because I swear; we had a rock star trying to go to college with us.

It wasn't because of the way he looked that I knew he would be right for Serenity. It was something in his eyes and I don't mean the whole black ring of darkness either. That was there alright, but there was this wounded look he had when he didn't think anyone noticed and it just reminded me of her. So of course I pushed him at her. If I couldn't find true love then I was gonna make damn sure Serenity would.

What they have, it's so epic I don't even think there's another love story quite like it. They really have been through hell and back and somehow, they're still standing. The devil wasn't enough to tear them apart and he tried, a lot. That's what I want. Am I crazy enough to think I'll find my one epic love on a college campus? Definitely not, but it doesn't mean I'm not going out of my way to find it and getting attached to every douchebag along the way.

Graham's different. He isn't like Cody or any of the others. He's pure, untainted. Well, at least that's how he was when I first met him. There was something so good about him and it was hard not to notice it. The guy was and is head over heels in love with my best friend and there I was checking him out. Classic Emma Daniels move, at least that's what the rest of the college would say if they knew about it.

The things he's doing now, that's not the Graham I know. He's more like Cody and the others than he ever was before. This is what the other guys are supposed to do with girls, not what Graham does. I'm not the only one that feels this way, Serenity does too, but for whatever reason, she's keeping her distance. Watching Maria leave his room now, I'm starting to wonder if maybe I should do the same thing.

It should be easy to do what Ryan told me so many months ago. Walk away from him, giving him time to get his shit together and finally get back on the right track. As easy as it seems though, it's not. I've never been one to give up on anyone. My relationship with Serenity proves that. I've been lied to, had things hidden from me and I'm still standing by her. It's what I do because I can't take another loss like the one I felt when my dad left.

I didn't give up on him, I won't ever give up on Serenity and I can't walk away and leave Graham either. I might not hold much stock in what the angels tell me, but I think Michael was right. Even after everything that happened between us, I do think I'm the one person that can break through. It's the reason I'm standing outside his door right now.

Ever since I learned everything from Ryan, I've done a whole lot of research into angels, vessels and what happens when you allow one to take you over completely. They need permission first. At first I thought it might be a problem but since Lucifer had tortured a yes out of him once before, I'm starting to think that's why Ryan pointed me in his direction. He knew it would be easier for the fallen one to get through than Michael.

With Maria gone, I only hope he does his normal routine. As much as it hurts watching other girls leaving his room, especially after what almost happened between us a couple of days ago, I can't let it detract me from why I'm really here. He's not even mine anyway, so what he does with other girls shouldn't matter. What does matter is ending this once and for all.

The rest of the world is moving on as if nothing's happened. It's time that Graham gets to do the same. Thanks to Kyle, I know he'll move to the memory blocking portion of the evening any time now. With no distractions around him, he'll want to drink until he can't feel the pain anymore and as I stand only a few steps away from his door, prepared at any second to enter, I pray that he does just that.

I only hope when we do go through with this and he's brought back, he doesn't hate me too much for who I had to go to in order to make it happen. With as bad as he is right now with the way he treats me and everyone else around him, I can't imagine what it will feel like to get him back only to lose him again.

Michael

"Well little brother, you're looking mighty human today."
"Oh Michael, if only you realized how much I missed this."

It's no surprise with what is about to take place that I am recalling the first time I came across Graham. It is true that I had known him before, but not in this particular lifetime. This one was different, as it belonged to Gabriel and not me. Seeing Gabriel enter the gates, having completely taken over the boy, I did not realize at the time the warrior that stood before me.

He had proven himself during our time in Hell, but that day with Gabriel, it had been only about ribbing my brother about wearing his meat suit home. It is not often we bring our vessels home with us, but given everything Gabriel faced at the time, it had not been all that surprising. It is a memory I look back on fondly and not only because it is one that my brother and I shared. It is because it was my first glimpse at the man that despite everything he has endured since; is one of the purest humans ever created.

I often wish I had paid more attention in those days, that in doing so I might have been able to prevent what is now taking place below.

He is the throws of another nightmare, this one even worse than the last and I am again reminded of my earlier talk with

Lucifer. If this did not cease, it would only be a matter of time before Graham Hudson was lost to us forever. We would not lose him to the dark side as it no longer exists, but we would lose him inside of himself and then to death. It is something that I cannot allow a second longer, despite Father's insistence that we let it play out the way it is meant to.

"She's called for Lucifer. It is only a matter of time now, Michael."

"Do you believe this is the right course of action?"

"There is no other way for it to play out, my son."

"I could easily be the one there to heal him. What I am asking is, are you positive that Lucifer needs to be the one to do this?"

"Is this more sibling rivalry I am sensing?"

"No, it is merely me making sure you have thought all of this through. It was not all that long ago when Lucifer had you wrapped around his finger. He manipulated you as easily as he did Gabriel in the beginning."

"I am well aware of what the old power did to your brother. I am also aware of what that meant for me. This time is different Michael. I know you are still coming to terms with everything that has happened, but you must trust not only in me, but Serenity and your brother. She did the right thing."

"You misunderstand me, Father. I am not questioning the choices made previously. I am concerned about Lucifer's readiness for this undertaking."

"I do believe you also want to be the one there with the Hudson boy because you see a bit of yourself within him. Am I correct?"

There is truth in that statement and I cannot deny it. I do see myself in Graham, though he has experienced far worse than I ever have. Whether that is because I am an archangel and made for battle, I am unsure, but what he is experiencing now is a level of darkness I am not accustomed to. He is stronger than I am, of that I am sure.

"Yes, Father. I want to be the one to heal him. It is not only because of the similarities between me and the boy, but I feel it would be the right thing to do by Gabriel."

"Lucifer wants the same thing. We must give him a chance sometime. The Daniels girl was right when they spoke. This is his chance to right his wrongs in a way that will be felt for years to come. This is his undertaking."

It very well might be Lucifer's undertaking, but it did not help the unease I felt about putting Graham through this with the very person that made it happen to begin with. When Graham woke up, he should be surrounded by the parts of the light that had never hurt him, not the darkness that created it.

"Father, I mean no disrespect with what I am about to say, but I fear if I don't say it, it will do us all a great disservice."

"Speak your mind, Michael."

"The humans have a saying. A leopard never changes his spots. Lucifer is the leopard in this case. I know that you want to readily accept that he has changed and I do as well, but I am not there yet. It will take quite some time before that happens. I want to make sure that moving forward with this, Graham Hudson is protected."

"Then what are you waiting for?"

"What does that mean?"

"If you are concerned about Graham and I can see that you are, then there is only one place that you need to be and it is not here standing with me."

He motions to what we are witnessing below and the moment he does, a relief washes over me the likes of which I have never known before. He understands my place and he is allowing me the chance to be where I need to be.

"You were always meant to be there, Michael. I may believe in Lucifer more than you, but it does not mean I am completely trusting in him, especially as it pertains to the other half of Serenity's soul. So you need to be there and you must make sure that in doing so, everything goes exactly the way it is supposed to."

"How is it supposed to go, Father? What do you know that I do not?"

"It is time to bring Graham Hudson back into the light, right where he belongs."

Chapter Ten

Emma

There's something about this that doesn't feel right.

Michael is here, which should put me at ease, but it's not having the desired effect. Lucifer is standing over a very passed out Graham and despite saying he's here to do the right thing, the look in his eye says otherwise.

I could be blowing this entire thing out of proportion and the look I see could only be one that Gregory himself is making, but I think there's more to it than that. His eyes are lit up and even though I've seen that same look in Serenity's eyes before and been ecstatic because of it, it's not having the same result now.

You know when you tease a dog with a treat or something equally as tempting that it wants and it starts whipping its tail around, tongue hanging out and an almost delicious gleam appears in its eyes? That's what Lucifer looks like now as he stands over Graham wearing a smile; eyes deadlocked on his sleeping form.

Yes, there is something definitely wrong about this. I'm not sure I made the right decision going to him and now Graham is going to pay for it.

I know how it appears Emma, but I am asking you to trust me if you cannot trust him.

Is it too much to ask to have an actual thought that isn't seen by some higher being? It's not the first time it's happened, but I can already tell I'm going to hate it. Sometimes I just like to have thoughts and have them remain my own, with no other input.

My apologies, Emma. I know how uncomfortable all of these changes can be for a human and it is not my intent to make them worse. I can sense your distrust of my brother and I only wish to make it better.

"I think you should've been the one to do this."

I want nothing more than to heal the man lying before us now, but as hard as it is to admit, it is not my place. This is Lucifer's task. I am merely here to make sure it goes the way it is meant to.

"Will this make him better? Like, for sure?"

Yes. After speaking with Father, it appears as though that is exactly what will transpire. You must have faith in that.

"What if he's healed, but isn't the Graham from before?"

I know it's a stupid question and it shouldn't matter, but when I went to Lucifer to begin with, it was to bring Graham back to the way he was before. Nothing else is acceptable to me.

Graham will never be the man he was before this happened to him. Change is inevitable, Emma, as is growth. He will come back to the very light that has guided him thus far, but he will not be exactly as he was.

Well that didn't sound good at all. I mean sure, everyone changes, hell, I've changed a lot over the years, but for Graham, with what he's already been through, I'm not entirely sure change is a good thing.

He will be better, Emma. When Lucifer finishes what he is meant to do, you will see it for yourself and all of your worries will fade away.

"You sound so sure—"

Have you forgotten who I am? I am not as all seeing and knowing as my father, but when I do speak, it is in truth and fact only.

"I just want this over with already. If he wakes up before Lucifer is finished with him..."

I cut off, knowing that the angel knows exactly what I'm getting at. Graham wants nothing to do with Lucifer, no matter how good he's attempting to be, and if he ever gets wind of just who had been the one to help him, he would never get over it. He would never forgive it, which means, he would never forgive me.

There will come a day when Graham will learn of exactly what has been done here, and by who, Emma. You must accept that day when it comes and own the choice that you made in reaching out to my fallen brother the way that you did. Despite what you believe, you have done right by Graham and even if he doesn't see it at first, he will eventually.

"I wish I could be as secure as you seem to be."

I am not as secure as I appear, I assure you. I have questions and doubts where Lucifer is concerned, but I have to put them in the background if I want to move forward in the way that we are all meant to. This is all about peace for all and no one deserves that more than the man in that bed now.

I don't feel as alone in the way I'm feeling after hearing Michael tell me how he feels. If his own brother can't trust him, then the doubts I have with what's about to happen seem okay. It's natural for all of us to doubt the fallen angel given what he put all of us through.

"Thank you, Michael."

For what? Speaking the truth?

"Yeah, I guess so."

May I ask you something?

"Sure." I answer easily, not sure what he could possibly want to know that's not already public knowledge, but more than willing to answer.

Seeing Graham in this state, wanting to fix it, it's about more than just your feelings for him, is it not?

"I don't know what you're talking about."

I apologize. What I mean to say is, seeing him in this way, it's reminding you of your own hardships, which only makes your need to fix it that much stronger.

I gotta admit, I've never really thought about it like that before, but the angel makes a good point. It's not a secret that I care about Graham, probably more than I've cared about anyone other than maybe Cody, but there's definitely more to it.

After spending years in the center, all the while believing myself to be a broken mess and not worthy of anyone's attention, much less love, I sympathized more than I wanted to admit with what Graham is going through. I also get the stubbornness. He wanted to handle it on his own because he didn't want to put anyone else through the darkness he was experiencing. Until I met Serenity, I was the same way. I kept all of it inside, not daring to let anyone see what really lied underneath.

I guess Michael has the answer to his question, or rather, statement. I'm doing this because this reminds me of what I experienced.

"Yeah, it's eerily similar to what I went through."

What you are still going through.

Way to get right to it. "Yeah, that too."

It is not my intent to make you uncomfortable, Emma. I am merely making an observation. As healed as you appear to be, there is still loneliness under the surface that has not been handled.

"Anyone ever tell you that you're too observant for your own good?"

Every day it seems.

"Well, alright then."

Michael, Emma. It is time.

Lucifer

The last time I was in this position, I had broken the man down until he was only a shell of his former self. It appears now, as I stand beside him, preparing not only myself, but him for what is about to happen next, not much has changed.

That shell of his former being is the way he remained after my time with him, though as evidenced by the way he appeared during his time in Hell standing before me, he tried desperately to appear as normal as possible. He is anything but the Graham Hudson of old and it is up to me now to rectify that.

Michael, Emma. It is time.

The Daniels girl may have no issue speaking out loud as she stands in the room with us, unafraid of the man sleeping soundly before me waking at the sound of her voice, but I did not feel the same. It is evidenced with Michael's choice to speak within her mind that he feels the same way. If we want this to work the way we have planned it to, then we must not do anything that could risk it.

Graham waking up to find me standing above him in the manner at which I am now would spell disaster, not only for my brother and me, but for Emma. He would look at her with different eyes than he has in the past and I cannot afford to let that happen. It is obvious that both of these humans need one another and care a great deal so it has to come to pass that they get to enjoy that. They must not have it torn apart before it even begins.

I am not sure if she is aware of it, but Emma is deeply troubled by something that pertains to the man I am now here to heal and it is so strong within her that it is making focusing on anything else nearly impossible. Whether it has to do with something that has taken place between the two of them recently or something completely unrelated, I cannot be sure without reading her thoughts. There is no denying its power to distract from the primary goal.

"Emma, please free your mind of all thought. With what I am about to do, I cannot be focused on anything other than healing the damage I have done."

Confusion is evident in her eyes, but she listens because within seconds, my mind is clear again and I am able to completely focus on what must happen next.

Placing my hand in the center of Graham's chest, I watch as the light appears and I watch with wonder as it grows until it is covering not only the man I am here to heal, but me as well. It has been so long since I have used the power for good that seeing it now in its true form, takes my breath away. This is the way it was always meant to be used despite the way I had turned it and it pleases me to be able to access it again.

As my form melds together with his, I am fused with a power and strength of which I have never known. For all of the pain and darkness evident within him, it is obvious that he is still very much the warrior he was in times past. He has not been stripped entirely of that which made him great. I am reminded of why he had been chosen in the beginning, not only by me, but by Gabriel. It was this very force within him now that drew beings both of light and darkness to him. I only hope that I can harness that very strength and bring him back to a much better state of mind.

Stepping into his mind is not a pretty sight. Even in his comatose slumber, he is haunted by our time together. It is these fragmented pieces that I not only need to heal, but bring together with happier times in order to lift him out of this mind numbing haze he has found himself in.

When I captured him, he was meant to be a means to an end and it was my hope that I would only have to use memory control over him. That is not how it turned out in the end. I used not only that method of torture, but physical torture as well. I had destroyed him, inside and out and despite knowing that I am the only one that can see this through to its end, I also doubt my ability to make all of this right.

Spending as much time as I have living in the darkness, letting it guide me and all of my decisions, it is not surprising that there are doubts about my ability to do the right thing. It has been centuries since I have had the chance to do the right thing and with that much time between my last good deed, I have to wonder if I can do this at all.

Remember what you are here to do, brother. Do not even think of turning back now.

Serenity has been trying for weeks to bring Michael and I back together and it appears to have been working, at least it had until I stepped foot into this room a mere hour before. He has been untrusting of me ever since and while I do not blame him; I do wish he could see that my intentions in this regard are only pure. I want to do the right thing by Graham, even if the rest of the world believes otherwise.

It is not doubt that you are feeling from me, brother. I only mean to keep you on your assigned goal as it pertains to the doubts you are having.

I can do this, Michael.

Then get on with it. Time is of the essence.

It is with those words, reminding me again that I only have a limited amount of time in which to do this, that I begin the arduous task of cleaning up what remains of Graham's mind. Putting every ounce of my remaining power into the task, I piece together the parts of him that are clearly torn apart and I watch as the light fuses around it, tightening the hold. I am repairing him from the ground up and the light is again guiding the entire process.

What had been covered in haze before is now shining in brightness. It will only be a short period of time before he awakens to find himself feeling better. It will be his first experience with that particular way of being in two years.

It has been done, Michael. I will now begin to extricate myself from him as promised. It is now up to you what happens next.

With his mind now clear, I begin work on his body, healing his very human liver as it appears to be damaged from the sheer amount of alcohol he has been pouring into it over the last few months. Struggling under the weight of my own light and power, I set to work cleaning up every part of him that my darkness has changed. It is only when I allow myself to be completely at rest within him that I see that all my work has not been for naught.

Graham Hudson has been healed.

Graham

There's been one thing I can always depend on when I wake up in the middle of the night. It's been that way for months, but where I expect it now, it's not happening and I have no idea why.

The deeper into my despair I go; the more I seem to take it out on myself. Waking up now though, there's no new marks, no blood, not even the faint trace of the rusty smell I've come to recognize easily. In fact, I don't feel much of anything at all.

Where I expect to feel the after effects of the singular drinking party I took myself on a few hours ago when the girl, Marcia, Marie, whatever her name was left, it's not there. I don't have a headache for the first time in forever and it's like I never drank at all.

Honestly, if I didn't know for a fact that I did it, as evidenced by the empty bottle on the table beside my bed, I'd think I imagined everything that happened. There is no way I can feel this clear after everything I've done tonight. It's impossible. Yet, that's exactly what's happening.

For the first time in months, maybe even years, I feel alive.

Michael.

The warrior angel that pretended not to care when in reality he cared a lot more than even he realized wanted nothing more than to put me back together. In fact, he tried to get through to me only a few days before. Is it possible that he went against his own training and did something to me without my consent?

It's entirely possible. Gabriel had done things, years before that didn't exactly go along with what his father wanted from him, so of course Michael could do the same. The only problem with thinking that way is, Michael is even more of a stickler for rules than God himself is. He wouldn't go against his family or even Serenity to do this. As much as he wants to heal the damage done to me by Lucifer, he wouldn't have gone through a back door to do it.

There's no other explanation though. I know I drank ninety percent of a bottle of Jack Daniels tonight, feeling the warmth all the way through my body before and after I had fun with the girl I brought back to my room during my trip to the liquor store. I shouldn't even be able to think at all right now, much less this much.

I can't deny it though, whether he did something to me or not. For the first time in two years, I feel like me again and it feels pretty damn good.

Sliding out of the bed, I stand and stretch, waiting for my body to in some way to react to the violation that even moving at all often brings, but I'm met with nothing. I'm completely limber, able to bend, stretch and move without the slightest bit of pain to any of my limbs that before would be screaming in agony.

The marks that have run up and down my arms for weeks, breaking open after each and every nightmare I faced, are now healed to the point where they don't look as though they'll ever break open and spill blood again. They are fresh of course, so I know that whatever is happening to me isn't because of actual healing, but the fact that they look as healthy and clean as they do is surprising.

Everything about this is startling and I don't know what the hell to do with it. I want answers, but I don't even have the questions to ask in order to get them. I want to call Michael and demand the truth about why I feel so good, but something tells me he won't be able to tell me. Whatever's happening to me, it couldn't have been him because he needs permission to even touch me at all.

This is all wrong. I'm not supposed to feel this good. I'm not supposed to walk around without my heart racing out of my chest, craving the next time I can be alone and drink the pain away. Where the sunlight spills through my curtains now, it shouldn't be. I've spent months going out of my way to avoid all things pertaining to the light, even in its most basic form and here it is now shining through as if it's a new day and I am a new me.

As wrong as I believe all of this to be, I can't help feeling happy about it at the same time, which just confuses me even more. For the first time in so long, I feel like I can get up out of bed, out of the room and enter the world again, doing the complete opposite of what I've been doing all these months. I want to live again.

There's more though. It's not only about the need to live for me. It's about who I want to share the living with. There's only one person that even at my darkest point, didn't walk away. I might have scared her, done things to her that I can never take back, but she never left despite all of it.

I only hope as I make my way to the closet in search of the cleanest thing I can find that when I finally do make my way out into the world, with one clear destination in mind, she doesn't shut the door in my face the way I deserve.

Emma.

I need to see Emma.

Chapter Eleven

Emma

I've been through a lot of things in my life, but there's nothing I've gone through so far that compares to what I went through six hours ago.

Walking out of that room after what felt like hours of prodding from Michael, was singlehandedly the worst experience of my life and that's saying something. I couldn't do as he asked. My feet were planted firmly in the carpeting of Graham's floor and they showed no signs of moving at all. I couldn't leave him, not after what I just watched him go through.

I wanted to be there when he woke up. It might be selfish, but I wanted to be the one that experienced the way Graham felt when he opened his eyes and realized he wasn't shrouded in the dark anymore. I wanted to see his face shining with light.

I'm starting to sound a lot like my best friend.

Up until six months ago, I never knew a thing about what she was going through. I'd had an angel screw with my memories in order to keep it from me. I was blissfully unaware of the real supernatural beings that are a part of this world. I was so naïve and stupid, but not entirely, because somewhere deep down I always knew Gabriel was an angel, even before I learned about it.

I was your average human girl, screwed up by the hand life dealt her and just going on my merry way, faking it as much as possible at every turn. Now, I know everything and I swear knowing it has turned me into Serenity. I see things in terms of light and dark, good and evil and there's no amount of blocking it out that I can do that changes it.

Watching what I did as Lucifer worked on Graham a few hours ago, it changed something inside of me. I no longer want to block out everything I'm being shown. I want to embrace it because that goodness that I knew was in him from the start, well, I know now it's actually light. It's the same light Serenity is made of and knowing it makes it call to me even more.

My heart ached for him when Lucifer took control. There was a brief moment where I thought he would possess him and do what he had before, but once that passed, it just ached and hurt because I could see the random movements he was making under the angels control and I hated that he had no idea it was happening at all. All of these changes were happening inside of him and he had to be completely out of it. He should have been able to experience everything with Lucifer and because he didn't, it hurt me.

I should be on cloud nine right now, but I'm not. I have no idea if what he did even worked because Michael wanted us out of there after it was over. I couldn't stay to check on him because in doing so, I would have tipped him off to what actually happened and he would hate me forever. I understood the logic of making myself scarce, but it didn't mean I had to like doing it.

I'm the one that put this in motion. Knowing that I'm the reason someone might be themselves again should make me beyond happy and deep down, it does, but I'm not sure I can live with the fact that it's all happening in secret.

When I see him again, I need to act as though I know nothing about why he's the way he is and play a role flawlessly based on his own reaction to whatever changes happened since Lucifer put him back together. I'm not the only one that's going to have to play a role. Michael, who is still guarding over him, will have to do much the same the minute Graham brings it to him and I've got no doubt he'll do that.

Michael will be his first stop. There's no way he would wake up, feel different and not take it right to the angel. He's going to go there and do the same thing I did when Ryan told me the truth about everything. He's going to accuse Michael of being the one that changed him.

I'm happy I'm not an angel right about now, even though I'm pretty sure Michael can handle himself just fine. It's like Gabriel all over again.

"So is it true?"

There's been a set of girls behind me since I left the dorm and they've been talking back and forth the entire time. It's easy to ignore what's going on around me with everything I've got to think about, but it's only when the one girl repeats herself that I realize they're actually talking to me this time.

"Is what true?" I ask as I turn around to face them.

"That you and Graham Hudson hooked up at the Pi Sig party?"

I don't know exactly when it happened, but the guy that wanted nothing more than to go under the radar when he got here two years ago is now king of the campus. I've been hearing girls talk about him for awhile now, but I blocked it because if they were talking about him, it meant they would leave me alone.

When you make your way through half the girls on campus though, I suppose it lifts your popularity a little. He had it coming and I can't help but get satisfaction from it because Graham is the last person that wants that.

"Rumor, just like everything else you've heard."

"You're such a liar Emma! Sarah totally saw you two go into one of the rooms!"

Sarah. Of course. I have no idea who Sarah is, but with the way they're making it sound, she's the go to person for all the Pi Sig hookup news.

"Don't believe everything you hear. Nothing happened with Graham and me."

"Sarah never lies."

"Well she is this time. Sorry to burst your bubble, but Graham Hudson means nothing to me."

"Really?" A new voice interrupts and my stomach drops. I don't even need to turn to see who it is. I know the sound by heart already.

Graham. Here and overhearing everything I just said.

"Oh hey, Graham! That was such an awesome party wasn't it?"

I'm ashamed to admit that I'm a girl right now. With the way these two are batting their eyes in his direction, the devilish grins all over their faces, letting him and the rest of the world know exactly what they want from him, it's just a sad day to be a woman.

"I didn't stay long, so I wouldn't know. Look, as nice as it is to see you both, you think I can steal Emma here for a minute?"

Great. I tell them that there's nothing going on with me and him and now he wants to talk to me. I'm happy to see that he's up and among the living again, but he's seriously making me look like a big fat liar right now.

You were lying.

Both girls nod, gushing at him, but doing exactly as he asked and making themselves scarce. It's only when I know we're alone that I finally let myself look at him.

The Graham I see the minute my eyes connect is one that I haven't seen since the day I caught him in my bed with Serenity. His eyes are shining again, the green brighter then it's been in months, which only lightens the peach color of his skin that in recent weeks had looked almost dull and grey in comparison.

It worked.

Whatever Lucifer did to him put everything right again. He's gorgeous.

"So, we're nothing to each other, huh?"

"They were being nosy. I wasn't going to add to it. It's like Gossip Girl around here enough already or have you not noticed?"

"I've been out of it, not blind, Ems. I know what it's like around here."

"Yeah, I figured as much." I say with a nonchalant shrug, pretending not to care that he's standing in front of me and looking better than ever. "So when are you bringing those two back to your room?"

I know I sound like a total bitch, but I can't let him believe for a second that I'm taken in by the change in him. I need to act like it doesn't get to me so that he never finds out I had something to do with it.

"Um, that would be—never?"

Oh god, that's such a good answer.

"Okay then. Well, it was nice to see you. I need to get to class."

"Emma—wait!" he calls as I turn my back to him and as much as I want to will my legs to walk, they totally betray me and stay completely still. Have I mentioned I really hate being me?

Do not be that girl right now. Do not turn around.

"Something happened to me."

Shit. Now I really can't turn around.

"I know I'm not making any sense and I'm sure you wanna be anywhere but here right now, but I needed to share it with someone. I need to share it with you."

I'm going to give in. I can't stand here with my back to him when he's saying things this way and not react. I know that I need to just move my feet and walk into class, pretending that I don't care about anything he has to say, but I'm Emma Daniels and I don't ever do that. I always turn around and listen.

"What does that even mean?"

"Um—what part?"

"Something happening to you?" I answer easily though it's not entirely the truth. I want to know what he means by needing to tell me, but if I open myself up that far, I'll never be able to come back from it. So, this way it is.

"I feel stronger, lighter somehow. Emma, I feel better."

"That's great. I'm happy for you." I say, again turning my body away from his, even more desperate to get the hell out of here before I spill my guts. It's only a matter of time before it happens. I've never been good at keeping secrets.

Before I can do it though, he reaches out and just like the day outside his room, he turns me back to him, preventing my getaway.

"About the other night—I'm sorry. I wasn't myself. I know it's no excuse, which is all I've been giving you lately, but I mean it."

Yeah, he's most definitely not the same guy from a couple days ago. He's not even the Graham he's been for the past three months. He's the one that my best friend fell in love with five years ago.

"Forget about it. I already have."

"I don't believe that."

"Well, not sure what to tell you then. What happened that night, it's not something I'm spending all my time thinking about."

"I know I was a dick to you, but why are you acting like this?"

"I'm not sure what you mean."

"You're acting cold, like you don't give a shit about any of it, when I'm pretty damn sure you do."

"So you're all better now and it gives you the right to make assumptions? You know what they say about assuming, Graham."

Yanking my arm out of his, not waiting for him to release it nicely, I turn again and this time I walk as quickly as I can for the door that will take me safely to my class and away from him. It's bitchy and it's crazy, but the longer I stand there, that close to him, the more hazardous to my health it becomes.

"Emma!" I hear him yell across the grass at me. "You're gonna have to stop running sometime!"

Graham

I've got a lot of work to do.

If it wasn't so damn serious, I'd laugh at how my life seems to be a cycle of repeated moments. Having a girl run from me, should be a first, but it's not. When I showed up here under Gabriel's advice, Serenity had seen me and taken off too. I know they're best friends and all, but did they really have to be this alike?

The fact that she even said two words to me makes me happy. I'd been dreading seeing her even though I spent the first part of the morning going first to her room, then the coffee shop she frequents in an effort to find her. I didn't lie when I said I needed to share things with her, but I knew it wasn't going to be easy.

The way she deliberately went out of her way to act like she didn't give a shit though, that was new. That is not her at all. I admit, most of the time I've spent around her lately has usually had something to do with Serenity, but even then, she never acted like she didn't care. The truth is; Emma cares a whole hell of a lot more than she lets on. It's written all over her face every time I'm near her.

Ryan told me that I need to fix my shit and that's exactly what I intend to do. However it happened that I feel the way I do now doesn't matter, it's only important that I do. It means that all the crap I put my friends though, people I genuinely love and care about, I can now work on rebuilding. Emma has to be my first stop with it. I hurt her worst of all.

She wanted to be with me that night because she liked me, but I can't blame her for the way everything went down even though I wasn't alone in it. This is on me because even when she wanted to slow down, I still pushed myself at her, just like I did before. All of that's over though, it won't happen again and I swear, this time when I promise her that I'm going to fix it, I mean it.

Most guys would give up, seeing the girl run away from them the way Emma did, but I know why she's doing it so I'm not going anywhere. I won't be like every other person she's had in her life. Now that I seem to be back on solid ground, I'm not giving up on her. I've never done that with anyone and I don't plan on starting now, even if it's what she wants me to do.

It's time for her to meet the real Graham, the one she should have known from the start. Not the one that's possessed or head over heels hung up on the girl next door. I want her to know the real me, what lies underneath and I want her to trust me again. At one point she'd done it, even when I lied to her best friend and tried making her believe something that wasn't even remotely true. She'd seen the darkest parts of me and never left and that's what I want to earn back now. I want the Emma that's just like me. The one that never gives up, even when everything in her tells her to do otherwise.

I don't have the first clue how to fix all of this, but I do know what the first step needs to be. She's been bringing me my work for weeks and that's the class she's running into now in order to get away from me. The class we share. If I want to show her that I really am different the way I claimed, then the first step is to get my ass into English Lit, in my spot right behind her and make sure she knows beyond a shadow of a doubt that I'm here to stay.

It's time to show Emma that she's not the only one that likes someone, because the very person she likes; just might like her back.

Chapter Twelve

Emma

I'm not sure what's worse. Having Ashley shooting me death glares the entire class or feeling Graham's eyes on me at the same time. I figure both are equally bad, but since my awesome plan of changing seats managed to fail, I'm gonna say that everything with him is far worse.

Death glares are familiar. Graham's eye on me so often that I feel the hairs on the back of my neck standing up, is most definitely not.

When I got into the class, I saw my seat and took a detour. If he's up and around that means he's coming back to classes. I want him to come in, go for his seat and once seated realize that this time he won't have me in front to keep him company. That was supposed to serve him right, except it didn't.

The minute he came in, he scanned the room. That was my first mistake. Believing that he would just head right for his normal seat. The second mistake was choosing a spot that had am empty chair right behind it. If I'm going to try and be shifty, the least I could do is think it through all the way before putting it into motion. He spotted me and immediately threw himself into the seat behind and it's been hell ever since.

"You wanna tell me what the point of learning about the 16th Century Renaissance is?" he whispers, his body angled into mine so closely I can feel his breath against my skin.

"To make Neanderthals more cultured?"

"Are you calling me an ape, Emma?"

"If the shoe fits."

He laughs and despite every attempt not to let it affect me, it hits its mark and I shiver. I really wish he'd just move back in his seat. Having him this close is going to drive me crazy pretty quickly and I need to keep my wits. I can't let yet another guy get to me, even if it's Graham and not someone random.

"If I spend my life painting the way I want to, do you think I'll need to know any of this?"

"If you don't want to be here, why'd you take the class at all?"

"Serenity."

"Yeah and she's not here anymore. So I guess that was a big fat fail huh?"

Shit. That came out a lot worse than I wanted it too. I know Serenity is a sore subject for him, especially now that she's off married to Ryan and even worse, sickeningly happy. Even if Lucifer healed him, there's no way in hell that my comment wouldn't sting.

"The biggest fail ever, I think."

Well, that's unexpected.

"You can still transfer out. I mean, it's not like you spend much time here anyway."

"I would do that, but it's not a total fail after all. I think I might actually like learning about the Renaissance."

I might not be the most experienced when it comes to sex, but I am damn good at picking up on cues, especially flirting and that is definitely what Graham is attempting to do right now. The thing is, as lame as it could have been, coming from him, it works. I can feel my heart start to pump faster the minute the words slip.

"Have fun with that."

The professor chooses that minute to speak and I silently thank the academic gods for the reprieve. As easy as it should be to sit here and banter back and forth with Graham, it's anything but. I've never wanted a class to start so much in my life because the way I'm feeling is something I don't want to think about, much less acknowledge.

It's obvious though that whatever plans I had to focus on the class and not the guy behind me will fail as epically as my choice of seating did because he speaks again and this time he's even closer then he was before. So close not only do I feel his breath on my ear through my hair, but I can also smell him and boy, does he smell good.

Graham's smell is deadly for girls. He smells like chocolate and as far as I know, other than people that are allergic, there isn't a female alive that is repulsed by chocolate. In fact we're the whole reason that holidays involving it sell so well. We enjoy it almost as much as we enjoy breathing.

"So, after class, you think we can meet up and go over everything I've missed?"

Is he actually suggesting a study date?

"You don't need help, Graham. I've seen the work you've been handing in when you give it to me. It's perfect."

"Maybe so, but I have a feeling with what he's talking about now, I'm going to need all the extra help I can get. So what do you say?"

There was a point a few days ago where I would have killed for him to be this way with me. To let me past the darkness burning so deeply in him, allowing me to get close, even if only to study or something equally as boring and mundane. Now though, I'm not sure how I feel about it.

Going back to his room isn't something I'm looking forward to considering what happened the last time we were alone in a room together. Add that to all of the girls he's brought back there over the last few months and well it's not all that inviting. It's not like my room is any better though. As safe as I feel there, it's lonely as hell without Serenity and right now being alone with Graham isn't high on my to-do list.

"I don't think that's such a good idea."

"It's studying, Ems and considering what you've been doing for me the last few weeks, I figure it's something you should be more than okay with."

Bringing his work to him and having the door slammed in my face and going to our rooms and studying alone together are two completely different things and he has to know it.

"Why don't you ask Ashley? With the way she's looking at us right now, I'm pretty sure she'll help you with whatever it is you need help with."

"I don't want Ashley, I want you."

I want you.

Why does that simple statement have to get to me so bad? My body shivers again and I hear him laugh lightly. So not only am I reacting, but he's witnessing it. Can I be any more transparent?

"If it's about what happened at the party, we can grab coffee and study there."

Of course he's going to give me a safety option. Doing that makes it impossible to say no. The guy you have a thing for breathes in your ear, making your skin crawl in a good way, suggesting that he wants you to be the one he studies with and in an open area no less and you'd have to be completely out of your mind to say no.

"Fine," I answer with a sigh. "On one condition."

"Name it."

"For the rest of the class you keep your mouth shut. If I'm going to help you, I'm going to need to know what the hell I'm helping you with."

"Deal."

I feel the air around me shift and I realize it's because he's leaning back in his seat again and I'm finally able to breathe. I have my doubts that he's going to do what I ask of him, but the more time that passes without another word, I realize that again, another plan backfired.

I'm going to have to study with Graham and the worst part is, I'm actually happy about it.

Graham

My freshman year of high school, while everyone was trying to figure out their place and exactly what it is they're good at, I did something completely out of character.

I've never been much of a sports guy. In fact, I pretty much blow at any sport I've ever tried to be a part of. I'm not athletically inclined or whatever they call it and I'm okay with that. In ninth grade, I had no idea just how bad I sucked, so I tried out for track and found the one thing I was actually pretty good at.

Hurdles.

Yeah, I know its funny right? As big a guy as I am, you would think I would be Quarterback of the football team or maybe even a super fast soccer player, but nope, I sucked at both of those and busted ass to be the best damn hurdler that Green Haven High ever had. It's embarrassing as hell but relevant to what I'm facing.

Working my way back into Emma's good graces is a lot like hurdles. The sprint that you take at the start as you prepare your legs for the inevitable jump and the prayer that comes along with it that you make it over and not trip and fall flat on your face. It's definitely a lot like that.

I don't want to fall on my face with Emma. I want to jump the hurdles, one at a time and at a pace where I don't end up destroyed by the end of it. I need to do right by this girl, which is where the sprint comes in. The first hurdle was getting her to agree to even speak with me once I showed up behind her.

The first one is always easiest and my ability to get to her and have her answer me despite her attempt to hide from me proves it. The second one, well I have to admit I was prepared to fall flat on my face. Once the momentum's hit, you're still praying, but you're also a little cocky at the same time. I didn't go into this one cocky, but man, I did pray a whole lot that I'd get over this one too. She had to agree to spend time with me.

The thing is, she's right. I don't need the help. I could pass this course blindfolded, no lie. It's a whole lot of reading and discussing, but there's not much else to it. I mean there is the course work, the written portions, but I can write and read better than anyone. Before Serenity came into my life, that's pretty much all I did. Well, when I wasn't going to parties just to shut people up. I don't need her, but if studying is the thing that opens the door so I can make up for everything, I'm going to use the hell out of it.

She minute she agreed, I hit the cocky portion of my hurdle jump. I was literally flying from it. It's been a long time since I've felt this excited about something, but there's no denying how fucking amazing it feels.

It's like I'm back in high school all over again. It's not a game to me, but with the way I acted in high school and the way other guys and even girls did, it kind of is a game. It's a game of back and forth and one-upmanship. She is trying to get the best of me and I'm fighting back doing the same thing with her. We're trying to one up each other and it's hilarious.

I wasn't like most guys in high school, only loving one girl my entire time there, but I have to figure what I'm experiencing now is how it felt for the others back then. Things haven't felt this good in a long ass time.

She's waiting for me to break and talk to her. I want to do it too. Sitting back here, with no one around me but her and a couple of people on her left, I mean there's not much else to do besides talk since I'm bored out of my mind. I won't do it though. She wants it to happen so that the condition she gave me can be broken and she can get out of what she agreed to.

It's one-upmanship at its finest. The thing is, I can play this better than she can. I'm a guy for crying out loud. I don't need to talk. I can just sit here and watch her drive herself crazy, smiling the entire time, not a care in the world. So that's exactly what I do.

By the time the class ends and I successfully fulfill her one requirement, I'm more than ready to talk to her again. Even the look she shoots my way as she gathers up her books and starts making her way from the class can't deter me. She's disappointed that I can play the game better than her and all I want to do is laugh.

She has every right not to trust me, but with the looks I get, I can tell that she's starting to see that I'm not the same guy I was that night and she hates that I'm not a total asshole after all.

"So do you wanna go to Java Hut?"

"It doesn't matter to me. You pick the spot, seeing as you're the one helping me out here."

Studying is the last thing on my mind and even though I love a good cup of coffee lately, that's not making the list at all. I want to get her alone and talk to her about what happened between us at the party. It might not be the smartest move right away, but it's a hurdle and it's one I want to deal with at the start because by the end I'm gonna be too winded to get to it.

I've been doing a lot of thinking about that night, with not being able to talk to her during the class and I think I've sorted it all out in my head. I don't mean I've sorted out what I want to say to her because I don't have the first clue what I'm going to say, but how I feel about it and why it even happened at all, that's what I've sorted.

I can blame possession and darkness on a lot of what's happened between me and her, but it's got nothing to do with it. I've found Emma attractive from the first time Serenity showed me her picture and we all might have gotten a bit older and been through a lot more shit since then, but it didn't go away. She's gorgeous. Finding her gorgeous doesn't lead where we ended up though. That's a whole other bag of nuts and ones I'm not sure I'm ready to admit to even though it's staring me in the face.

There is a whole lot more to Emma then her beauty. Sure, she looks like she should be attached to some blonde haired California surfer with her light hair and crystal blue eyes, but underneath the body and the sun-kissed skin, there's a soft hearted girl that loves hard and deep when she allows herself to. It's obvious in the way she is with Serenity.

I've heard a lot of things about her since I moved here and I gotta admit, I bought into a lot of it, but the more time I spend around her, I know I was wrong to do it. She's not what other people make her out to be and I'm a heel for believing it for a second when the only side I've ever been shown of her has been one that makes her one of the sweetest human beings alive.

That night at the party, wanting her as badly as I did might have been because of the alcohol a bit, but it was more than that. I wanted her because I like her. I like the way she makes me feel when I'm around her and just like that day outside my room when she wanted to walk away and I wouldn't let her, I can't let her run away now. That light feeling I had playing along with her demands in class, I couldn't get it anywhere else.

It's only with Emma.

It's what makes talking to her about everything important. I want to put it out there. Do I think the best way to get her to look at me differently is to tell her how I feel about her? No, but I do think that she needs to know that I didn't bring her into that room solely to screw her and leave.

"I'm starting to see it now."

"See what?" I ask the minute I hear her voice again.

"You and Serenity."

"What about us?"

"The whole soul-mate thing. Two identical pieces split apart."

I have no idea what she's getting at, but I'm curious.

"Explain?"

"She does the same thing you just did. You zoned out on me and had the same expression she gets when she does it."

"Oh, okay."

There used to be a time where any mention of Serenity would cause a few different reactions in me. Most of them were good reactions, but after she married Ryan, it was always just an ache. Emma bringing her up now though, it doesn't do anything, good or bad. It is what it is. It's another way I'm different, but one I'm thankful for. Any time I can spend without an ache in my chest is welcome.

"I keep doing that. I'm sorry."

"Okay, I was curious before, but now I'm just confused. What are you apologizing for?"

"Bringing up Serenity. I know it can't be easy for you."

"Serenity is my best friend and yours too. Of course you're gonna bring her up. It's fine, Emma."

"Really?"

"Yeah. It doesn't hurt the way it used to. I told you, I'm different."

"Seems like it."

We're close to the coffee shop now, which reminds me how close I am to actually having to study with this girl and something shifts in me. I can't let her think I want to study or even that I need it. I'd be lying to her and after the huge lesson I learned about lying not all that long ago, I can't repeat it. As much as my life repeats, this is the one place I can't let it.

"Ems, I need to be honest with you."

This stops her in her tracks and by that I mean, she's completely frozen in place, rigid body language and all. I hate that my words cause this. Being honest with someone should never cause them to shut down. It's just further proof that I don't know as much as I should about her. Something I definitely have to rectify soon.

"Be honest about what?"

"I don't want to study."

"I already knew that, but thanks for telling the truth."

She already knew? What?

"You knew?"

"Oh please! You don't think I actually bought that stuff in class did you? I mean, don't get me wrong, you were kind of convincing and even better with the whole 'keeping your mouth shut' thing, but I saw through it. All of it."

Well damn. Maybe I'm not as good at playing the game as I thought, but its obvious Emma sure is.

"You knew but you're still here?"

"Yeah, Graham, I am."

"Why?"

"Because there's really nowhere else I need to be."

That's the moment I jump hurdle three.

Chapter Thirteen

Emma

What started that day when I agreed to the fake study session continued on the same way for the rest of the week. Almost like a routine, we met outside class every day, talked back and forth when we should have been focusing and then we grabbed coffee together.

You would think that all this talking, hashing things out would be a dream come true for me, but for the first couple of days it was anything but. I didn't want to be reminded of what happened between us and I didn't want to talk about how much he changed after what happened with Lucifer. I know what I'm like and every time he brought up how great he felt, I knew I was only a few seconds away from spilling my guts.

I'm not much of a secret keeper. I'm human, so I've told lies before, hidden things but for the most part I hate doing it. That's a lot of the reason Serenity and I got along so well. As much as I hated lying or keeping things from people, she was even worse. It made our friendship stronger than most.

I like to think of Graham as my friend and because of that, the time we spent together became increasingly hard on me because I was keeping a secret of the worst kind from him. I have no doubt that if he found out exactly what it is that I'm keeping from him, the last week together would be obliterated and he'd never speak to me again.

By day four in our week long attempt to spend as much time together as possible, I finally let go of the worry and just embraced how fun it was spending time with someone. It wasn't even that I was with Graham; it was just being with someone and it not having anything to do with dating and expectations that made it so great. There was an expectation, sure, but it wasn't about what should be said or done between us and more the expectation of meeting up with him every day. It became routine.

A few months ago, I couldn't tell you what was going on inside his head, but from that first day on, he opened up with me in a way I hadn't expected and I know so much more than I ever did before. The way he had been mean and hateful when we interacted after Serenity's wedding, now he was baring his soul and I liked it. With him, I always knew where I stood.

*****

"I know what you said earlier, but Ems, we need to talk about that night."

"Yeah, I guess we do."

"I'm pretty sure it wasn't obvious considering how fast I booked it out of the room, but what happened in that room with you, I wanted it to happen."

"Usually when someone wants something, they don't run from it."

"In most cases that's true, but that night wasn't most cases."

"I don't understand what you mean."

"I'm just gonna spit it out." he says and I wonder what he means by it. There are a million different things he could say right now and I'm pretty sure a lot of them I'm not going to want to hear.

"I drank before I met up with you that night. When we got to the party and you went off, dancing with other guys and even some of the girls, I was left on the sidelines with nothing to do but watch. I wasn't ready to experience the party lifestyle. I don't think I'm ever gonna be ready for that to be honest. I just watched you and as much as I want to blame the alcohol, I can't."

"Blame it for what?"

"How bad I wanted to be the one you were grinding against. Shit, grinding isn't the right word. It makes you sound bad. I wanted to be whoever the guy was that you were dancing with."

I hear the words and in times past, hearing them would have made me jump, but I couldn't do it this time. As hard as I try to fit in, make people like me, be the outgoing girl that the entire campus knows me as, it seems I'm learning things now that I ignored before. Where someone saying they wanted me would normally make me happy, this time it just makes me uncomfortable.

"You could have danced with me."

"It wasn't really about the dancing, Emma. That was just what started it."

"Started it?"

"God, this is awkward. Ems, you were sexy as hell that night. You're sexy all the damn time if I'm honest about it, but that night, I've never wanted something so bad in my life."

"You wanted me?"

He laughs and I can't help it, I feel annoyed. Like he's making fun of me for trying to make sense of what he's saying.

"Considering where we ended up not twenty minutes later, I'm pretty sure it's a safe assumption that I wanted you, yes."

"Graham, what happened that night, it wasn't all on you. I know you're taking a lot of it on as your fault, but at first, I wanted it too."

"You wanted what?"

"You—us," I stop, knowing that as right as that sounded, there was still more. "I wanted that connection. I wish I could tell you why, but there's just something about you and that night, the way you looked at me, everything you wanted, I wanted to give to you."

"A connection..." He says, replaying my own words back to me. "I need to ask you something."

"Okay."

"Why did you stop? One minute, we were close to something and the next; there was this look in your eyes. You were legit scared of me. What happened?"

I blush because I know why I stopped. Why I decided halfway through that it wasn't right and needed it to end. It's just not something I ever thought I'd have to explain. It was my secret and no one else's business. This wasn't just anyone though, it was Graham and he deserved the truth, at least the truth that I could admit too.

"I've never been with a guy that way before. What happened with you is probably the furthest I've ever gone, despite what everyone around here believes."

"You're a virgin?"

Ugh. That word. I hate that word.

"Yeah, that's exactly what I am."

"Shit."

I've spent a lot of time around guys and I do mean a lot. I know the signs. You can always tell a good guy from a bad one in how they react to the whole virgin thing. A bad guy won't even blink at the admission, while a good guy, well, he always will. The good guy will hear it and immediately feel bad for pushing something on a girl that should be cherished and special. Graham is proving he's one of the good guys. He feels bad for pushing it that far.

He doesn't need to though, because until reality swept in, I wanted him to be my first.

"Why didn't you stop me sooner?"

"I didn't want to stop."

I study him as I say the words and I can tell that he's surprised. I don't think he ever expected that answer from me. Virginal Emma not wanting to stop must come as a shock. I did want to stop eventually, but until that moment in the room, I was riding the wave the same way he was.

"Emma, I like you and what I did that night, I can't ever take it back. Sorry isn't good enough to make up for how far things went. That's not me. I don't do that kind of thing, despite what you've probably seen and heard. When I choose to be with a girl, I only want to be with that girl."

"Okay…"

"That didn't make sense did it?" he stops, and his eyes lift, like he's searching his mind for the right words before he speaks again. "What I'm trying to say is, I wanted you that night, not because of the alcohol, but because of you. You weren't a conquest or one of my so called 'girls'. You were different. I'm just not sure how to deal with the news that you wanted me enough to let me be your first."

"Someone was your first at one point, so why is it strange when it's about me?"

"It's just different."

"Not from where I'm sitting."

"It's different because when you're with someone for the first time, Emma; it needs to be driven by desire, need, attraction and all of that stuff, but something more too."

"Like what?"

"It should be about love. When you're finally with someone, they should be making love to **you**, not fucking you. That night, I tried to fuck you and it was wrong. I did everything wrong."

I understand that he wants to take the blame, especially now that he's learned my most private secret, but I can't let him do that. I was in the room just as much as he was and even though he pushed himself on me near the end, it didn't change the facts.

I wanted him to be my first, even if it was fueled by alcohol and even days later, I feel the same way.

"Emma," he says, the silence on my end obviously getting to him. "I like you and it's because I like you, that what happened that night can never happen again."

*****

His words hurt, but not enough to send me running they way it normally would have. He wasn't saying it to hurt me, he was doing it because it's just the kind of guy he is. I spent years listening to Serenity tell me how good Graham is and with those words he was proving it. Not only was he back to being himself again, but along with it, the light that I started to realize was inside of him was back in full force too.

There was this second when he said that I should be made love to and not fucked with that my heart started beating super fast, wishing that he'd tell me that he wanted to be the one to make love to me, but it never materialized. That's how much that first conversation got to me and it's only gotten worse the more time we've spent together since.

A week together and I'm even more positive than I had been at the party. When I finally do feel comfortable enough to be with someone, there's only one person I want it to be with.

Graham.

The one person in the world I'm not allowed to have.

"I wondered how long it was going to take for them to shove romance down my throat."

All of this thinking and I completely forget that we're hanging out. It's a good thing he didn't need me to study with because I'm turning out to be the worst study partner in history. He could have been talking the entire time and I missed all of it, preoccupied with the past as I was.

"There's nothing wrong with romance."

"No, there's not, when you're a girl. "

"You shouldn't make gender generalizations, Graham. It's a cheap shot."

He sticks his tongue out at me and I laugh. Conversations like this one have happened a lot this week and whenever I'm right, he enjoys sticking his tongue out. It's become so frequent that I actually go out of my way to be right more than I ever have before just so I can see it.

"It's not a gender thing, it's a factual thing. Sure, there are guys like Ryan that are on the same level emotionally as women, but that's not me. I can't believe that we've got to read and study this book."

"*The Odyssey* is about more than just romance, Graham. It's brilliant."

"It's brilliant because of the romance though right?"

"No." I answer back quickly though he's right and it's the romance of the story that makes it such an interesting read. There's something about the couple and what they face that I can identify with. If you think about it, it's actually the reason I'm still a virgin. The real deal is worth waiting for.

I really need him to read this book.

"You know, if you want me to believe you, it's probably a good idea not to crinkle your nose up like that. God, you'd be a horrible poker player."

"From romance to poker? Who's the transparent one now?"

"What's that supposed to mean?"

"That's such a *guy* thing to say, Graham."

"Well played, Emma. Well played."

There's a look in his eyes when I look up and meet them that makes me smile. It's almost as if he's appreciating my attempt to banter back and forth. I know I've seen the darkest parts of him over the last little while, but now that he seems to be back on solid ground, I'm left with the same feeling as before.

Is there anything about Graham Hudson that's not jaw droppingly perfect?

Chapter Fourteen

Graham

After spending a week jumping imaginary hurdles with Emma, getting her to open up a little bit more with each passing day, I'm starting to notice something. Not only am I repeating instances in my life over on a seemingly endless loop, but I seem to be doing it as it pertains to actual people as well.

Emma is a lot like Serenity.

When I first met Ser, she deviated between the tough exterior because of her abilities and this innocence to the world around her. It was the combination of both that drew me to her and made me even more determined to break down her walls to what really lied underneath. She was trusting, yet guarded at the same time and as confusing as that was at first, it only made me like her more in the end.

It's that exact way with Emma now. She's trusting, I can see it the more she opens up to me, but she's still guarded. The thing that sets Serenity and Emma apart though; is by now Serenity would have seen through my bullshit and Emma is completely unaware of it.

The Odyssey. I've read the book; honestly, I really like the book. It was one we studied freshman year of high school and as much as I hate admitting it, I haven't forgotten about it. I rip on Ryan for being the emotionally driven one of the two of us, yet I'm the one that can remember a romance novel like I read it yesterday.

Not telling her that I read the book is lame, but the way she reacts to it and the way I remember feeling when I read it, that's what drives me to keep up the charade. She's so vocal about her opinions on it that I can't help but push her. As timid as she's been with me lately, it's doing things like this that bring out the real fire that's buried inside her and it's when that happens that I'm happiest.

Just like I did with Serenity when we were teenagers, I'm doing with Emma now. I'm building a relationship with her that has nothing to do with feelings. I like her; I have no problem admitting that, even though I still believe she deserves someone a whole lot better than me. I just don't want to make that what we're about. I want to break down her walls, get to know the real her, not the one she's displaying for everyone else on campus and once that happens, then I can act on whatever is going on between us.

Ryan telling me that she likes me gives me an advantage that she doesn't have, but I'm not going to use it to further an agenda. There is no agenda when it comes to Emma, at least not one that is in any way devious.

When she told me our first day together that she was a virgin, she knocked me on my ass. Then before I have a chance to adapt, she drops another bombshell and if I hadn't been sitting at the time, the girl would have brought me to my knees right there in the coffee shop.

"I didn't want to stop."

Five words and I was done.

Sure, things eventually stopped and I'm thankful they did because what I told her that day I meant, but when a girl sits there and tells you that even though she's never been with a guy before, she still wants to be with you, it's deep. It's not just deep, it's huge.

Despite the way I've acted with the girls on campus, both when I was possessed by Lucifer and also since I got back from Hell, that's not the way I want things to be. I've never been the screw 'em and leave 'em guy. I mean up until I realized I like Emma, I only had feelings for one girl my entire life and we didn't even sleep together. I'm definitely not that guy.

I've turned into a pretty big asshole over the last year or so, someone that I never even knew I could be, but it didn't change the way I am underneath, the way I picture my life going. I want to be with one woman and one woman only for the rest of my life. When I sleep with someone, it means something. Honestly, it means everything. Whoever the person is, they're the only one I want to see and experience. The one night stand shit can be for everyone else. I'm content being a one woman man.

That's the kind of guy Emma deserves. That doesn't mean I think I'm that guy. Up until a week ago, I was the asshole that screwed his way through the campus, one willing girl at a time, so I'm definitely not the guy for her, but someone like the way I want to be is.

My first time, it happened during my possession period, so what I told Emma about the way her first time should be, wasn't exactly accurate. I didn't get to experience it that way, but that's the way I wish it happened for everyone, especially her because of the way I feel. What she doesn't know, that I didn't tell her that day because I know it wouldn't have been right, is that I really want to be the guy to give it to her.

I want to give her the experience of making love, not what almost happened between us.

There's more that she doesn't know.

When I said that what happened between us could never happen again, I know she took it to mean that I didn't want to be that way with her, but she's wrong. I really meant that I didn't want to repeat the dark period again. I never want to be put in the position with her where my real feelings are overridden by some dark desire to take advantage of her. I don't want to screw her and treat her like I did the other girls. It's just another thing I can't tell her.

I have to let her believe I mean it the other way, at least for now because I can't let anything stop me from doing all of this the right way.

There's something in her past that's causing her to hold back on me. I don't think she's aware that I can tell, but with as close as we've been getting over the last few days, I can see it clearly. I'm pretty damn sure it's what caused her time in the center too. Whatever happened in her life changed her. It made her change into the person she tries to be for everyone else and not the person she is when she's with me or Serenity.

Asking her about it would be the easiest way to get it out there, but just like with Ser years ago, I need to let her bring it to me in her own time. If I push her, she'll run, the way she did that first day and no amount of begging and pleading will bring her back. She's already having a hard enough time dealing with the things that people say about her when they don't think she can hear, I'm not going to add to it.

That's another thing that's starting to eat at me. She knows what's being said about her. I've seen her roll her eyes so many times now when things are said; that I've lost count, yet she won't stand up and say anything in response to it. It's almost like she's accepting the way people believe her to be and well, I can't do that as easily.

I'm a defender. Every time someone says something, whether it's about her or someone else I care about and it's false, I have to resist the urge to confront about it. I'm not a violent guy, but that doesn't mean I can't use my words to put them in their place. I want to do that with Emma more than anyone now, but it's just another way I'll push her away if I do.

During the last week or so, at least when I'm not with her, I've been doing a lot of thinking. From the time I was sixteen and that angel moved in across the street from me and swept me up in her tidal wave, I've wanted only one thing. My life had a purpose because of this girl and I would have died for her. Our lives are always going to intersect in a way that isn't exactly normal, but where I had a clear path before, everything isn't so clear now.

Liking Emma and my need to go out of my way to be around her, making things right with her, it's given me a lot to think about. I've made decisions over the last couple of days that if you asked me a year ago, I would have told you weren't mine to make. Serenity carved out her own path, despite everything that was placed in front of her and I'm doing it now too.

It's this new path, the choices I want to make moving forward, that bring me here now.

I made sure Emma got back to her room, the way I've been doing every day for the past week and I knew the minute she was safe inside that this is where I was going to end up. I'm pretty sure that no matter where I go in life, what I want from it, I will always end up here even though lately it seems like the last place I should ever be.

It's time to see Serenity.

Serenity

The first thing I notice when I open the door is just how much things have changed in such a short period of time.

There's only been one thing missing from my life since everything happened three months ago. I have had so many things happen that I'm happy about, marrying Ryan at the very top, but it didn't change the fact that there was still something missing and seeing the person standing on my doorstep now, I'm reminded again of exactly what that is.

Graham Hudson will always mean so much to me. He is the first boy I ever loved, one of two people on the planet that saw the real me underneath all of the stress of my abilities and who made me want to be who I was always meant to be. He is my best friend and no matter what happens to us in our lives, he will always be that and more to me.

He's been missing for a long time. I don't mean that he's missing the way he was when Lucifer kept him hidden from us, but something far worse in comparison to it. The Graham I grew up living across the street from was gone and in his place was a person that try as I might, I just couldn't seem to get through to even with the very real bond that exists between us. He was lost to me, lost to everyone.

Being around him, during his darkest moments did nothing good for either of us. Despite the way it looks, I never walked away from him or gave up. In fact, I made a point of visiting him a lot, especially after the wedding. The reality is though, that what should have been a good thing for him, only did more damage so I had to stop doing things the way I had been.

Graham being my soul-mate, the other half of my soul, strengthened us in the past. It was the one thing that carried us through his time with Lucifer and in the end, connected us on a level that we had previously not known. We are the best parts of each other and there will never be another human alive that can speak straight to me the way he can. Ryan shares a bond with me, but despite that, he will never be the other half of my soul. That is reserved for Graham alone.

Where the bond made us stronger in the past, it seemed to do the opposite after I married Ryan. I don't know if it's because the two bonds collided and twisted it somehow, but Graham seemed to struggle with reality and the very real darkness inside of him more when I was around then when he was alone. So in an effort to do right by the first boy I ever loved, I stayed away.

Seeing him standing here now, something is different. He's alive again. His green eyes are bright and shining under the sun and even though his cheeks are wind burnt from the chill in the air, they're rosy where before they had been dull and lifeless.

He's been healed.

"Are you gonna stand there staring at me like you've seen a ghost or let me in?" he asks laughing.

"Oh, you know me. I'm so blinded by how gorgeous you are, I seem to forget about everything else."

"See! I told you I was right about that. You're still as shallow as always."

He winks at me as he makes his way past my place in the doorway and I laugh. This is definitely my Graham standing here now. There's no doubt about it. There's also no doubt about how much I've missed him either. I was starting to think I'd never experience moments like this one again.

"So, you're here to rub your sexiness in my face, is that it?" I ask as we both end up in the kitchen. It occurs to me as he seats himself, that this is the first time he's ever been here since we moved in. It's amazing to me just how comfortable it is having him here, despite our history.

"You know it, Ser."

"Swimming in bullshit over here, Graham Cracker. So, how about you tell me the real reason you're here?"

"Well, as you can see, I seem to be pretty damn close to perfection again." He winks at me again but before I can respond, he speaks again. "And there's some stuff I need to talk to you about. I think it's time."

"What kind of stuff?"

"Us."

This moment, it was inevitable. I wasn't sure we would ever get to the point where we would have the conversation with the way things had been going, but I knew that at some point it would come and I'm pretty sure I know the reason why.

"Well, I think we need to talk about it, but are you sure you're ready to?"

He laughs, but where before it had been natural, it sounds awkward now. He's not comfortable.

"If you asked me that a week ago, I would have said no, but Ser, a lot of shit's been happening and I think I'm finally ready."

"Why don't you tell me about what's happened and then we can talk about us?"

"I think Michael went against Heaven and healed me."

"Why do you think that?"

"The other night, I woke up in bed and had some girl tell me I was bleeding. After I kicked her out," he stops almost as if he senses that I'm going to go off on him about the way he treats women, holding his hand up to stop me and again I find myself laughing. Some things never change.

"I wasn't gonna say it, Graham Cracker. I know you've heard it enough by now."

"Yeah, you're right I have. Anyway, I kicked her out, drank a bunch and passed out. I should have woken up with a really bad hangover and even more cuts. It's been that way for a really long time. I didn't wake up that way though."

"How did you wake up?"

"Healed. I'm not joking Ser, it's like I was all screwed up when I went to bed and when I got up, I was completely okay. The cuts were still there, but they weren't open and bleeding anymore. I could breathe easily. No headaches, no haunting memories. I didn't even wake up screaming the way I normally do. It was as if the few months didn't even happen."

Graham is one of the toughest guys I know, but hearing him talk about the horrors he's been living with breaks me inside. It doesn't matter if I moved on from him or not, I would always care.

"What makes you think Michael had anything to do with it?"

"He's the only one that could have."

I need to be careful with what I say next because I know the truth and even if he's feeling better, he's not ready for it yet. It will not go over good. Michael played a part in what happened to him, but not in the way he thinks. That was all on Lucifer.

"That's true, but do you think that maybe you just went through the worst of it and all of this happening was your doing and not of the angel variety?"

"You're kidding, right?"

"No. I'm dead serious. You're one of the strongest people I've ever met Graham. If there is anyone that could go through what you did and come out on top of it on his own, it's you."

It's times like this where I see how we're the same. I know I didn't believe it in the beginning, but over time, things started happening and now I can't deny it. Neither one of us deals with being complimented in the right way. In fact, we both hate it. The pink tinge creeping across his cheeks proves it. He's blushing because I complimented him and I'm pretty sure underneath that, he doesn't believe a word of it.

If the roles were reversed, I would be the exact same way. He's the other half of my soul alright.

"You don't think it was Michael?"

"No, I don't. If Michael went against God that way, he wouldn't be kicked from Heaven, but we'd know it. You know how loyal he is and also what a complete ass he can be when he's angry. We would know about it."

"Did you just call your brother an ass?"

"Yeah," I smile. "I did. It's not like he doesn't already know it."

"That's true."

"Look, I know you think that you weren't strong enough to come out of what you went through on your own, but I think you need to accept that in this case, you did it."

"I don't think that's possible."

"Anything's possible, Graham. You just have to believe."

"Thanks, Gabe."

As much as I want to respond to what he said, the minute I hear Gabriel's name, I'm frozen. Like I said before, even though there are so many things I have to be thankful for, there are still parts that are missing. Gabriel will always be a tough subject for me even if I'm sure he's watching over us somewhere. I may not know where that is or even if it's possible at all, but after what happened at my wedding, I believe it.

"So, you wanted to talk about us?" I ask, deviating away from thoughts of Gabriel and focusing on the real reason he's here.

"Yeah, I do. With me as out of it as I've been, what's between us has just sort of hung in the air ever since and I think for both of our sakes, we need to focus on it now."

"No time like the present huh?"

"Something like that." He says, and the crack in his voice doesn't escape me. This isn't going to be easy for either of us.

"I want to go first if that's alright?"

"Truthfully, I wanted you to. As sure as I am that this needs to happen, I'm not quite ready to do it, if that makes any sense. There's something so damn final about it."

"It's not an ending, Graham. It's a new beginning. There is nothing final about this conversation other than that we're both going to walk away from it stronger than we were before."

"You really believe that?"

"With all of my heart. What we are to each other speaks to it. We're never going to end. We're always going to be connected in the purest way possible."

We are two unique yet similar pieces of energy and when our lives are through, we will join together again the way that we're meant to and everything in that moment will be right. All of the struggles we dealt with during our time here and everything that happened in our past lives will cease to exist and we will be one again. It is the purest bond there is and I mean every word of what I say to him now.

"What we share, you and me, it's a lot like what's happened between me and Lucifer. I know you're not going to like being compared to him and I get it, I do, but it doesn't change the facts. I cared about him during the time I spent alone with him and just like with him, I care about you too, even more so. I had to adapt to a new and even better relationship with him and that's what needs to happen here. "

"A new relationship?"

"The bond we share will always be there between us until we're joined together again. There's nothing we can do to change that, but you know where my heart calls home and I think I know the same about you. We can never be together, not in the way our hearts seem to want with the call they make to each other. It means we need to carve a new path, one that still keeps us close, but in a way that works for both of us and doesn't hurt the people we love."

He makes a face the minute I mention the people we love and again, I'm aware of why. He's not quite there with it yet, but if his response is any indication, it won't be long until he is.

"What kind of relationship can we have where the bond doesn't hurt people or even each other?"

"We put the focus back where it belongs."

"Not following, Ser."

"Before we knew about the soul mate connection, even before I kissed you the first time, what were we to each other?"

"Best friends."

"There's your answer."

"You want us to be best friends?"

"We never stopped, Graham. We got taken in with the bond and all that comes with it and then the weight of the world on our shoulders, but that was the one thing that never changed. It's incredibly easy to be your best friend, but not easy at all to be your soul mate."

"You never stopped being my best friend? Even after what I put you through?"

I know what he's getting at. When I was rescued from Hell, I came back without my memories of the last couple of years and Graham had been the person I latched onto because he was the one I remembered. Seeing an opening to get what he needed and wanted so badly, he lied to me and while it upset me for awhile, it never tore us apart so far that we couldn't recover.

"It's precisely because of everything we've been through that I know we've never stopped being best friends. Look what we faced head on and tell me you don't see it."

"I can't. I just can't believe that after all the lies I told you that you'd want anything to do with me. It's only because of the bond that you stuck around at all."

"And again, you're making me wade through bullshit. That's not true, Graham. I stayed because of you, not the bond."

He opens his mouth to say something and there's this way his eyes go from bright to dim and his head bows that tells me he's struggling with it. Whatever he's about to say is causing him pain and it's taking everything in me not to reach out to him. He's the last person that deserves to struggle.

"I don't want to say goodbye to you."

"Well, that's an easy fix. Don't say goodbye."

He looks up and the minute his eyes meet mine, I know he's starting to get what I've been trying to say all along.

"Graham Hudson, I will always love you, just as much as I did when I was sixteen and no matter what path I take in life, it's the one thing that will never change. It's fact. There was never meant to be a goodbye in our lifetime together, only hello."

"I'm ready to take a chance, Serenity. For the first time in forever, the chance I'm about to take, it's not one I'm taking on you. I love you so fucking much and it hurts like hell to say this, but if I don't say goodbye now, I'm going to betray you, betray us and I can't do that. I won't let you down in another lifetime."

I want to tell him everything. He deserves to know what's really going on, but it's not time yet. He's not where he needs to be. Hearing him speak of our past lifetimes, it makes me want to spill it all because he needs to understand the truth. This isn't like the lifetimes before; this is different because unlike what we went through then, we're not going to lose each other.

"You're never going to lose me and you don't ever need to say goodbye. Two years ago I took a chance and now, other half of my soul, it's your turn. So instead of thinking about me, it's time you think about yourself. It's time for you take a chance, Graham."

Chapter Fifteen

Emma

There's been one thing I've loved since I came here three years ago and it's got nothing to do with the people or even the opportunities to learn. It's something much more basic.

It's the weekends.

When I first got here, I was insistent that this would be the time my life changed for the better. I was completely out of my hometown and away from the people and places that loomed over me. I could officially have the fresh start I'd been craving since before I got bogged down under all the official labels. I could be whatever version of Emma Daniels I wanted and there's nothing anyone could say or do about it.

What's strange is, the outgoing girl I'd been in high school, or at least the one I wanted everyone to believe I was, she's what I became and the weekends became my salvation.

It started off small, just me going to a few mixers around campus. There were some I even dragged Serenity too, at least in the beginning, but it quickly became obvious that the party lifestyle wasn't her thing and no amount of reinvention would change it. From the mixers, I went to all out parties, meeting people, kissing people and overall just having a good time.

All of that worked pretty well for me; at least it did for the first couple of years. It's only lately that I'm starting to see that there's more to a weekend than just the parties that happen all over campus. There's more than getting drunk and hooking up.

The weekend can also be relaxing. Staying in your room, reading, studying, listening to music, watching old movies that even three years after you've watched them can still make you cry. There's enjoyment in all of that just as much as there is the parties. So for the first time in forever, that's exactly how I spend my weekend.

At least that's how I was spending it until the supernatural came calling.

Nothing can rip your relaxation and peace away quite like a couple of angels that just don't seem happy considering what they are.

It started out just the way I planned. I did a little reading for English Lit, wanting to be prepared for the class come Monday, switching over after awhile to having a solitary movie watch, while trying my hardest not to miss my best friends commentary. I was about to start the second movie in my marathon when the light literally blew apart above me.

It didn't take long after that to realize exactly why it happened.

I might not have much experience when it comes to them, but I don't think I need to, seeing as their way of interacting with us is so obvious you would have to be blind to miss it. What Michael wanted to talk about, I had no idea, but it didn't take very long to find out. As soon as the knock came on the door and I saw just who was waiting for me on the other side, he opened up and spilled pretty quick.

I'm not sure if it's because I've developed a tolerance for things that are out of this world or not, but I wasn't nearly as affected by their presence as I would have been six months ago. All they are now is two beings that stood between me and a Christian Slater fix.

"So, I know I'm new to the whole, being able to talk to angels' thing, but do you guys always show up like this?"

"I am not sure what you mean." Michael asks as Lucifer just stands silently in the corner with a smile on his face. A smile that a few weeks ago I would have found evil, but now looks funny.

"Brother, I do believe we've interrupted something pertinent."

"She was doing nothing of consequence. I made sure of that before my arrival."

"You must excuse Michael. He doesn't get out much." Lucifer replies, causing me to laugh in response. I never thought it would be possible, but it seems I'm starting to like the fallen angel more by the minute. He just gets it, where Michael seems lost.

"I get out more than enough, thank you."

"Michael, he was being sarcastic."

This stops the angels in his tracks, which only makes me laugh even more. Maybe being taken away from my movie wasn't so bad after all. It was like watching an improv show with the way these two carried on. There was no doubt about their relation to each other even though they couldn't be more opposite.

"So, you obviously need to talk to me. You wanna tell me what about?"

"I wanted to speak with you. Lucifer just wanted to tag along as an annoyance."

"Glad we cleared that up, so again, what do you want?"

"I have been keeping tabs on Graham and it would appear as though everything that was done has worked according to plan. I am here to find out when you have decided the right time to tell him the truth would be."

So here's the thing. I know I need to tell Graham the truth. It's obvious considering how much time we've been spending together lately. I won't be able to hold back on the truth much longer, but it doesn't mean I've actually come up with a right time to tell him.

It's not as if I can just walk up to him on Monday morning before class and say something like 'Hey Graham, the reason you feel like yourself again is because I asked Lucifer to heal you'. It's not right.

"If telling him is so important, why haven't you done it?"

"I was unaware that you wanted me to be the one to do it. If it is indeed what you require from me then I can handle it right now."

"No, that's not it at all. I told you both that I wanted to be the one to tell him, but every time I feel like I'm about to, it never seems right and I chicken out."

"You do what with chickens? What does poultry have to do with the current conversation?"

"Lucifer, I can't believe I'm gonna ask this, but can I get a little help here?" I ask, shooting him a pleading look and praying he'll indulge me. I know how easy it is to confuse Michael, I saw that with my own eyes when he interacted with Ryan, but I don't know if I've got the patience to explain something that should just be common sense.

"Michael, it is a human saying. It means she is too afraid and will back down from her original plan."

"Thank you."

"You are welcome."

"Well now that we have gotten all of that nonsense out of the way, why is it that you chicken out?"

"Emma, if you do not mind, I wish to answer Michael's question."

"Yeah sure, have at it. I'll just go back to watching my movie and dreaming I'm Mrs. Slater if that's cool."

I turn back toward the television but not before hearing the baritone of Lucifer's voice as he laughs at me.

Yeah, he's definitely the angel with the brain.

"Michael has a brain, of that I assure you. He is just selective on when he uses it."

"Lucifer, you are dangerously close to crossing a line with your humor. If you want to answer the question for her than I suggest you do so. Wasting time is not an option."

"The reason she does not want to tell him this, or as she said, she chickens out, is because of the way she feels for the boy, brother. You have been privy to their times together. They have grown closer over the last couple of days. It is only natural that dropping the truth on him now would create a rift between them. It is one she is afraid can never be fixed. You would know all of this if you just paid attention."

"How are you knowledgeable as it pertains to them?"

"I've run wild over this planet for generations, Michael. There is not much about the human condition that I do not understand. "

"It does not change the fact that he needs to be told."

This time there's no reply from Lucifer and I realize that Michael is again talking to me. I'm the one that's supposed to have an answer for this and I do, but it's one he should already know. I agree with him. Graham does need to be told, but it doesn't change the fact that I don't really want to be the one to do it. Lucifer's right. I don't want to wreck whatever it is we've been building over the last week. It's become a lifeline for me.

"I understand your feelings Emma, but the boy needs to know the truth. If you feel you cannot tell him than it must come from me. I will not spend the rest of my time watching over him being dishonest."

"May I make a suggestion?" Lucifer interrupts and we both turn to face him. I'm all for anything he wants to add here because I definitely don't have the answers Michael wants to hear.

"Go ahead, brother."

"Graham has only been himself for a week. Why don't we give it a little bit longer before dropping the weight of this on him? In a weeks' time, we can revisit this if Emma hasn't already told him and go from there."

Score another like point for Lucifer. If he kept it up, my hatred of him would be gone in no time. As much as I still have reservations about him, he's been doing as he said ever since we talked things through and it's getting harder to hate him.

"As much as I would prefer we do this now, in case the boy calls to me, I can see how this plan also works."

"So you'll give me another week?" I ask, hoping that's what he's getting at. Maybe if I have the looming threat of the angel off my back, I won't feel the need to spill the truth to him quite as badly as I do now. I meant what I said. I don't want to ruin what's been happening, at least not yet.

"You have one week and then if you do not tell him, Lucifer and I will take the choice away from you and do it ourselves, regardless of the fallout. "

He doesn't seem the most thrilled with this and his tone honestly scares me a little, but he's giving me time and right now that means more to me than his attempt at appearing stern.

Michael disappears from the room, leaving Lucifer and me completely alone. Given his place, joined with Gregory, it's no surprise he hasn't done the same. It's only when he doesn't make a move toward the door that I realize that while Michael is finished with me, he's not.

"Something else you want to add?"

"What was obvious the day you visited with me is even more so now. Emma, moving forward, tread carefully. For it is not only your heart on the line, but the heart of the very man I spent hours healing only a few short days ago."

"What are you trying to say?"

"You care a great deal for Graham Hudson and after the damage that I caused both his heart and his mind, I would hate to see it repeated."

"I would never hurt him the way you did."

"Of that I am aware. You would not do it intentionally, but there is always the unintentional and even though I agreed to give you more time, not telling Graham the truth is definitely a case of the unintentional. As I said, tread carefully."

He turns and is out the door before my mind can conjure up the perfect response, not that there was one. The truth in his words only makes me feel something even more for the fallen angel. Where I only had loathing, hatred and misunderstanding before, now with the like was also something I'm not at all familiar with.

I respected him.

Even though he was the reason Graham turned away from the light and even now struggles to come back from it in not so subtle ways, he's doing everything in his power to make up for it and do right by him and that alone earns my respect.

I would not hurt Graham. When the time felt right, I would tell him the truth about what I set in motion the day I went to see Lucifer and I would deal with the fallout, whatever it was, in the only way I knew how. Graham deserves that much.

In fact, he deserves a whole lot more.

Chapter Sixteen

Graham

"Take a chance, Graham."

It's those words that stay with me, more than any others that were said for an entire day after Serenity said them. She knows me better than anyone. I'm not a thrill seeker, a risk taker and I'm definitely not the guy that takes a chance. With as long as it had taken me to admit to her that I wanted that kiss the night of the party, I've more than proven that.

The thing is, this time, the words have more meaning. I went to Serenity to begin with because I know what's happening to me and I owe it to her and even to Emma to do things this way. She was right, we'll never say goodbye to each other, but we are destined for different directions and that's okay.

I can move on from the standstill I've been finding myself in and it has nothing to do with the dark cloud that followed me around for months. I've been frozen in place because despite the way everything turned out, I hadn't allowed myself the chance to move on from her.

It's not exactly a secret that I've been in love with Serenity Richards, well McGregor now, since she moved in across the street from me when we were sixteen. We're twenty-two now. I spent the last six years, even with our time apart, fueled by that love and when she married Ryan, despite that picture in my mind that I would be the one she was marrying, I left myself at a standstill.

A weight has been lifted off my shoulders. She told me to take a chance and it's those words that guide me now. Whatever path I take from here on out, she's going to be there for, even if it's not in the way I imagined her when all of this started. She'll be there supporting me every step of the way, just the way I need her too.

I'm going to take my chance with Emma Daniels.

Well, I would be, if she'd open the door already.

I feel like I've been standing here for an hour when in reality it's only been a couple minutes. It's the nerves I think. I'm not used to doing things like this, but I've got to if I plan on following through with what I promised myself.

For as long as I can remember, I've always been a certain way and for the most part, I don't want to change a thing about that. It's only the last few months I'd like to erase completely. I definitely don't want to be that dark person anymore, but the way I was before isn't working for me either. I want to be something better than both of those versions of me and it starts here.

I came up with the idea last night after mulling over the conversation with Serenity and now as I wait for her to open the door; I pray that she won't think it's stupid. That might be the one thing I miss about my all night drinking binges. I didn't give a crap what anyone thought. It's much easier to do things when you don't have that nagging, doubtful voice in the back of your head.

"Graham? What are you doing here?"

This is where things are about to get tricky. I'm standing on her doorstep, it's before noon and judging by the way her hairs all over the place, it looks like I just pulled her straight out of bed. I'm starting to wonder if this was such a good idea after all, but there's no turning back now.

"Did I wake you up?"

"Well considering it's not even seven in the morning, yeah, I'd say you did."

"I'm sorry about that, but this couldn't wait."

"What couldn't wait?"

"Do you think I can come in?" I ask, motioning past her into the room.

"Yeah of course, but the minute you get in here, you're explaining exactly what you're doing here."

"I know its super early, but since it's the weekend I thought we could do something fun." I say the minute I've stepped past her into the room.

"What's your idea of fun at this hour?" She asks, running her hands through her hair in an attempt to untangle the obvious tangles. It's a move that's not lost on me. She's worried about the way she looks, but what she doesn't realize is, even with bed head she looks amazing.

"The zoo."

"Excuse me? What?"

"You heard me. I'm here this early because I want to take you to the zoo."

"Uh, Graham, are you sure you're feeling okay?"

"I feel amazing, actually. Thanks for asking. So will you do it?"

"You're serious?"

Most guys, when they're asking a girl out, they'll plan to take them to dinner and a movie or something and there's nothing wrong with that. I'm just not most guys. I don't want to wine and dine this girl. I want to enjoy time and space with her and what better place to do that then at a public zoo? We can walk around for hours, checking out the animals and when we're done, we can eat or go our separate ways and there won't be the awkwardness of what to do once the dinner and a movie concept is over.

I don't want to take Emma back to my room or even come back here to hers. I want to enjoy her company. That can't happen though, if I can't sell her on it. Getting shot down isn't an option.

"I'm as serious as a heart attack, Emma."

"Well, that's a first." She says and there's this moment where I feel elated that I've come up with something to do with her that will be a first.

"So no one's ever shown up at the crack of dawn and asked you to go to the zoo with them before? Yours is a lonely existence, Ems."

Her lips rise in a smile and I know I've jumped another hurdle. I don't know why I keep looking at everything with this girl as a hurdle I need to jump, but there can be no mistaking how awesome it feels when I realize I've done it.

"I guess it's a good thing I have you then, huh? You're obviously in the *know* about these kinds of things."

"Exactly! So, Emma Daniels, will you do it? Will you come to the zoo with me?"

There's this unease floating around inside me while I wait for her to answer, but it's quickly being overridden by the sheer happiness I feel at knowing she's going to say yes to this, even though it's probably the lamest attempt at a date ever.

"I'll do it, but there's one condition that you gotta meet first."

It's like we're back in class and she's trying to get me to stay quiet again. This time's different though because over the last week I've gotten under her skin and now she's not doing it as a test. I'm not sure how I know that, but it's just something I can tell. It might have something to do with the smile she's wearing though.

"Name it."

"If I'm going to step foot outside this door before noon, I'm going to need coffee and not just a cup of it. I might need a couple pots."

"Well, what are you waiting for princess? Your wish is my command."

Emma

When he showed up on my doorstep a few hours ago, I honestly had no idea what to think. Opening the door, expecting to see one of the girls on my floor or even Serenity and coming face to face with a very awake and smiling Graham Hudson, well that was just the farthest thing from my mind.

After the angels had taken off, I'd settled back into my movie marathon until I passed out. I had no plans for Sunday so falling asleep somewhere between two and three in the morning seemed adequate. It wasn't like I needed to be awake for a class so I was completely content with just sleeping the day away.

Looks like life had other plans.

When I told him that it was a first for me, I meant it in multiple ways. Showing up the way he did and asking me out, well that's just never happened. Sure, I've been asked out, but it was usually at the end of class or randomly coming out at the parties I went to, never like what he did.

The zoo was also a new experience for me. I've gone to a lot of different places since Serenity and I came to school here, but that's one place we never went, together or alone. I'm not sure what's gotten into Graham since the angels worked their magic on him, but whatever it is, I like it and I don't think I want it to change.

Walking around the entire zoo with him took four hours and it was the most amusing four hours of my life. The way he reacted to some of the exhibits, I swear I was walking around with a four year old. His eyes lit up and he rambled with facts he would bring up. I watched him a lot more than I did the animals we were supposed to be looking at, but it wasn't awkward, the way I expected it to be. Seeing him this way was like seeing a whole other side to the guy that up until now I had only ever known as my best friend's first love.

About halfway through our walk, his hand brushed up against mine and while I tried not to read too much into it, the warmth that appeared just from the barest touch made that impossible. It's only when it kept happening the more we walked that I ended up finally leveling him with a look. I wasn't looking for him to stop, but the frequency of it happening demanded some kind of response.

*****

"I'm sorry, that keeps happening doesn't it?" he says as he catches my questioning stare.

"Yeah, I guess."

He starts walking backwards and he doesn't stop until he's about six feet away from me. I don't want to admit it, but him even backing up a little feels like I've been stabbed in the chest. It's only when I look up and catch the huge grin on his face that I feel the sharp pain start to dissipate.

"Is this far enough?" he calls to me and I can't help but laugh, thankful that my less than stellar reaction to his touch didn't change anything between us.

He jogs back over and falls in line with me again, only this time before I can come up with some kind of response, his arm brushes against mine and as I look down, I see that he's locked our fingers together.

We're holding hands.

"There, that's better, don't ya think?" he asks and I open my mouth to respond but am met with nothing but air. I really don't know how to answer that.

"Emma, I'm not really good at this kind of stuff."

What the hell does that mean? What kind of stuff is he talking about?

"What do you mean?"

"I wanted to hold your hand."

"You are holding my hand, Graham."

"I mean, I wanted to hold it earlier. That's what all that brushing up against you was. I was trying to let you know. I just suck at all of this, so of course you didn't read my mind."

It's the stupidest thing ever, but I swear the way he says that he wanted to hold my hand makes me go light headed. I feel like right now, standing here in the middle of the zoo, I'm twelve all *over again and this is my first date. Well, this is how it would be if I had a complete do over for that time period of my life.*

I'm not familiar with any of this. He's not the only one that's not good with it. I've never had trouble getting the attention of guys, but to have one genuinely want to hold my hand and do things the way Graham's doing them right now, that's never happened. I have no clue what to do or say. All I know is that I don't want the feeling to end. I want whatever this is.

"Why didn't you just ask?"

"Ask to hold your hand? Is it really that easy?"

There's something in the way he says it that makes my stomach drop. I'm pretty sure he wasn't calling me easy, but I can't help but get the feeling that in letting him hold my hand this soon, it's exactly what I am or at least what I am to him.

Easy.

"You're scowling, Ems."

Of course I'm scowling. What the hell does he expect? I have no idea what any of this even means. I'm twenty-two years old and even the most basic attempt at human interaction is throwing me for a complete loop. Maybe it wasn't such a bad thing being someone else the way I have been since I came here. Acting like myself is getting me nowhere.

"Sorry."

"You don't have to be sorry; you just have to tell me why you're doing it. Was it something I said?"

I nod and he bows his head. The last thing I want to do is make him feel bad for what he said but I'm also not going to lie to him either.

"It was the easy thing right?"

I nod again but instead of keeping his eyes trained on the ground the way they had been a second before, he looks straight at me and I'm locked in place with the intensity shining in his eyes.

"I don't think you're easy. I was ripping on myself. That's it."

"Okay."

"If I asked you to hold hands, would you have done it?"

"Yeah, Graham, I would've done it." I answer as I look down and see our hands still locked tightly together. There's something about the way it looks, seeing it this way that makes me blush and before I have a chance to hide it, he catches it.

"Wow, nice shade of pink there, Ems."

"Shut up, jackass."

He beams that smile of his down at me and I blush again which only causes him to laugh before pulling me along to the next exhibit on his list.

"So, I was thinking we'd hit up the tigers next, but the more time I have to think about it, I'm pretty sure there's somewhere better that we need to go first."

"You're afraid they'll eat you, admit it."

"Uh, no. I don't have enough meat for them, but nice redirect there."

I blush again, what feels like the hundredth time in the last couple of minutes and he bends in close, his next words sending shivers straight through me.

"As much as I can identify with the primal nature of the tiger, especially watching you blush that way, it's not the right place for you."

"Where's the right place?" I whisper, his words hitting their mark and turning my insides to liquid.

"With your own kind."

"Where's that?"

"With the other butterflies."

*****

True to his word, he'd taken me to the butterfly exhibit and we even made our way around to see the tigers before eventually calling it a day. I really can't imagine a more perfect day and it's made even better by who I'm spending it with.

It's only when we've left and we're heading back to the school that I realize I have no experience with what's happening between us. I've been with my share of guys over the years and even dated quite a few of them, but none of the other times or my guy expertise prepares me for what I feel whenever I'm with Graham.

The way it feels holding his hand, hearing him laugh, the way his entire face brightens when he smiles and god, the way his eyes look when he's dead serious about something, it's enough to throw me off completely.

This is new territory for me, but frightened as I am by it, I can't back away.

I want more.

Chapter Seventeen

Graham

The off-handed comment I made about her being a butterfly was supposed to be just that. A random comment, but after spending the last hour dreaming of nothing but the flying insect, I'm beginning to think there's a whole lot more to it.

It's a nagging thought so strong in my mind that any hope of going back to sleep is pointless. If it means something, then I have to know what. Though, getting up and searching the internet at three in the morning, for information on butterfly symbolism, is enough to have me classified crazy.

I find a lot of information that matches with what the guy at the zoo explained to us when we'd travelled through the exhibit, but after scanning a few pages, I finally hit pay dirt.

Some believe the butterfly to be a spirit animal, and more than that; one with multiple meanings. The more I read, the more I see the reason why I called Emma that to begin with and why I can't seem to escape them, even in my dreams.

It's an animal that speaks to personal growth and transformation. It's through the butterfly that you are given signs of rebirth, something that over the last few days I know better than anyone.

I woke up a few days ago and expecting to be stuck in the darkness forever, found myself living the complete opposite. In a way I was reborn, this time surrounded by the light and not what had plagued me for the better part of a year.

The butterfly can mean finding joy in life again, being light and playful. All things I've been experiencing with Emma. It isn't a fluke that I told her she needed to be returned to her own kind, because in giving me all of that joy, happiness and a feeling of being completely light, she really is a butterfly.

I don't know if it's the time or the fact that I'm still acclimating back to the land of the living after living apart from it for so long, but all of this sounds insane. After everything I've been through, you would think this would be the least crazy of the things I've had to think about it, but it's not. Angels, demons and even heaven and hell I can get behind, but believing that a girl I happen to like might be a butterfly, yeah that's crazy.

With as crazy as it might be, I won't turn away from it. For so long now I've wanted a release from the pain and anguish I was living with and I have it now. I'm still not sure how it all turned around, but maybe I'm not supposed to know. Maybe it's what Serenity said and I was strong enough to beat whatever it was, it just took longer than I thought it should have.

Closing down the browser windows and heading back to bed, I focus on the way the day went with Emma, but more than that, what I can do next to make the next day even better. There's no mistaking it, our time together earlier was perfect and I want more of it. I want more of her. There's only one thought that stops me from pushing forward making plans.

There was a moment, before the butterflies where I didn't feel like myself. A split second in time where I felt the way I did the night of the party. When she blushed at me, I tried to push it down, but it built up inside of me and wouldn't be ignored. I craved her just like I did then. It's that craving that stops me now, worries me moving forward. I don't want to make this about sex, but it seems like my body won't agree with my mind.

I don't think I'm as healed as I thought. If that part of me can still creep in and make itself known then what else will come? Will I get close to her and have everything that for the past week I've been enjoying come tumbling down around me? Will I make a move on her and ruin what I've been trying so hard to rebuild?

Am I really okay or is all of this just an elaborate illusion?

I want to take this chance, I think I'm deserving of it, but I won't put anyone in danger. I can't go back and do all the things I did before. I need to be better than that. I just don't know if I can be.

What you are experiencing has nothing to do with the darkness that haunted you before.

I should be used to this by now, but it still amazes me that there's never a time where I'm completely alone. There always seems to be an angel just hanging on the periphery, waiting for the right time to make its presence known.

"You seem pretty sure about that."

It is because I am sure. What you are experiencing now is human in nature, not something of my fallen brother's design.

"Are you really gonna tell me that what I'm feeling is normal?"

That is exactly what I am saying. You humans—are some of the most primal beings I have ever known, so it stands to reason that you would feel that way in regards to the Daniels girl. It is natural.

So basically, what he's saying is, I'm just a horny bastard. Great.

I am not here to call attention to your human impulses, Graham. I am merely here to explain to you that the darkness you lived with is gone and you have nothing to fear.

"Yeah, darkness you lifted from me."

Are we still on that misguided notion? I did nothing of the sort. If I had healed you without your consent I would have been severely punished. Not only by Father, but all of Heaven. As much as I was tempted to go against what I know in order to fix what had been done to you, I did not do it.

"So I'm just supposed to believe that one day I woke up from a bender and I was completely okay, without your intervention?"

I do not care what you have your mind believe. I only care that as it pertains to me it is based in fact. I did not heal you. That is fact.

Before I can think of anything to say in response, I can feel his absence. He's gone. Despite his claim that what I'm going through is human and has nothing at all to do with the supernatural, I still can't believe in it. The way I just started a fight, accusing him of things I know deep down he's telling the truth about proves that it's not human.

I've never been that confrontational before.

I need to sleep. Now that I'm finally able to do it without being haunted, I should be enjoying every second of it, yet here I am, first waking up because of the butterfly nonsense and kept awake by the worry that in some way I'm going to end up blowing everything before I've even started.

It needs to stop. If I don't put it out of my mind, I have no doubt it won't be long before I'm right back where I started again. In the darkness. Now that I've had a taste of the light again, there's no way in hell I can let that happen.

My future depends on it.

Emma

The more time I spend with Graham, I'm starting to see that he doesn't like to do anything in the conventional way.

Movie dates, dinners, walks around campus, football games, parties, those are all things that I know and I've experienced both in my time in high school and also since coming here almost three years ago. With Graham though, none of that is happening and as strange as it is, it's a nice change.

His first attempt at a date was the Stephenville Zoo and his second attempt is shaping up to be just as different.

When he picked me up this morning, again at the crack of dawn, wanting to do it before classes started, I had no idea what he had in mind. I only had the same request as I did the day we went to the zoo. We needed coffee, and a lot of it.

He delivered and here we are now, standing on the dock of the marina. It's another place I've never been, but it's an experience I never want to lose. I want to remember it, just the way it is right now for as long as I can.

The sun is breaking through on the horizon, turning the sky above us into this beautiful shade of peach. It's a mixture of orange and red but softer somehow and as I take it in, I realize I've never seen a more beautiful sight in my life. It's made even better by the person standing to my left sharing it with me.

Under the rise of the sun, there are boats moving in, after being out all night and some going out. It's not a known fact, but Stephenville is known for its fishermen. As much as we have all of the more popular fast food joints, we also have a whole lot of restaurants that cater strictly to a seafood variety and taking in the picture before me now, I'm getting to see how that all comes to be.

Despite my hatred of it before, I'm starting to become a fan of the early morning rise. The world is completely different at this time then it is at every other point. It's more alive somehow.

"This is weird isn't it?"

His question has a whole lot of different meanings, at least with the way we're standing, what's taking place between us and where we are, so I'm not entirely sure how to answer.

"Define weird."

"Bringing you here like this. It's weird right?"

"Honestly Graham, weird is the last thing that comes to mind right now."

"Well, what does come to mind?"

"It's beautiful."

"The girl finds waking up and heading to a marina as the sun rises beautiful. I definitely gotta remember that."

"Yes, do that. It seems you're not as crappy at this as you thought."

"Nah, I still am. It's just the company that makes this work. I'm not sure anyone else would find being here right now all that beautiful."

He's so unsure of himself. That's the one thing I don't enjoy about the way he is now. He might be right about most girl's not enjoying being out here, but it doesn't mean it's a bad idea or it's not beautiful and right. It's actually perfect. I just wish he could see that instead of questioning every step.

"Well I guess it's a good thing that I'm the one you brought here then."

"The thought never crossed my mind to bring anyone else."

He does this a lot too. He says things that have the ability to melt my heart. Right things. The only problem with it is that it makes me speechless at the same time. All thought process just seems to evaporate and I'm left staring at him wearing nothing but a 'duh' expression.

I really need to get my brain in check.

"So, I did something this morning. It's kind of weird…"

As far as I can tell, there's not a whole lot about Graham that's weird, but if he wants to share with me, there's no way I'm going to say anything to stop it.

"Is this where you tell me that you had a dream about me and woke up so turned on you had to do something about it?"

The minute the words tumble their way out, I blush and slap my hand over my mouth. Apparently all the coffee in the world doesn't block the brain to mouth filter. That is definitely something better off thought and not said.

"No, but wow, Ems does that happen to you often?"

More often than I'm going to admit to.

"Kind of, yeah."

He laughs and I breathe a sigh of relief. I also make a mental note to start filtering the crap that I let slip. The last thing I need to do right now, with everything he's done so far this morning is slip up and say something even worse.

"Well, my thought process was more pure than that, but I'm definitely going to keep that other bit locked away for future reference."

It's not lost on me, the way he smirks as he says it. He's making light of the fact that I just attempted to put my own foot in my mouth.

"Alright Graham, what did you do this morning?"

"I spent about an hour on the internet looking up butterflies."

"A little late night reading, huh?"

"Something like that, yeah."

"Well, you got my attention. Why did you spend an hour looking up butterflies?"

"Do you remember what I said at the zoo?"

Like I could forget even if I wanted to.

"Yeah, what about it?"

"I dreamt about them and when I woke up, it wouldn't leave me alone. So, I looked it up and I actually found some things I didn't know."

"Like what?"

He goes silent and watching, I can see that he's lost in thought. That whatever he's about to say next he wants to be sure he says right. I recognize it so easily because I've made the same facial expression before. His brow furrows and his eyes, lighter seconds ago seem to go dark under the determination it takes to focus his thinking.

"I know what the butterfly stands for now. I also know why it seemed so right when I called you one."

Catching his gaze as he looks up and locks on me, I sense how unsure he is even though I don't understand why.

"Well, I'm all ears."

"Waking up that day, everything different, feeling better than I ever have, I knew there was only one thing that I needed to do."

What this has to do with butterflies and why he called me one, I'm not sure, but his words are dripping in truth, I can see it. The determination is back in his eyes, the insecurity of before gone.

"I needed to make things right with you. I knew you wouldn't trust it, trust me, but it didn't matter. I had to do it."

"Okay."

"Emma, I know none of this is making any sense, and a lot of that is because I've got literally no experience with this kind of stuff. I've been in love with one girl my entire life and stepping away from that, taking a chance on something new, especially when I'm not even sure what it all means, it's confusing as hell. I just know that being around you, calling you a butterfly, it all means something."

"What does it mean?" I manage to push out even though with everything he's saying, I'm losing all ability to cognitively function. He's turning my brain to mush.

"The butterfly is a sign of change, transformation, being reborn. I feel all of that when I'm with you. I did in class, yesterday at the zoo and standing here now. It's like everything that's been weighing me down for months, it's lifted and I'm light. I'm free."

"Graham..."

"No, don't say anything yet."

I nod my head and as I do he moves closer to me, our hands still locked together the way they've been since the minute we got out of his car. It's only when he breaks the contact to wrap his arms around me that I wonder what he's about to do next.

I've kissed guys before, I've done a lot of different things in my effort to be someone other than myself, but right now, in this moment with him, I'm not that other version of me, I'm myself and I'm scared about what this means. If he's going to bring me this close to him, is he going to want more? And if he does, am I going to be able to deliver or will it all just crash and burn around me the way it always does?

"You're my butterfly, Ems. You fought the darkness and beat it. You're the reason I'm better now. You wouldn't walk away when that's all I wanted you to do. You gave me back the light. You're the reason I'm standing here now, reborn."

Whoa—Holy shit.

I'm about to say something when his hand comes up around and I feel his fingers brushing against the skin of my now flushed and overheating cheeks. The words fall flat as I just listen to the sound of his breath as it escapes through his nose, the both of us so close now there can be no doubt about what's about to happen next.

"I'm not right for you, Emma, and this, whatever it is between us, it's dangerous, but I can't do things like this with you and keep denying it."

"Denying—what?" I whisper as his face moves even closer in to mine. We're a hairs breath away from our lips touching now and the pounding in my heart has reached a fever pitch. I only hope with the way it's exploding inside of me isn't noticeable to him. I don't want him to know how being this close is making me lose all control.

A control I've done my best to maintain for so long, I don't know how to handle it breaking down.

"How badly I want you."

His lips crash into mine and all rational thought is lost in the air around us. We grab onto each other so tightly, the need so desperate between us, fueled by a desire previously unknown. I push my lips back against his, struggling to take control back from him, wanting to taste him on my terms, controlling the speed and the strength of what's taking place.

He's not the only one that's been denying and even now as we stand here, hanging on for dear life; I still fight the need to deny it. Despite everything I've done in an attempt to keep myself separate from him, away from the feelings I knew were building in me, it's been completely impossible.

The way his lips feel as they're pressed on mine, there are no words for. Completely absorbed in the way all of this feels, there's only one thing that breaks through and the reality of it is startling.

I'm falling in love with Graham Hudson and there's not a damn thing I can do to stop it.

Chapter Eighteen

Graham

If someone would have told me months ago that life could be this good, that I could feel this alive, happy, complete, I wouldn't believe it. There was no way with everything I faced, how broken down I'd become, I could ever be deserving of what's happening to me now.

I've gone toe to toe with some of the darkest demons hell has ever created, yet finding peace, happiness even, with somebody else; it's a luxury I never thought I would be afforded. When you spend your entire life believing that things are meant to be one way and its turned on its axis, there really isn't much hope to be had in something more.

Emma is my something more and the way I felt the minute my lips connected with hers proves it. I'm not even sure what I was thinking doing it the way I did, but I wasn't about to turn back. Not when it felt like the right thing to do. In fact, it's the first time in months that something has felt right. There wasn't anything waiting around the corner this time, nothing that would break us.

Things may have started when I was under the devil's control, but nothing that's happened since has been and what's driving me now isn't darkness, or even the voice of an angel pushing me in the direction I'm meant to go. It's just her. The way she stands in awe of the horizon when we show up at the marina, the smile she wears as she watches the boats coming in. The way she turns into me when I speak to her, more than willing to hear what I have to say. It's everything about her.

The kiss must have lasted a total of two minutes, but it was the most peaceful two minutes I've experienced in months. It started slow, me just pressing my lips to hers, not entirely sure where I wanted to take it next, but the minute her lips answered back, it became so much more. We gave into the need we both had to feel more. We pushed each other deeper, farther than I'm pretty sure either of us were expecting.

We connected.

That feeling of something more that I gave up on, the one I never felt deserving of, especially with the way I handled Serenity's return from Hell, was being offered to me and I did what any undeserving man would do, I grabbed on to it with everything I had, preparing to never let it go.

Nothing could ruin the moment, even though it did cause me pain when she broke away first. There was a second, when I caught her eyes as they opened and locked on me that she looked sad, as if something about what just happened between us was wrong.

"Graham," she says, my name starting off quiet but gathering strength the more air she breathes in. "I need—"

"Don't say it." I answer, thinking that I know what she's about to say and not wanting to hear it. I don't want anything to ruin the way kissing her felt, not even if she's completely right.

"You don't even know what I'm gonna say."

"I think I do. This is about Ser, right? I mean kissing me, knowing how I felt about her, shit, how I might always feel about her. It's wrong."

She's shaking her head, disagreeing with me, but she doesn't realize that her eyes are giving her away. The truth is in them, even if in shaking her head she's giving me the answer I most want to hear. I don't want this to be about her best friend, our best friend. I want what just happened to just be about us. It won't get tainted that way and what I just experienced, should never be tainted.

"Graham, there's something I need to tell you—"

Her voice fades off again, almost as if she's unsure of what she's saying and I take that as my chance. Whatever it is she thinks she needs to tell me, I don't need to hear right now. Especially if it's something that could possibly ruin this moment. I put my finger to her lips, before bending my head down again and bringing my lips to hers softly. It's nothing at all like the kiss before, this time used only as a means to hush her, but it still has the same effect. It's as if the minute I in any way touch her, my body comes alive.

She is definitely my butterfly, no doubt about it.

"I want to hear everything you have to say Ems, I do, but right now, can we just enjoy this for a little while longer?"

I can see that she's struggling with whatever it is she feels we need to talk about, but she nods her head in agreement, giving into what I want. I know what all of this must be doing to her but with the limited amount of time we have before we've got to head back for classes, the last thing I want to do is spend it talking about how wrong this is because of who our best friend happens to be.

Emma's right though, we do need to talk about what's happening between us and what it means. She needs to know that I've been to see Serenity and that where I go from here has nothing to do with my best friend and everything to do with the advice she gave me. In a way, her telling me to take a chance was her way of saying that being with Emma is the right thing. I refuse to believe otherwise.

For now though, all I want is to enjoy the few remaining minutes I have with my arms around this beautiful girl. Everything else can wait.

She's turned again, facing the water, her face giving away nothing as to how she feels about everything I've said and what I've done kissing her, but I'm comforted by the fact that she hasn't made a move to leave my arms.

"You're not the only one who feels reborn, Graham."

Enjoying the silence of the moment and the way her body feels being this close to mine, along with the hushed tone of her words, I almost don't catch them, but there can be no denial of the way hearing them makes me feel. I wasn't sure what the hell I was trying to tell her earlier, explaining about the butterfly and what it meant to me, but it seems I didn't have to because she did.

"What do you mean?"

"When I'm around you, things are different. There's no pressure to be someone else and as scary as that is, I like it."

"You shouldn't be anything more than what you are—who you are, Ems."

"It's not that easy."

"Why do you think you need to be someone else?"

It's a question I've wanted to ask her for a long time, but no matter how many times it's come up, it was never the right time. It seems like now, holding her here, after sharing something with her I never thought myself capable of experiencing again, it's the right time. Maybe now I can get her to open up to me.

"I need to be someone different because spending any amount of time around the real me, would scare people away pretty quickly."

"That's crazy."

It's obvious with the way her body pulls away from mine that I've said the wrong thing. With all of this being so new to me, let alone what it must be like for her, it's inevitable that this would happen. If she would let me in, let me get to know the real her, I might be able to avoid this kind of screw-up, but until that happens, I can see it happening a whole lot more in our future.

"You know I don't mean it the way it sounds right?"

"How do you mean it then?" she asks, turning her body around and leveling me with what are probably the saddest eyes I've ever seen.

"I've been around you for two years, off and on, and I haven't been scared away yet."

"You don't know the real me."

"That's not true."

"No, Graham. It is true. Not even Serenity has seen the real me, at least not entirely. The parts she has seen, she had to go searching for answers for, because the show I put on, the role I played was so well done that she couldn't see the broken mess that really lies underneath. She couldn't and you can't either."

"I see a lot more than you give me credit for."

"What does that mean?"

"You're running from something. You've been doing it for a really long time, so to you, it doesn't even feel like running anymore, but you're doing it. Something happened to you, I don't know when or what, but it changed you. It made you believe that the only way you can ever be happy is to be someone other than the person you are and its wrong."

"Are you sure you're not taking Psych classes on the side?" she asks, her tone lighter as a laugh escapes her lips.

"I don't need a class to tell me what I can see clearly. I just wish you would trust me enough to tell me what you're running from."

"It's got nothing to do with trust."

"Then what is it?"

She lowers her head and I don't need to hear her explanation to know why she's so afraid to open up. She's already told me as much before.

"You're afraid the minute you tell me, I'm going to bail."

She nods and my heart drops. I have no idea what she's been through in her life, but if it's so hard on her that she believes people will leave once they find out, it's wrong. Anyone worth having around would never leave just because of something that may have happened in the past.

"That isn't going to happen. There's nothing you can tell me that would ever make me bail on you."

There's distrust in her eyes, maybe even disbelief that what I'm saying could actually be real. Whatever's happened to this girl in her life, it's preventing her from believing in anyone and I want to put an end to it. She'd opened up enough to believe in Serenity, and now I want to show her that she can do the same with me. My feelings for her aside, she needs to know she's not alone.

"How much has Ser told you about my problems?"

"Not much. It wasn't her place."

"You know my diagnosis right?"

"Yeah, but it's not like you've ever kept that a secret."

"I walked in on my dad screwing around on my mom when I was a kid. I held onto his secret for him, for a really long time, until it ripped me apart so bad I finally broke and told my mom. That's when everything started."

It's no secret I don't have a relationship with my father. That the only person there for me growing up had been my mother, so I'm not exactly the best one to talk to when it comes to daddy issues, but I do know one thing. What she walked in on, what she held inside of her as long as she did, it's not something anyone should have to deal with, let alone a kid. It's no wonder she's at the point she is now, not trusting anyone. The person that she should have been able to trust above anyone else had let her down.

"When what started?"

"Holding on to all of that, that's when the depression started. I pulled away from everything and everyone and for a really long time, made no effort to live my life. I was just moving moment to moment waiting for it to end."

"Is that when your Mom put you in the center?"

"Yeah, it was around then, but some other stuff happened leading up to that."

"Like what?"

"I'd go to school and in an effort to hide what was really going on with me; I'd act out in ways that were nothing like me. I would go out of my way to appear to be having fun, faking it until finally I started believing my own hype. I literally became someone else entirely."

"The way you are now?"

"Exactly like that. The thing is, I hated every second of it. I hated being the person I was when I was at home with my mom, watching her go through the motions of her own pain, and I hated the way I was at school, because both versions weren't me."

I know I wanted her to open up and I'm not regretting it now, but with the sadness in her eyes, the truth that lies underneath it all, I feel like I pushed her into something again that she just wasn't ready to face and I have no pretty words I can say that can take it away or stop it now that it's started.

"I told you that being around you is like being reborn because for the first time in years, I'm not putting on a show. The person I am when I'm with you, Graham; that's the real me. I think the reason I fought so hard when you were sick was because I saw myself in you and it scared the hell out of me. I didn't want you to become someone else."

She doesn't know how close to the truth she's hitting right now. I want to tell her that what she didn't want for me had already happened, but I can't do it. I'm sure she already knows it anyway. I did become someone else, and just like she hated every second of being someone else, I did too.

We're a lot more alike than either one of us wants to admit. We're both broken and in desperate need of repair.

"I don't ever want you playing a part, Emma. Not with me or anyone else. You should always just be yourself. The people that really care, they'll see past all the things you're afraid to show."

"You really mean that don't you?"

"Every word of it. All you have to do is look at the way you interacted with me, even when I was at my worst to see the truth. I did horrible things. I used women, I treated my friends like shit, I pushed people away, I even did physical and emotional damage to myself, but you never walked away. Why is it okay when you do it, but for anyone else to do it with you, it's not possible?"

"Because you're worth it and I don't think that I am."

It's in her words that I feel the connection that formed earlier grow stronger. It's as if in those few seconds of silence where she thought about her answer, she'd stepped inside my head during the darkest point of my life and pulled out exactly how I felt. She's not the only one who didn't think they were worth fighting for, because numerous times I thought the same thing. It's why it's so amazing that I'm even standing here with her at all. I never expected to live through it, that's how deep my lack of self worth went. I didn't believe I was worth it.

I didn't think I was worth anything at all.

"You're worth it, Emma. We're worth it."

Chapter Nineteen

Emma

There was this moment when I opened up to Graham on the dock, that I anticipated him seeing the real me, the parts of me that I've been trying so desperately for years to hide, and running from it. It was like waiting for the other shoe to drop, but all of that anticipation, waiting for him to turn his back on me, the same way my dad had done years before, it never came.

The opposite seemed to happen. Where before we had been comfortable, but with this underlying nervousness, he seemed more secure after I opened up. In fact, he grabbed on to me tighter, never once letting our bodies separate. Even when he mentioned needing to head back for class, he made sure in some way that we still touched. Holding my hand, brushing his side up against mine as we walked, it was like he was proving his earlier words to be true.

Graham really does believe that I'm worth it, that we're both worth it even though I'm pretty sure he's reached the same point I have before, where it seemed like nothing was worth it at all anymore. He was also holding true in his statement that he wasn't going to walk away just because there might be things about me that were a little hard to handle.

It's him being this way with me that made me realize what I've been trying so hard to deny for the past few months. The way I feel about him, even though it started out in the beginning purely as a physical attraction or even a reaction to the way he had been while under Lucifer's control, is so much more than that now. I'm falling in love with him and with each second that passes, the knowledge of that rips me apart inside.

We get back to campus with enough time to make it to class and the entire time, I keep thinking about what I'm still hiding from him. I was finally able to open myself up enough to tell him the truth about my past, and even about my issues and what putting me in the centre had really done to me, but there is still something he doesn't know and it's something he needs to.

I should never have let him stop me from telling him, especially after the kiss and the words spoken after the fact, but that's exactly what I did. The one thing he needs to know; deserves to know more than anything and I'm still keeping it from him, which I know will only make everything that much worse when it does finally come out.

I made a promise to the angels. It needs to be handled and I do want to be the one to do it, but with the way he looked at me, wanting to enjoy the time with me, needing me to open up so that he could learn about me, in an effort to be close, I couldn't bring myself to do it. I chickened out at the last second and I can't help but feel that in the end, that's what's going to cost me the most.

We've gotten through English Lit together, this time sitting beside each other and finding ways through the entire class to continue the physical contact we started a few hours before and we're now about to go our separate ways, but just like I've come to expect of him over the last couple of weeks, he's not going to let me out of his sight without some promise of seeing me again.

If I didn't already like him, this would definitely be one of the times where he makes it happen.

"I've got an idea."

"Okay."

"I've got back to back classes today and a whole shit ton of work I need to catch up on, but have dinner with me tonight?"

My heart wants to leap out of my chest at the possibility of spending more time with him, but I do my best to gain control before he's able to notice. Yes, I'm sure it's not a secret after what we shared that I like him, but there's no need for him to know just how much.

"Won't that distract you from the 'shit ton of work' you need to do?"

"Yeah, that's sort of the point." He laughs. "With as much as I've got to get finished, I'll be barricaded in my room for another few weeks. Who wants that?"

"Good point. I think you've spent more than enough time in your room."

"So you'll do it?"

"Yes, Graham, I'll do it."

"Awesome!"

"Not really sure how awesome I am keeping you from getting your work done, but I can't resist that smile."

"Well then it's a good thing you put it there, huh? Resistance is futile when you're the cause of it."

Before I can respond to his words, he's bridged the gap that leaving class caused and he's wrapped himself around me, my body curled so tightly in his that I'm sweating from the heat occurring between us. As strange as it is for me, being this close to someone, especially not putting on a show, I'm enjoying it. It's the most comfortable feeling in the world.

"Do me a favor?" he asks, as he breaks the hold and I'm met again with the chill that separation between us causes.

"Sure."

"As hard as I know it will be, don't spend your entire day thinking about me. Try and pay attention to your classes too."

He backs up and ducks as I reach out to slap him and I can't help laughing as I watch him jogging away and in the direction of his Art History class. It's only when I see him turn around and face me, waving as he keeps walking backward that I'm taken by just how much everything's changed.

It wasn't all that long ago that I was afraid of this guy. That what I experienced with him during his time with Lucifer put a fear in me so strong I thought I might never recover. Yet, here I am now, watching him walk away, a smile all over my face matching the one I see on his and I'm excited about dinner with him in a few hours.

Even knowing that once he found out the truth, everything would come crashing down around me, I still can't tame the excitement level inside me. I want this. For the first time in years, I really want something and more than that, I want someone and there's no one better than him.

There's no doubt about it. I'm in love with Graham.

Graham

When I texted Emma and told her where to meet me, that I wanted to take her to dinner somewhere that had nothing to do with fast food and everything to do with the entire date like experience, I expected her to back out.

That's something I'm learning that I could only assume about her before. When I first met her, I always thought she was high maintenance, that she was one of those girls that no matter how hard you tried; nothing would ever be good enough for. As it turns out, I was dead wrong. She actually hates getting dressed up as much as Serenity, though her closet would probably argue with you. She prefers the comfort of staying in more than going out, and that's why when I dropped the location on her, I expected a text back saying that she couldn't make it.

She surprised me again because not only did she text back and let me know that it was okay, but she got there before me and she looks amazing. There's nothing overly fancy about the way she's dressed, it's just that she owns what she is wearing. She owns it so well that she's had my full attention from the second I walked in the door.

Looking around, I can tell I'm not the only person she's captured the attention of. The only difference between me and them is, I actually get to experience the girl behind the baby doll dress and they only get to ogle from a distance.

"I feel slightly underdressed now."

"Why?" she asks me as her lips lift.

"Well, I'm sitting here in jeans and you, well shit. You know how you look."

"Actually, I don't think I do. You should probably tell me."

"Emma."

"Graham."

She smirks again and it takes all the self control I've got not to reach across the table and grab her. As hard as it's been fighting my urges whenever I'm with her, it seems I'm beginning to lose the fight. With the way she looks right now, especially when her eyes are leveled on me this way, bright and alive, it's killing me.

"Ems, you're gorgeous and you know it. It's why half the men in here are staring at my date instead of their own."

She blushes and I feel like the luckiest guy alive. I was beginning to wonder if the confidence she seems to exude could be broken. Seeing it happen fills me with a happiness I don't think I've ever known.

"You know how to make a girl feel good, don't ya Hudson?"

Just when I think the need to have her can't get much worse, she has to go and say something like that. I can easily tell she's joking with me, especially with the way her eyes continue to sparkle, but there can be no denial of the implication underneath. It's almost more than I can take. She has no idea how good I want to make her feel, in every way imaginable.

I need to change the subject, but my mind's a complete blank.

"If I wasn't seeing it with my own eyes, I wouldn't believe it. Graham doesn't have a comeback."

"Enjoy it while it lasts, princess. It won't last very long."

"Awe, well that's no fun. I kind of enjoy seeing you unhinged."

"You're killing me here, Ems."

"I have no idea what you're talking about."

She laughs and that's when I completely lose it. I'm up and out of my seat, coming to rest behind her, my lips as close as possible to her ears so that what I'm about to say can be for her only.

"As badly as I want to have dinner with you, I'm willing to skip it in favor of dessert, princess."

Her breath catches at my words and the sound drives me crazy. I already knew I was affected by this girl, but it appears it's not just her words that have the ability to get to me anymore; it's every single thing about her.

"So, dinner—right. We both need to eat." She stammers, which makes me happy as I again make my way around the table and take my seat. Emma may enjoy seeing me come unhinged but I'm pretty sure I enjoyed her doing it more.

After we've ordered our food, the conversation takes a turn to how the rest of our day apart went, both of us going back and forth effortlessly talking about our classes, the people in them, and just what the point of all of it is. It's the first time in awhile where I've been able to sit across from someone and not have to worry about what comes next.

With as primal as I seem to act whenever I'm within a foot of this girl, it's moments like this one right now that mean the most to me. Everything about our time together is natural, nothing is forced and I couldn't ask for more. I even find myself enjoying myself as I watch her dig into her food.

The way she moves her fork across the plate, wrapping the spaghetti around is fascinating to me, as are the noises of pleasure she makes as she takes her first bite and then the subsequent ones after it. I don't have much experience being around a lot of people when they're eating, only having my mother and Serenity to fall back on, but none of my previous experiences can compare to this one.

She's even beautiful when she's eating.

"Is everything okay?" she asks, and as I look up and catch her eyes on me, I realize I've been caught staring.

"Yeah, I'm great. Why do you ask?"

"You're quiet."

"Just taking it all in."

"What does that mean?"

"I can't remember the last time I did something like this. I'm not even sure I've ever done something like this. It's just nice."

"If it's so nice why aren't you eating?"

"Because watching you eat is ten times more fun."

She blushes again and just like before, I feel like I've won some kind of award. Her cheeks are so pink now that they're almost the same shade as the flowers on her dress. It's only when she puts her fork down on the plate that I realize I might have made her feel uncomfortable with my admission.

"I didn't mean to make you stop."

"You didn't. I'm just done."

"Why don't I believe that?" I ask, smiling in an effort to put her at ease. Even I have to admit watching her eat might have come off a bit stalker like and that's the last thing I want.

She shrugs, but before I can open my mouth to say anything more she speaks.

"I've never done anything like this either. I've been on dates, sure, but not like this."

"No one's ever taken you out to dinner before?"

She shakes her head and I feel bad. It's another way I think I've made assumptions about her. I always just assumed that most of what I would want to do with her, she'd have already done with other guys given her track record. Hearing that what we're experiencing right now is new for her, it's shocking.

"I've gone to movies with guys before and even clubbing, but not this. I'm not the girl most guys want to date or haven't you noticed that?"

"Most guys are stupid, that's why."

She blushes and this time she must be aware of it because she tries to hide it from me, something I'm just not having any part of. I reach my hand across the table and touch hers, pulling them one by one away from her face. She shouldn't hide her reactions from me, no matter what they are.

"You don't have to hide from me, Ems. I like the blush. It matches your dress."

She smiles but makes no move to slide her hand out from under my own, both of which are now resting back on the table in front of us.

"Graham..."

There's a lift to her voice that tells me there's something she wants to ask, but the trepidation in her tone also shows how uncertain she is doing it. With as comfortable as I feel, there's a part of me that hates the uncertainty. She should feel the same way I do.

"Just say it Ems."

"What are we doing here?"

"Eating? Enjoying each other's company? Having fun?"

"Not what I mean."

"I know it's not. I just don't know what to say. What do you think we're doing here?"

"You know what? Forget I even asked. I don't even know what I'm trying to say."

"Emma, I'm not going to forget it. I'm just not sure how to say what I think I need to say. All of this, it's still really new to me."

"Me too."

"I like you, I told you that. I want you, Emma."

"Want me like you did at the party or something different?"

Any reminder of that night, the way I acted at the party, it stings. I don't even want to remember that night, let alone compare it to what's going on now. This has nothing to do with that kind of wanting, though as much as I want to deny it, that's definitely a part of it too. The desire I have for her now, the way I did that night, it's still there. I just can't act on it.

"I want you to be mine. No one else's, just mine. I want you to be my butterfly."

She's silent after my admission and it's scary. I worry that I said too much too soon. She may have opened up to me this morning, but that doesn't mean she's in any way ready for the gravity of what I feel for her. I'm having a hard enough time admitting that to myself, let alone laying it out for her to accept.

I want her to accept it though, because I mean every word of it. I do want her to be mine. No more waiting around, playing games or feeling her out. This is me jumping the last hurdle. This is me taking my chance. I just hope I don't end up regretting it.

"What about Serenity?"

"Serenity who?" I know how it sounds, so before she can come up with a reply, I hold up my hand in an effort to explain. "This isn't about her, Emma. This is about us. I like you. I've liked you for a while, despite my attempts at denying it. I want you. I want us."

"Graham—"

"Emma, just tell me what you want. All the wanting in the world on my end doesn't mean shit if we're not on the same page. So just tell me what you want. I swear to you, I'll be okay with whatever it is."

"I want you, Graham. I just want you."

"Then you've got me. I'm not going anywhere, Emma. Not ever."

Michael

It's a risk appearing this way, knowing that at any moment, we could be interrupted, but with everything I've witnessed this evening alone, there can be no more time wasted. I know that it has not quite been a week since we entered into our agreement, but there can be no denial that it is time to revisit this.

"Jesus, Michael. Are you trying to give me a heart attack?" she asks as I waste no time appearing in front of her. It's obvious from her reaction that she had not been expecting me, though how she could go on believing we wouldn't find ourselves in this very spot after everything this evening is beyond my comprehension.

"I assure you, it was not my intent, but it should come as no surprise to you why I am here."

"Is Lucifer gonna walk through the door any second?"

"No. This time I believe a visit from one angel is more than adequate."

"He's going to be back any second, so what do you want?"

"It is time. You must tell him."

"I know."

"I have to admit, I expected more of an argument about this."

"You seem to think that I want to keep this from him. Like you think I enjoy it or something when it's really the complete opposite."

"I believe no such thing. I have seen the struggle you have maintaining this secret. I have also been privy to the times at which you have wanted nothing more than to admit the truth. I am also aware at how human emotion works Emma, despite my claims to the contrary."

"What's that supposed to mean?"

"You are in love with the Hudson boy. It is clearly evident. It is my understanding that in situations such as this, love makes you do the wacky."

She laughs and I am at a loss as to what is so humorous. For every step I take in trying to understand these beings, it appears I continue to take one step back.

"Love makes you do the wacky? Really Michael?"

"You act as though you've never heard the statement before."

"No, I've heard it alright, but I didn't take you for a guy that steals lines from movies to get your point across."

"I do no such thing."

"You just did."

"It matters little. The point I am trying to make is, you are in love with the boy and when in love, it can sometimes block you from doing the right thing."

"Well, it's not doing that with me. I know that I need to tell him."

"That is what brings me here to you. I am aware that he is merely parking the car and will be back in the room in a matter of minutes. I am also aware of the magnitude of this secret and what it will cause. I want you to be aware that I am here for you, for the duration."

"You want to be here when I tell him?"

"Do you have a better idea? I have the power to make the boy understand the choice you made going to Lucifer and asking him for help. In fact, I do believe I am the only one able to make him see the truth."

"What truth are you supposed to make me see Mike?"

It takes me a second to realize that Graham has indeed made his presence known, despite my ability to be able to sense his arrival ahead of time. For whatever reason he had gotten past it and in doing so had walked in at a most unfortunate time.

"What's he talking about Emma? What does he mean by you going to Lucifer and asking for help?"

His words are choked, the pain he feels even having to ask evident. I want to go to the boy and erase it from him, but I cannot. That is not what I am here to accomplish.

"Can someone please tell me what the hell is going on?"

"It is time that you are made aware of the truth as it pertains to your healing, Graham."

"Michael—"

"Emma, the time for the truth is now. I know that you wish it could have taken place in another way, but this is the way we've been given."

"What's he talking about Ems?" Graham asks again, this time turning to the woman he loves, his eyes pleading with her for answers. "What truth is he talking about?"

Silence weighs heavily in the room as Emma struggles with the gravity of the situation before her. She is aware that she must tell him the truth, but she's also aware of what's going to happen the moment she does and is doing her best to drag it out as long as possible in an effort to spare the both of them any more pain.

I sympathize with her plight, but if she does not tell him soon, she will leave me no choice but to do it for her.

"That last night, the one where you were drinking and passed out with the girl in your bed, I was here, Graham. I saw her leave, and I called for Michael and Lucifer."

"You what?"

"It started before that actually. I was scared for you. I could see you getting worse instead of better, and I saw how close you were to giving up. I couldn't let you do that, so against my better judgment, I went to Lucifer and I asked him for his help."

"Emma, this isn't funny."

"She is not attempting to be funny, nor tell you some kind of a joke, Graham. She is merely trying to tell you the truth. What you have been due now for the past week and a half."

"You went to Lucifer?" he chokes out and my heart breaks at the sound. Gabriel was right all along, I do feel for these humans despite my claims to the contrary. I hate seeing any of them in pain, especially when I can feel the pain as if it is my own.

"Yes. That night when you kicked the girl out, you passed out and that's when I called Lucifer to come. Michael was here with me, making sure that nothing went wrong."

"What did he do to me?"

"He healed your mind—and your heart the way he should have a long time ago."

"Michael, what does that mean exactly?" he asks, turning toward me and away from Emma and her truth.

"Lucifer joined with you in an effort to heal what he had broken."

"That son of a bitch was riding around inside me again?" he screams, this time, the reality setting in and the betrayal rising to the surface, pushing him forward.

"In a manner of speaking, yes, but not in the way you believe. It was nothing at all like the previous time the two of you joined."

"Yeah, because that actually matters." He spits out before turning his rage back toward the woman now frozen in place in the middle of the room. "Why Emma?"

"I needed to do something."

"So, the only reason I'm okay again is because of Lucifer?"

Both Emma and I nod at the same moment and that is when he turns his back on both of us.

"Michael, get out of here. I need to talk to Emma and I need to do it alone."

I do not feel right agreeing to his request. The last thing that feels right about this situation is me giving in to the boy and walking away. I meant what I said to Emma, I want to be here for her during this process. She is going to need support for what I know would come from this.

"I am not leaving the two of you alone. I do not believe that is in anyone's best interest."

"I don't really give a shit what you believe in."

"Michael, it's alright. Go. I'll be fine." Emma cuts in and despite my earlier reservations in leaving her alone, I can tell that it is exactly what she wants, or at least it is what she feels needs to happen now. I still do not feel right about it, but I will not take away their right to privacy.

"Graham, I have no doubt that right now you are feeling betrayed and you have every right to feel that way, but what

Emma did, with the blessing of Heaven behind her, was the right thing to do. It brought you back to us where you belong and that will never be wrong."

Chapter Twenty

Graham

This is all a sick dream. I need to just wake the fuck up because there's no way that any of what I'm hearing and seeing right now can be real.

Emma, my butterfly, the girl I damaged more than anyone else during the darkest period of my life, she wouldn't do this. She knows better than anyone what something like this would do to me, so she would never take the risk.

Except that's exactly what she did. She did the unthinkable.

I want to be angry that Serenity, Ryan and even Michael had been a part of this, playing along, lying to me the same way that she's been doing for the past two weeks, but I can't be. All I can see is that she did. The one person that I trusted not to make a decision like this had been the very one to plunge the knife in.

It hurts like a bitch.

All the suffering and pain I went through, they all made me believe I was the reason it ended. That I somehow used the strength inside me and beat what Lucifer had done. The reality is, I was never strong enough to beat it on my own and I knew it. I don't know what hurts more. Knowing I was right all along about my own abilities or knowing that everyone worked together to make me believe otherwise.

After watching Serenity marry Ryan, I'd been prepared to never feel anything ever again. If I couldn't be the one standing up there with her, joining with her in the way I always believed we were meant to, than I didn't want to have it at all.

Emma Daniels changed all of that. She'd given me my life back even though I'm pretty sure she wouldn't agree. She would want me to believe that I saved myself, but it's not even close to the truth. She had done it by staying with me despite all of the horrible things I put her through and showing me a side of life that I had long since forgotten about.

Sure, we had this unspoken connection between us, that's been going on for awhile, but we both fought against it. We did the right thing by Serenity first, then by ourselves because between the both of us, we were both too damaged to believe we could actually mean something good to another person. That we could impact someone else's life in a way that really matters in the long term.

It's only in admitting to that connection, that we became free. I was free to love again, to feel something other than the self hatred and darkness, something other than broken over a bond that was never meant to last. She was able to open up to someone, let them see the real her, instead of the painted picture she'd been living for so long that it was hard to tell where the real Emma began and the fake one ended.

That connection, the one I felt so completely, the one tangible thing in my life that was real, is nothing but make believe. It was all an elaborate plan by the very person that had turned me to the darkness in the first place.

Lucifer won again.

"Graham, say something please."

"How long Emma?" I spit out, my voice so rough I don't even recognize it. "How long were you planning on keeping this from me?"

Her head lowers to the floor and it takes every bit of self control I have not to walk to where she's standing and yank it back up until her eyes are deadlocked on mine. There is no way in hell she's going to turn away from what she's done. No, I deserve answers.

"Not long. I planned on telling you. It was actually a deal that I made with Michael and Lucifer. I had a week to tell you the truth."

"A week? You didn't think to tell me when I brought it up with you that first day!" I scream at her, my anger getting the better of me, but too lost in it to care how it appears to her now. She brought this on herself when she took my choice away.

"Of course I did! I hated keeping it from you. Every time we were together, it took everything in me not to tell you the truth."

"Yet, you didn't tell me."

""No, I didn't tell you. I wanted too, god, I wanted to tell you so bad, but I couldn't do it. Not until I knew that whatever he did, actually worked and you were okay."

"He never should have done it at all! That wasn't your decision to make!"

She flinches from my tone, which isn't helped by the fact that my hands are flailing out at her in anger at the same time. As angry as I am with her, I don't want to scare her, but the rage inside is building in me so much, it's cutting off my ability to think logically.

"You're right; it wasn't my choice to make. It was yours, but you weren't getting better Graham! You were just getting worse. I know all about what you've been doing to yourself in your sleep. It was only a matter of time before you cut yourself so deep that you'd be dead! I couldn't let that happen."

"So you go to the one person that you know I want nowhere near me? The person that did all of this to me to begin with, and you ask him to fix it? Somehow, asking the devil for help seemed like the way to go?"

"No! Not at first it didn't. I wanted it to be Michael, but it couldn't be. He couldn't break his oath to Heaven, to his father. It had to be Lucifer."

"You really are the stupidest person I've ever met if you believe Lucifer was the only choice."

She flinches at my words and where it should have affected me, it doesn't. I mean every word. Emma is as stupid as Serenity is. They both want to see the good in a being that doesn't have a good bone in his body. He might be able to make them all believe he could be different, but I know better. I spent time with him, closer than even Ryan was. I know what really lies underneath.

Before I realize what's happening, I feel her as she attempts to wrap her arms around me. The minute her hands make contact with my body, I feel my stomach turn and I push at her, as hard as I can and as I watch, she falls to the ground in front of me, her eyes now streaked with tears.

She's crying for what she did to me, for what I've done to her and will still do to her and I feel nothing. I'm completely numb to it. The feelings I have for this girl, the ones that I thought would be the thing to set me free are gone and there's just nothing left in me. I'm completely empty and devoid of everything.

I never want to feel again. Feeling is what got me into this mess to begin with.

"I couldn't let you kill yourself—"

Bending down to her position on the floor, I place both hands on the sides of her head and I bring my face as close as possible to hers, so that she can't look anywhere but at me. She needs to hear me now, more than ever, and more than that, she needs to understand because once I've said what I'm about to say, I never want to see her again.

"I was ready to die. You took my choice away. You can sit here and think you did the right thing, the unselfish thing, but you did the complete fucking opposite. Just like I did when I made Serenity believe she was mine and not Ryan's. You did it too. You were selfish, you *are* selfish. Which makes you no better than the bastard you went to in order to heal me."

"You don't mean that..."

"I mean every word. You wanna know the worst part?" I ask. "Not only did you do this, knowing full well this is how I was going to react when I found out, but you turned every single one of my friends against me in an effort to do it."

"I didn't turn anyone against you." She chokes out through her tears, something I can't bring myself to feel anything for. "They're all still your friends."

"That's where you're wrong. The only friend I had is dead."

As the words fall I realize how true they are. The one person that's innocent in all of this is the one person no longer here.

Gabriel.

"You don't mean any of this—you're just angry and you have every right to be. I should never have done it without your permission, but Graham, it wasn't the wrong thing. I did do the right thing, even if you can't see it."

"I've never meant something more than I do right now. Emma, what you did, I can never forgive you for. You not only took my choice away, but you brought my friends into it, all in an effort to keep it from me. I don't think you would've ever told me the truth and that's what hurts most of all. If I didn't want to be with you so damn bad, after the day we had, I never would have come back here tonight and you would have just gone on keeping your fucking secrets."

"No," she answers, shaking her head for emphasis. "I would have told you—"

"Well that can be what keeps you warm at night because from now on, it won't be me. I'm done. I'm done with you and with all of this."

I turn from her again, backing away and making my way toward her door, never once turning around to see what my final words do to her. For the first time in two weeks, I can feel the headache beginning its slow rhythm pound in my head and instead of fearing it, being turned inside out by it the way I would have in the past, I welcome it. I want to feel the pain because in focusing on that, maybe I can block out the betrayal I feel at everything I've learned here tonight.

With the way Serenity felt for me at one time, I would have expected this from her, especially given how she feels about Lucifer and his supposed redemption, but Emma? Emma knew the parts of me that I wouldn't let any of the others see. She even admitted as much in saying she knew what the nightmares were putting me through.

She knew going to Lucifer would have been the last thing I wanted and she had done it anyway. There's a part of me that sees her point. She wanted to do right by me because she didn't want me to suffer or die, but she could've found another way. More than that, she could have still told the truth about it, and she didn't.

I meant what I said. I'm done with her, I'm done with all of this, supernatural or otherwise. I'm done with everything. They might have put me through all of this in an effort to bring me back to them, giving me the light back, but all they did was push me further into the part of myself that I knew would never truly go away now that it had been embraced.

They pushed me straight into the darkness, right where I belong.

Chapter Twenty-One

Lucifer

The road to hell is paved with good intentions.

It is not the first time that the statement has made itself known to me and I am sure with each step I take moving forward in my bid to earn my redemption that it will not be the last, but it has never been more apparent than it is in this moment.

Doing the right thing by someone is not an exact science. It remains a risk even when it's driven by the purest intention. In answering Emma's request the way I did, I know I was doing the right thing and for that I harbor no regret, but there is no doubt, especially with the fallout that has come from that very action, it may not have been handled in the best way.

It is no secret the way Graham feels about me and he has every right to feel it. Just as I have to earn my entrance back home, I also have to earn my redemption as it pertains to the very beings I did the most damage to. Graham is one of them, as is my counterpart in Gregory Richards. I altered both of their existences for my own selfish gain and that is not something that can be easily erased or fixed overnight. It will take time, of which I now have an unlimited supply.

The minute Graham woke after being healed by me, there should have been a conversation. I am not naïve enough to think that in having said conversation it would have alleviated all that both Emma and Graham feel now, but it would have gone a long way to rectifying all that has been done. There would be no secrets between them and they would have had an easier time with recovery then it appears they do now.

Michael had been right the day he visited Emma, wanting to know when she planned on telling Graham the truth. It should have been done long before that meeting, but we all wanted the same result. We were driven by the same thing. We wanted to be sure that Graham woke up and adjusted to the changes that having his human body healed would bring. We wanted his mind to adjust just as easily as his body and not risk him sliding further back into the despair that it had taken a great deal of power to erase.

It was the right thing to do, but in the long term, it has done damage that I am not sure can ever be healed. Graham isn't being driven by the darkness anymore, despite how angry he is and how dark his thoughts are. He is experiencing a very human reaction to the betrayal he feels and because it is very real, it is not something that I can take away from him. He has to go through this even if it is the last thing any of us want. He was not meant to live in the darkness and he never will again, despite his claim otherwise. The darkness no longer exists. He is grasping on to the one thing that right now seems real. It's a state of consciousness that he knows well because it's still so fresh, but the depths he reached before, can never be reached again. Serenity saw to that when she completed her undertaking.

His belief that Emma is in some way a symbolic butterfly to him is not wrong. It is what I believe she was always meant to be. Just as Michael believed in it before and even Father himself, I see it as well. Where Serenity may have been able to get through to him at one point due to the bond they share, it was never her place to do so. That particular destiny fell on her best friend. She was to be a beacon of light for Graham and one had to look no further than the changes in him over the two weeks they spent together to see the truth of it.

It is my belief in that, and my sense of loyalty to Emma that brings me to where I stand now. I have requested through my brother, a meeting with Father. I need to know what is to happen moving forward and there is no one better to ask than the seer of all things. He has the answers I seek and it is my hope that in seeing the damage that has been inflicted now, that it is answers he will give me now.

"You are right to question where we go from here, my son."

"Was it supposed to happen this way, Father? I am aware that healing him was part of the grander picture, as both you and Michael have spoken of it previously, but was it really meant to take this turn?"

"There is no other way it could have happened and deep down I believe you know that Lucifer. It is in our darkest moments, the times where we feel the most alone, broken off from the world and all it contains that the strength inside of us, our will to survive, is in its purest form."

"So in order for Graham to reach his full potential, he must travel this road now?"

"Yes."

"Has the boy not been through enough? What I did to him alone was more than any human should ever have to endure. Surely he is due a reprieve."

"That he is, Lucifer and just as you were the one to strip him of what remained of the darkness, you are also the one that will bring about his reprieve. You are the only one that can set all of this right."

"When the boy hates me as much as he does, how can you believe me to be the one to rectify this?"

"It is not something that I believe. It is something that I know because I have seen it happen. Lucifer, what has happened between Graham and Emma, it was written to be that way, not only for them, but for you as well."

"What does that mean?"

"It has always been about more than just healing Graham for you and if you look deep inside, to the very core of your being, I think you will be able to find the answers you seek."

My father; he is the king of word play.

"That is all I get? That the answers are inside me?"

"I never give answers when they are already known."

He is right. He said much the same to Serenity during our last meeting. He would not answer questions as they pertained to things she already knew inside, even if her conscious mind had not allowed the knowledge to come to light. It is the way he has always been, which means that any further help I need in determining what direction to take next, has to come from me and me alone.

"Lucifer, in forging ahead, you must promise me something."

"Anything."

"Do not let that which has befallen your sister and brothers in times past also have its way with you. You must not let the seed of doubt; of your own worth as it pertains to this mission take you away from what must be done."

It is not an easy request he makes. I am aware that Gabriel faced the seed of doubt on more than one occasion, especially in our history together; I had placed it within him to begin with. I am also aware that it has affected both Ryan and Serenity. I am sure even Michael has had his moments. We are all capable of doubt, whether we're regular human beings or celestial in nature. Doubt picks no favorites.

"I cannot promise you that, but what I can say is you have my word that I will try."

"The time is now Lucifer. Go forth and make this right."

Emma

What do you do when your entire world blows apart and there's not a damn thing you can do to stop it because you're the reason it happened to begin with?

If you're me, you do what you've always done.

You party your ass off.

It's been twenty-four hours since Graham learned the truth and walked away and even though I was content after that to stay barricaded in my room, not answering the door for anyone or anything, but after about twelve hours of it, something began to shift inside me.

I no longer felt sad about what happened, only angry. How dare he call me selfish when everything I did had been to save his life? How dare he call me stupid when it was through my so-called stupid move that he was able to be here now, happier than he's been in forever? How dare he believe that I would have kept the truth from him forever when it had taken everything in me not to spill it every damn time we were within a foot of each other?

No, I refuse to feel bad about this. Despite what he believes, I know deep down that going to Lucifer was the right thing. There can be no denial that the fallen angel was the reason all of this was put into motion in the first place. That was one thing Graham said that was the truth, but it didn't change the fact that the one that put it there had to be the one to remove it. It didn't change the fact that Lucifer did want to do right by the guy he damaged so long ago. Graham might think that in choosing the path I did that I destroyed everything, but I didn't. I saved it.

I saved him.

It's those facts that guide me to get out of bed, to throw off the agony I've been feeling for the past twenty four hours and push me out the door and back into life. At least it pushed me back into the life I've been leading since the day I walked in on my dad blowing my world apart.

Opening myself up, I always knew it would be a mistake. Showing the real me to someone, other than my best friend, who had thankfully seen and been through the worst of it with me years before, it was never supposed to happen. The world didn't need to see the depressed and broken Emma. No, they needed the girl that was full of life, willing to try anything and have the time of her life doing it. The girl that wasn't affected by what others thought of her and lived only for herself.

He thinks I'm selfish, well then I might as well make it reality.

I've been here for the last two hours. I've danced with at least five different guys, none I can remember the names of. All I know is that the last one, I want to remember his name because he was cuter then the others. He's also the only one that I wasn't repulsed by when he put his hands on me, bringing me close to him when we were dancing.

Yes, I definitely want to remember his name.

I grabbed a beer the minute I walked in the door and I swear my hand hasn't been empty since and I know I finished that first one off ages ago. It seems no matter where I turn, there's someone with a painted on smile, passing me another drink and I've got no problem at all taking them. In fact, the more I drink, the more I seem to block Graham Hudson and all of his issues out entirely. It's like he doesn't even exist.

Problem is, he does exist. He's the reason why I'm okay letting this guy touch me right now. The guy, Bill, or Will or whatever his name is, he looks like Graham. From the shaggy blonde hair covered by a beanie to the green glow of his eyes, they could definitely be brothers, if not something more. As much as I want to block him out entirely, it seems even in my drunken haze I'm searching him out through everyone here.

As he spins me around and I lock on his eyes again, this time noticing the differences, I feel dizzy. I don't know if it's the heat that's built up from all the dancing I've been doing, the amount of alcohol I've managed to funnel down my throat or just all my thoughts finally pushing me to overload, but whatever it is, I need to get out of here. I'm the queen of falling all over myself, especially at parties, but right now it's the last thing I want to do.

His lips are moving, he's saying something to me, but I can't make it out with the beating of the music in my ears. I motion to the other side of room in an effort to let him know I need to get off the dance floor and that's when his arms wrap around me. The way he smiles as he does it should make me feel secure, but it makes me feel anything but.

I don't think I want him helping me. I think I need to get away from him because the dizzy sensation is only getting worse and I'm starting to think there was more than just beer in that last red cup they passed me.

"I need—to—go. I'm sorry." I manage to garble out through my haze, but he doesn't release his hold on me. In fact, it feels like it's even tighter now. What have I gotten myself into?

"You can't leave yet, Emma. The party just started. Besides, I didn't think I'd ever see you again."

Wait, what? Why wouldn't he see me?

"Huh?"

"Well, with everything that happened with you and Hudson..."

"Nothing happened with Graham, is all bullshit." My words are slurring now, I can hear them and they aren't coming out at all the way I want them too, but it doesn't change the truth of my statement. Nothing had happened between me and Graham.

At least nothing happened for him.

"So, that means I might have a chance after all?"

I open my mouth to tell him no, that he would never get within ten feet of me, but all that comes out is the strangest sounding giggle, which only makes the hold he's got around my shoulders that much tighter. Apparently giggling like a twelve year old means that I'm interested.

Shit. What the hell was I thinking doing this? I should've stayed home.

"Emma."

At first, I think Will, Bill, or whatever is talking to me again, but once my name's repeated a second time, I realize it's not him at all, in fact it's the last person I ever expected to see here.

"Ser?"

"You know this girl, Ems?" he asks me and I shrug and giggle again, which makes him pull me even closer to him, the complete opposite of what I want. Now that my best friend is here, I've got my out. I need to get away from this guy, this party and the dizziness that's now so bad, I'm not entirely sure I can walk out of here on my own.

"Come on, I'm taking you home." I hear Serenity say as I feel her pulling on my hand, trying to break the hold that this random guy that looked so much like Graham a few minutes ago has on me.

"She's not going anywhere, are you babe? We haven't even gotten to the real fun yet."

There's something about the way he says *real fun* that turns my stomach. Now I'm more than a little sure there's more going on than just him wanting to dance and party it up with me.

Before I can answer him, tell him the last thing I want is to have any fun with him, I watch my best friend move forward and in one fluid movement, she wraps her hands around his wrist and twists until he drops his death hold on me. I've seen Serenity a lot of different ways, but right now, this is new. I've never seen her be the aggressor.

She really is an angel after all.

"You crazy bitch!"

"You're damn right I am, and if you know what's good for you, you'll get your buddies to stop drowning the drinks in GHB, or you'll find out just how crazy I can get." I giggle again and she turns to me, her face a mixture of sadness and anger. "Let's go Emma. We're getting out of here—now."

Grabbing my hand in hers and dragging my drunk ass along behind her, she maneuvers her way through the groups of people that seems to be standing around just about everywhere, and it's only when we're back out into the fresh air of the night that she stops and turns around to face me, her face this time betraying nothing. Or at least that's how it looks through the haze I'm still dealing with.

"What the hell were you thinking?"

"I wasn't."

"That's obvious. I do all of this work and for what? So you can throw it all away by going and doing something you won't be able to come back from?"

I've heard her angry before, but it's never been at me. We've been through so much since we met in the center and never once has she blown up at me like this. What's even worse is that none of what she said makes sense to me. What work is she talking about? What am I throwing away?

"Emma," she says, sighing before taking my hand in hers again, preparing herself for the trek we still had coming across the lawn of the frat. "There's some stuff I need to tell you."

Chapter Twenty-Two

Graham

"What you believe about yourself, it is accurate."

"You believe yourself to be dark in nature due to your experiences in past lives, and you are accurate. It is why you are the perfect vessel."

"I am sure that you would love nothing more than for me to end your suffering, but it is that suffering that will make you most viable."

"That strong façade you put forth will only last you for so long. The only question now is, just how much pain can you take before you break?"

"Just give in to it, Graham. The pain stops the minute you break."

It's been this way since I stormed out of Emma's room. It's as if learning about what she and the others had done has somehow thrown me right back into a time I'd much rather forget. I want to shut it off, but no matter how hard I try, how much I think about other, happier times in an attempt to break the constant barrage, nothing works. I'm stuck with the reminder and I know why.

This asshole has taken everything from me. He took the girl I loved and twisted her until she actually had feelings for him, he tortured my mother in an attempt to get closer to me, going so far as to ride around in my skin for months and now he's doing it again. He'd twisted yet another woman I let get close to me and made her believe in him until he got his way.

I can't say what his end result is this time, but the memories of my first time with him were more than enough.

They served as a reminder of what I've always believed to be true about him. Despite everyone's belief that he's changed, all he'd ever wanted was to see me break and now, he's getting his way because I am indeed broken.

It might not be all the way through the way it had been before, but it won't take very long to reach that point again. I can feel it in my bones, the way my body surrenders to the memories, and the very real agony I faced during my time with him. I spent what seems like forever being haunted by the fallen angel and with the way I feel now, the anger building more in me with each passing second, it's only a matter of time before it takes me over completely.

Emma had seen the worst of it. What I had become, she had seen it, lived it, experienced it. She knew better than anyone how serious I was about never letting another angel, whether fallen or not anywhere near me, even if it was in a healing capacity. She knew my hatred for Lucifer and everything he stood for, despite his claims that he wanted to earn his spot at home again. Everyone was aware of it, but Emma got to see it firsthand. I never hid it from her, because she wouldn't let me.

Why she did this is beyond me. She gave me reasons of course, and I understood all of them but it didn't mean any of it is right. I was right. She had taken my choice away. If I was meant to die from the onslaught of pain I was living with, then it should have happened that way. She never should have gotten involved and tried to change it. Even more than that, she never should have gone to Lucifer of all people in her bid to make everything better.

Every step she'd taken had been selfish and wrong, yet despite believing in that whole heartedly, I can't hate her. I want to hate her, in fact, I never want to see her again, but despite the betrayal and the hurt, I can't deny that one thing she said was right.

She did try and tell me. The more I focus on our time together, I can see her pained expression multiple different times and even her own words to back it up. She wanted to tell me something, in fact she kept pushing for it, especially during the time we spent watching the boats come in at the marina. At the time I thought it had something to do with Serenity and her concern about our bond, but I can see now that it wasn't that at all.

Emma had been living with this secret and it weighed on her so heavily, that she was willing to back away in order to tell me the truth. She never wanted to keep it from me. As much as I want to hate her, it's because of this that I can't. It destroys me that she kept this from me and I'm not sure I can ever trust her again, but I can't deny that she wanted to tell me the truth. Her admission that she would have told me, it's fact.

It doesn't change anything though. I meant what I said before I stormed out. I can't look at her the same anymore. Everything I believed about her and the type of person she is, it was all wrong. Where I believed her to be good, she had proven that in the end she is no better than anyone else.

I feel stronger than I have in months. I can breathe easier for what feels like the first time. I'm haunted now by Lucifer's voice, but before that, there had been no ill effects of the darkness that for months ruled my life. I had taken myself out of seclusion, throwing myself back into living again, enjoying the sunshine, the air, the world around me as a whole. I was me again and for the last week and a half I enjoyed every second of it even though I knew it was too good to be true.

Lucifer was the reason for it.

Emma choosing to go to him and putting everything she felt for me, and what could possibly happen between us on the line in order to save my life, might be something I couldn't forgive, but there was no doubt that the move had been a smart one. Ryan brought it up to me the day he verbally accosted me for the way I treated her and even though I'd made the choice in the end to not follow through with his idea, it didn't mean that for a split second I hadn't given it some thought.

Living with what I'd done to her the night of the party opened me up. I wanted to make things right, change the way I'd been and I had given it serious consideration. It would be crazy not to think about a positive outcome when all you're surrounded by is the negative, but the ending he gave my mother won out over whatever thought process that speaking to Ryan had brought to the surface. Honoring the woman that gave me life meant not accepting help from the person that had taken her from me.

What hurts even more is that before I learned the truth, I had been ready for a change. I was ready to take chances that normally I would never have taken. I was ready to love Emma with everything I had despite being pulled in another direction by the bond that seems to rule my life. Everything seemed so perfect.

The problem with perfection; is it's an illusion. When something appears to be without flaw, it shouldn't be trusted because there isn't a being alive that is without imperfections. True perfection is nothing but a mirage. In order to give me back what they thought would be perfect for me, they only thrust me into the arms of the darkness again. By allowing Lucifer to join with me and then lying about it, they did the one thing they claim to have been fighting against all along.

They made sure the darkness they were trying to eradicate from the world continues to live on. I'm so full of pain, betrayal, anger and disappointment that what did remain of the light Gabriel said I was made of; has now been obliterated and all that remains is what the devil has been saying all along that I'm made of.

Evil.

Emma

I'm not sure what I expected to see when I woke up from my coma sleep, but its most definitely not my best friend standing over my bed staring at me.

It's not that I don't remember what happened last night because I do, in painstaking detail, but I hoped most of it would turn out to be nothing more than a bad dream. It seems though, that with the way she's standing over me now, her face a mask of worry and concern, that all of it was very real.

"Were you expecting me to die in my sleep or something?" I say as I begin stretching my body out in the bed, allowing my sore muscles and hazy mind to go through the motions of waking up so that I can get this over with.

"Somehow I doubt I'd be that lucky."

"Wow. Thanks for not sugar-coating your hatred there, Ser."

"I don't hate you, Emma."

"So this is the kind of thing you say to the people you love now? Is that what being an angel means?"

She rolls her eyes at me and I can see that she still hasn't come to terms with what she is now. It's no secret that she accepted the changes that happened when she saw her destiny through to its conclusion but she still hasn't come to terms with it, at least not hearing it anyway.

"This has nothing to do with what I am."

"Right, this is about you coming to my rescue last night."

"One would think you'd be happy I showed up when I did."

"I am, trust me."

She sighs before throwing her body down onto my bed and I catch something in her eyes that reminds me of the last thing she said to me before I passed out. She mentioned needing to tell me something, but what that could possibly be, I have no idea.

"Last night should never have happened, Ems. It should've never gotten that far."

"I know that. I don't know what I was thinking even going to the party with the way I was feeling. I just couldn't be here anymore."

"You wanna tell me why?"

No, Serenity. I don't want to tell you that the reason I needed to get out of here so badly has to do with your soul-mate. I don't want to admit that I fell in love with the first boy you ever kissed. I don't want to admit to any of it because you'll hate me and I'll lose the only person I have left.

"Ems..."

"What?"

"I know all about it."

"Know all about what?"

"Graham." She sighs. "I've known about it for a long time."

How is that even possible? Did Ryan tell her what we talked about?

"No, he didn't tell me anything. He didn't need to. I figured it out on my own."

"Can you not do that? It's creepy. It's bad enough that Ryan does it and then Michael, but I can't handle it from you."

"Sorry Ems. I'm not intentionally trying to do it."

"It's okay." I answer with a sigh. "So, how long have you known about everything?"

"About a year. I wasn't entirely sure until right around the wedding, but I had suspicions. It all got confirmed when I talked to Graham though."

Well this is news. Apparently Graham had spoken to her about us and I had no idea. Not that any of it matters now of course, but it would have been nice to know.

"You talked to Graham?"

"That can't be all that surprising."

"It's not, I guess."

"He came to see me and even though I know it was a struggle for him, I got the sense that in some way he was looking for me to be okay with him moving on. I'm more than okay with it. Despite the bond we share, the one we're always going to share, he's always been my best friend and I want his happiness even more than I want my own."

"What does that have to do with me?"

"Emma, you know what it has to do with you. You're his happiness."

"Yeah, I'm not so sure about that anymore."

"You did the right thing and he's going to wake up and see that. Right now, he's hurting and he has every right to feel that way, but in time, he'll see that you did the right thing. He'll see that we all did."

"You're not the one that went to Lucifer."

"No, you're right. I'm not. What I did was far worse."

"What does that mean?"

"I went to God."

"Excuse me?"

"After the wedding, I went home. I spoke to God about you, about Graham and what I wanted to happen. Ems, you going to Lucifer, it was the right call because it's what was supposed to happen. If I hadn't gone to the big man himself, I would never have known that, but I did and I do."

"Is this where you tell me that it was all written to happen this way?"

"It's stupid right? I'm the first person to tell you that the destiny thing, is old and tired and I'm sick of hearing it, but yes Emma, all of this was exactly what was written to happen, at least according to God."

"So it was always written for him to find out the way he did and leave?"

"Yes."

"Why aren't you killing me right now? I went behind your soul-mates back and did something that I knew in the end would destroy him. Why aren't you angry?"

"Because you did it out of love, the same way that I would have if faced with the same decision. The thing is; what happens with Graham, it was never my decision to make."

"What does that mean?"

"It was always meant to be yours."

"That's bullshit. He's the other half of your soul, Ser. There's no way you can sit here and make me believe that I'm the one that determines his fate."

"He determines his own fate, Emma. That's not what I'm saying."

"God, this is confusing and my head hurts. What are you trying to tell me?"

"I was always meant to love Ryan, deep down you know that just as I do. It might not have started out the ideal way, but he was always meant to be my future. I think that's why I always believed saving him that day in Green Haven had been my destiny. It's the same with you and Graham."

"You're still not making any sense."

"Okay, the only way for all of this to make sense for you is to start from the beginning."

"That's usually where people start."

"Shut up. I'm getting to it."

I can't help but feel comforted with the way things are, even if I'm confused. It feels like old times, sitting here on my bed this way with my best friend. It's as if the last few months didn't happen at all and we've always just been here, right where we are now, together. It's the only thing that's keeping me level when all I want to do is fall apart.

"You were brought into my life for a reason. I didn't know about it, but when Gabriel couldn't be with me during my time in the center, he went to his father and appointed you to be my guardian. Once I got out, it stopped, but Emma, you were always meant to be in my life, especially as it pertains to my destiny."

"Gabriel had a real hard on for turning my life upside down didn't he?"

"You're not still mad about the altering are you?"

"No, but come on, really? He thought I was the best person to be your guardian?"

"You don't? It actually makes perfect sense."

"You're losing me."

"Emma, you found out I heard voices and you didn't even flinch. You're the reason I even found out as much info as I did about it. Of course you were the best person to be my guardian when he couldn't. Other then Graham, you're the only one that could do it."

I don't have the heart to tell her that every time she mentions Graham, my heart hurts. It's the reason I wanted to get out of the room so bad the night before, the reason I drank so much and almost let a random guy take advantage of me. I wanted to block him, his name and everything about him out of my system. The way she says his name so easily, causing her no pain just makes me jealous.

"The point I'm trying to make is, you were meant to be in my life for the duration Ems, and because of the way you were brought into it, that's when it was determined what your true calling would be. It was always meant to be this. I took my concerns upstairs and as it turns out, I was right in what I saw happening."

"It was always supposed to be me and Graham." I say, in statement rather than question. It's something I don't understand, but it's also something that for some reason I don't have to question anymore. It's just fact.

"Yes. You were right earlier when you said he's the other half of me, but that doesn't mean that we have to be together in every sense of the word. It's possible for it to mean that we both live our own lives, yet still remain connected, without the romantic entanglement."

"Do you really think that's possible?"

"It's entirely possible because it's exactly what's been happening since I met him."

"That's bullshit."

"No, it's not. Emma, think about it. Graham and I, we've never gotten together. We've had a couple of shady moments where it looked like we might, but we've never actually connected on that deep of a level. I love Graham, I think I'll always love him, but not the way that you do. We share a bond and a friendship. What you share with him, it's cataclysmic."

"So you think what we share is a violent disaster?"

"No. I think it's life altering because of the intensity of it. It's the same damn thing I feel for Ryan. I know the way all of this looks right now. You think that because of what you did, you've lost him forever, but I know Graham better than anyone, and that's not the case at all."

"How can you be so sure?"

"Because I've seen what's been written, Ems. I entered into a plan with God in order to make sure that in the end, the two of you didn't lose each other. There's no way in hell I'm letting that happen."

"You're the heavenly matchmaker?"

"Damn straight. I know it's crazy, but it was always meant to be the two of you together in the end. What you did, it's not destined to tear you apart. It's the one thing destined to bring you together."

"Ser—I—I love him."

"I know you do."

"You don't hate me for it?"

She laughs and there's something about it that puts me at ease. After everything she's already said, you'd think I would already see that she's giving me her blessing to love him, but there's still this part of me that doesn't believe in it. I need to be sure that falling for Graham won't tear what I have with Serenity apart, she means too much.

"No, hate is actually the last thing I feel for you, Emma Daniels. The way you feel for Graham, I love you for it. All this time I've needed one thing in order to be happy, and that's the security in knowing that you, Graham, Ryan and Gabriel were okay. You are what makes Graham happy."

"You really believe that don't you?"

"It's the first time in almost three years that my soul feels at peace, Emma. It's not about believing in it. I know it. Do you remember my vows?"

"Depends. What part are you talking about?"

"I told Ryan when I married him that he was the place my heart called home."

"Okay, yeah, I remember that, but what does it have to do with me?"

"You are the place that Graham's heart calls home Emma and I'm not the only one that knows it. The angels know, God knows, hell, even Graham knows. Now it's your turn."

"My turn for what?"

"To let Graham come home again."

Chapter Twenty-Three

Ryan

It's not exactly a secret that even with all the time that's passed, I still don't trust Lucifer the way everybody else does. I am the holdout, the one person besides Graham that isn't quite sure what to make of this newfound change that's present in the fallen angel.

What should have been alleviated when he joined with Gregory hasn't been, at least not for me. There's a lot of history, most of it dark, between Lucifer and myself and it would take more than just a few good deeds in order for me to entirely jump on board with him becoming one with Heaven again. It's not a secret. I don't hide it and I don't think I ever will.

As much as I love my wife, she understands that I can't stand side by side with her on this and despite the fact that it should easily cause some form of discord between us, we're making it work. We've made choices before that we haven't seen eye to eye on and this is just another one to add to the list. She's allowed to believe in him and I'm allowed to reserve my feelings on the issue until I see more. It's one of the reasons this works so well between us.

Standing here now, being summoned by the man that at one point I called Father; well I'm not sure what to make of it. I trust my wife and I know that she would never willingly put me in a situation that in the end could end up bringing about my very end, but my history with the man fights that every step of the way. He needs to explain to me what he wants with me, and he has to do it soon because I'm not sure how much longer my tolerance for him can continue.

"It is no trouble to see that you are conflicted."

"That can't really be a surprise to you."

"It is not. I just need you to realize that my calling you here, it is because you are my last resort. Knowing how you feel about me and everything I have done, both with you and apart from you, I want nothing more than to leave you out of this, but I cannot."

"You know I don't trust you, that I'm not sure I'll ever be able to trust you, so why does it have to be me that you call on?"

"There is no one else that can help me with what must happen now."

"Whose life are you meddling in now?"

"It is not meddling, Ryan. It is my attempt at making things right."

"What you call *making things right*, I call meddling. What's this all about Lucifer?"

"I need your help as it pertains to the Hudson boy."

Graham. Of course it has to do with him. Now that he's learned what Emma did, along with Michael and the very man standing in front of me, he's even more detached then before. It bothers me, knowing that he's pulling away again, especially after everything that had been done to fix it to begin with, but I couldn't fault him for the reason why.

I'm one of the first people to tell you that the only person that could've fixed this for Graham is Lucifer. In fact, that's exactly what I told the guy myself because I knew it as fact, but to find out that the person that caused everything to begin with was used to fix you without your consent, well walking away makes sense.

It's a betrayal to the extreme, but what Lucifer thinks I can do to help him fix what he broke, is beyond me. I'm probably hated just as much as he is.

"You need me to help you how exactly?"

"I need your help in making things right again."

"Honestly man, I think you've done enough. I think you need to take a backseat here, let Gregory run his own life and leave Graham alone."

"I would like nothing more than to do just as you have said but it appears that I cannot."

"I can't believe I'm gonna ask this, because honestly, the last thing I want to do is spend any more time with you and the mess you've created then I already have, but why can't you?"

"When I discovered Graham that day in Green Haven, there were some steps taken that weren't pure. As you well know, nothing I did back then was bathed in the light in any manner and it is one of those steps that I need to fix now."

"What did you do?"

"Graham's mother."

"What about her?"

"She did not perish. Gabriel knew it of course. It was why he could not pick up a trail of her on Earth or in Heaven. It is also why there was no mention of her during either of your visits to Hell."

Well, this is definitely not what I expected to hear today. Graham's belief that Lucifer killed his mother during the destruction he leveled on his home is one of the very reasons he hates the fallen angel so strongly now. To learn that it isn't the case and that the woman may very well be alive, it throws everything into further disarray.

There's no telling how Graham is going to react to this when he finds out.

"What did you do?"

"Much like I did with Graham, I hid her during my time controlling the old power. I have had a trusted individual guarding over her, keeping her alive and well despite her illness."

"And you're just now getting around to admitting that? Seems you haven't changed all that much after all."

"Father was aware of it. Where I had become singular focused on both you and Serenity during my time here and in

Hell, I put the woman out of my mind. As long as she was being guarded, there was no reason for me to think of it."

"So God knew and he what? Kept it to himself?"

"In a manner of speaking. It was not his problem to handle. It has always been mine."

"So, you kept her alive, but used her death as a means to control Graham?"

"Yes. It is not something I am proud of, but in order to use the boy in the manner I needed him at the time, I did what had to be done."

"No, you didn't do what had to be done; you did what you wanted to do. The sooner you accept that, the sooner more people can believe you're not the total asshole you've always been."

His head bows and I can tell that my words have hurt him. As much as I don't want to feel for this guy, especially after everything he put me through, that's exactly what's happening. I know what it feels like to be labeled as one thing and want so desperately to prove yourself to be something different entirely. As untrusting as I am where Lucifer is concerned, I can't deny that I sympathize.

"So, his mom is still alive. What does that have to do with me?"

"He will not listen to anything I have to say, I am sure you can agree with me on that. He has pushed Emma away and no doubt Serenity as well given that she kept the truth from him. The only one that has not done wrong by him is you."

"Again, what do you want me to do?"

"I want to bring her home. I want to reunite mother and son the way I should have so very long ago. I never should have separated them to begin with. With your help, I want to rectify that which I have broken."

"What makes you think he's going to let me get within two feet of him after everything that happened?"

"Michael, Emma and I, we all played a part in the mishandling of the current situation. The only fault that may lie at your doorstep as it pertains to Graham is that you were the first one to try and get him to come to me regarding his struggle. I do not believe he will fault you for that."

"You obviously don't know Graham as well as you think you do."

"That is where you would be wrong. I have joined with him on two occasions now and in doing so; I can sense what lies deep inside of him. He does not hate Emma for what she has done; in fact it is the complete opposite. He is just blinded by the betrayal and cannot seem to see past it to the reality of the situation. His mortality. If he can see Emma in that manner, it stands to reason that he will also see you in the same light."

"You think that because he loves Emma, even after everything she did, that he'll be open to talking to me?"

"That is my hope yes. Ryan, I know this is a long shot and that it is yet another risk, but you cannot deny that it needs to be done. I need to rectify this. I cannot let it go on a minute longer than it already has and there is no one more deserving of some sliver of light right now then Graham."

I couldn't argue with him. He was right. Graham has been through literal hell and back and considering the way things looked right now, needed a bright spot. He needs to know that Lucifer lied to him. He needs to know his mother is alive. No one should go through life believing their parent to be dead when it wasn't the case.

This really had gone on long enough.

"Will you help me accomplish this? Will you put your feelings for me aside in this one instance and help me make things right?"

What he's asking of me, it should be a decision that I struggle with given our history, but it's not that way at all. He's right. In order for the peace Serenity put in motion to be reached, for everyone both above and below, this has to happen now. With everything Graham had done for each and every one of us, it's only fair that it's given back to him in that same way now.

My answer is obvious and I can tell as I look to him, that he can see it clear as day written all over my face.

"Let's bring Mrs. Hudson home where she belongs."

Michael

This is a monumental day.

When I had been called off my guard of Graham, told that my presence was needed back in Heaven and that Father had something of great importance he needed to share with me, I will admit to experiencing a moment of fright at just what that might be. He had kept so many things from me over time that it has taken time for me to build back trust in him again and the last thing I wanted was for that already shaky cord of trust to be shattered.

It is only when I heard what Father had to say that I realize that this time there is no feeling of betrayal. Yes, he had kept another secret from me, but this time it was not the same way as it was with Gregory. This time the secret had not been his to tell.

This was all on my fallen brother.

Graham's mother is very much alive and if it was hard to believe hearing it from Father earlier, it cannot be denied as I stand before the woman and watch over her. This is my new task. Now that Lucifer has realized what must be done, he is taking steps to rectify it and in the meantime, I am to guard over the woman and make sure that no more harm comes to her.

Well, no more harm than almost two years away from her son can cause.

Lucifer had not been lying when he said that she was taken care of during her captivity. She was a captive, a pawn in a sick game that my brother had put into motion years before and no amount of fixing could entirely erase that fact now.

Where I expected the woman to look gaunt and disheveled, she looks remarkably bright and agile. She does not look happy, but given her current location and the details behind her capture, I cannot imagine her enjoying a minute of this. I am just thankful that even in his darkest moments; my brother had not done the unthinkable and ended this human's life, something he could have easily done given the power level he commanded at the time.

"Are you going to speak to me or just leer the way you have been since you got here?"

Despite my need to always make myself visible to those that I appear before, I had not done it in this case, choosing instead to forgo that option in order to guard her much the way Gabriel had done in the early days with Serenity. With everything that she has been through, the last thing she needs is the stress of an angel appearing before her, especially if she had no previous knowledge of us.

I may know what Lucifer had done now, but that did not mean I knew all there was to know. I was unsure if he had appeared before her, and if he had, if he used a vessel or come to her in his true fallen form. For humans that have not interacted with us, appearing before one can be quite the traumatic experience and I am of the belief that this woman has had more than enough of those to last a lifetime.

"You can see me?"

"I'll admit it's a little difficult with that light surrounding you, but I can see the shadow of a man buried beneath it all, yes."

"Are you aware of what I am?"

"Boy, I am more than a little aware of what you are. I do believe I spent a good portion of the last ten years of my life praying for you to appear just the way you are right now."

She speaks the truth. I am not the one that handled her prayers, that being left to Gabriel given his connection to Graham, but it is true that she had prayed quite a lot for heavenly intervention.

"What do you believe my being here now means?"

"I think it's my time. I'm being called home."

"You are going home, but not in the way that you imagine. It is not your time yet."

"It was my understanding that I didn't have much of a home to go back too."

"Who told you that?"

"I wasn't told. I was shown."

"Shown in what capacity?"

"He destroyed my home, but not before bringing me here and having me watch. I'm afraid there is not much left to go home to."

"What do you believe came of your son?"

"He died in the demolition of the house of course. I was shown that as well."

Jesus. Lucifer had used the same tactic on both Graham and his mother, making them believe they had perished in the same way.

"Graham did not perish in the explosion. He is very much alive. That is actually what brings me to you now. It's time for the both of you to be reunited."

"He's alive?"

"Alive and well, I assure you."

"Before you do as you've said and bring me home, can I ask you something?"

"You may ask me anything."

"How much time will I have with him?"

I know what she is getting at, though she cannot bring herself to say the words aloud. She has long since come to terms with her own mortality, believing that at any given moment it could be her time to go. She was prepared for it and even knew in the end where she would end up. It is not surprising that with all that I have said about reuniting her with her son that she is concerned about how much time she will have with him once they do come back together again.

"The illness, it should have killed me by now. I need to know that in going home, he won't lose me…"

"Mrs. Hudson, it is not your time and it will not be your time for many years to come, I assure you of that. It was never God's plan to reunite that which had been lost, only to take it away again. You and your son will have a lifetime together."

She does not realize this of course, but it may have very well been Lucifer's handling of her that kept her alive as long as she has been. She had been slated to die shortly after Gabriel visited with Graham that first time. What she is also unaware of is that this decision, the one in which I have promised her a lifetime with Graham, it will not come without a cost.

It is not Father that has decided what her fate will be once she is returned home. It is me. I may not have been able to help Graham when he needed it the most, but I can do this, regardless of what it will cost me in the end.

It is the only thing left to do. Graham will not lose his mother. I will not allow it. I will give her the life that Lucifer stole from her back.

It's the right thing to do.

Chapter Twenty-Four

Graham

I don't know how much more of this I can take. I've spent the last two days locked away in this bed, the voices of the past haunting me the same way they did before. The only difference this time around is, it's not only the voices of the past, but the ones from the present too. It jumps back and forth vividly between Serenity and Emma, both of their words and actions haunting me even more then the nightmare I lived with Lucifer ever could.

Serenity with her smile as she tells me that I need to take a chance, letting me know that despite what taking a chance really means, we'll always be in each other's lives. Then it switches to Emma and the way she broke down at the marina, telling me about her past and what turned her into the person she's spent the last ten years trying to be. The breathlessness in her voice when she tells me that I'm the one she wants, despite knowing my past and the damage I can inflict on her if we did take the chance.

It's torture, having them wrapped up in my subconscious, my time with Lucifer interrupting at the worst times and showing me again just why I'm never going to be good enough for anyone.

Why didn't she just walk away and let me die? I thought I was ready to die when Serenity saved me in the church that night, but nothing could have prepared me for the way it would feel living through the past six months. The headaches, the nightmares and the physical pain I put myself through because I couldn't let go of the very real nightmare I'd somehow lived through. That was the moment I made the decision to die. Not after Serenity saved me and was taken away the way I thought. I was only being melodramatic then. Now is a different story entirely.

My heart hurts. What Emma did, despite knowing that she did it for the right reasons, it's destroying me. The very person that had given me this second chance at life, had taken it away from me just as easily and it's left me cold, empty and alone. I feel nothing but numb, despite the fight inside of me to feel more. I want to feel again. I want to experience life the way I have been, not locked away in this room the way I am, repeating the way I've spent the last three months. I want more. I just don't deserve more.

In the past when I got like this, ignoring the world and classes and everything I should be focusing on, Emma would be at the door, banging on it until I finally acknowledged her presence. This time, it's eerily quiet and there's no sign of her at all. I don't want that to bother me because of everything she did, but it does. I want her on the other side of the door even though if she did somehow appear here, I wouldn't have the first clue what to say or do with it.

It doesn't stop me from wanting it though and I hate myself for that. I can't honor my mother's memory if I'm still pining after the girl that brought the devil back into my life.

When I hear the knock, I can feel the lift in my chest, the breath of fresh air that I feel and for the first time in two days, I feel myself scrambling as quickly as possible to get out from the darkness the covers of my bed afforded me. Is it possible that in wanting something so hard, I've made it materialize? Is the supernatural really that much of a presence in my life that I've got the power to make things happen just by thinking about them?

It's only when I see whose standing on the other side of the door when I swing it open that the uplifting feeling inside of me slowly begins to dissipate. It's not Emma the way I hoped, but Ryan.

"Well, I gotta say, that was easier than expected."

"What was?"

"I didn't expect you to even acknowledge I was here, let alone open the door that fast."

If I'd known it was him on the other side, I wouldn't have opened it and I'm pretty sure he knows it, if the knowing look he's giving me now is any indication. As much as I don't want to wear my feelings so openly, I'm pretty sure that's all I'm doing, no matter how shitty I feel.

"You expecting someone else?"

"No." I answer back easily because the truth is, I wasn't expecting anyone. I just foolishly had hope. "There's no one I want to see."

"You wound me, man."

"Whatever. What do you want? Serenity ask you to check on me?"

"Now why would she do that?"

There's a second where I start to think he doesn't know anything. It's only when he smirks before pushing his way past me and into the room that I realize he's bullshitting me. I've had Ryan show up here a lot over the last couple of years, but never once has he smirked at me like that. Seems now that he's married to the girl of his dreams, he's permanently showing emotions I was unaware he was capable of.

"She didn't make me come here. I'm actually here about something that has nothing to do with my wife."

"What does it have to do with? As you can see, I'm not exactly up for company."

"Lucifer."

"I don't want to talk about him."

"You see, I figured that, but I'm not giving you a choice here. There's some shit you need to know and since you've pretty much crawled back into your hole and pushed everyone away, it's gotta happen this way."

"Since when did you become Lucifer's errand boy?"

"It's about Lucifer yes, but I'm not even here for him. I'm here for you."

"What the hell does that even mean?"

I don't want to admit it to him but he's starting to sound as vague as Michael and Gabriel and I'm not a big fan. I want him to just get to the point already so I can go back to the supposed hole he assumes I've crawled into.

"It means that for the last year or so, you've thought something that's not true."

"Spit it out, Ry. I'm not really in the mood for reading between the lines."

"I'm not here alone, Graham. You need to go back and open the door. I could just tell you what's going on, but I think you need to be shown."

"Is this some kind of intervention?"

"Do you need one of those?"

"No."

"Then go open the damn door already."

I do as he says and the minute I do, I finally see what he's getting at. I'm just not sure I can trust it. My eyes have to be playing tricks on me, because the reality of this happening isn't possible.

"No, this isn't happening! He's playing fucking mind tricks with me again and he's using you to do it!"

My hand still on the door, I shove into it, believing that in shutting the door and blocking off the vision of the person standing on the other side, I can get back to the reality of the situation. Ryan, who I finally started to believe might be one of the good guys is proving just how truly dark he is.

"It's not a trick, Graham." He says as he catches the door before it slams. "She's real. Everything you've believed up until this exact second is what has been the trick."

"I saw it all man! I saw what he did to her, what he put her through and what he did to the house. There's no way in hell this is real!"

"Graham Michael Hudson, this is very real."

How many times over the last year have I dreamt about hearing my full name said that exact way? How long have I wished for this exact moment to happen because I couldn't imagine my life without her in it, despite spending years preparing myself for the inevitability of it?

"It's not possible."

"I said the same thing when the angel appeared before me too. I was shown what I believed to be your final moments, the same way you were shown mine, but Graham, this is possible. I'm here and this is really happening."

My mom, standing in front of me, taking steps through the doorway toward me, wrapping her arms around me. It's all real, I can feel that as her arms wrap themselves around me, yet I still can't allow myself to believe in it entirely.

"How?" I choke out and before she can answer me, Ryan clears his throat, reminding me of his presence before filling in the blanks that I need so desperately.

"You know the answer to that."

"I saw her die! There's no way he could have faked it."

"You also thought Serenity was dead, remember? He faked that easily and he did the same thing here. He knew what would impact you most, what would break you down and he used it."

"Where have you been?" I ask her as she pulls away from me and our eyes lock on one another, both of us obviously shocked to be standing where we are. It's a place neither of us thought we'd ever be.

"I'm not exactly sure where I was, but I was kept away."

"He kept her hidden in an abandoned building in Green Haven, Graham. He warded the placed pretty heavily with magic and old power before he lost it and she's been there ever since."

"And you thought I was dead?"

I watch as she nods her head and my stomach ties up in knots. Not only had he shown me what I believed to be her death at his hands, but he'd done the exact same to her. It only made me hate the fallen angel even more. It made me understand why Ryan had been sent to deliver this blow, because if he had come himself, I would have done everything in my power to kill him.

"Don't go there."

"Really Ryan? You know what he did, what he's been keeping secret and you're actually gonna sit here and tell me not to go there?"

"No one understands better than me where you're coming from man, but it's not going to solve anything thinking the way you are. I don't trust him either. I'm not sure I ever will, but wanting him dead, it's not right."

"Why's that?"

"Do you not see what's happening here? Your mom, she's not dead. She's standing right here in front of you. As much as you hate him, and trust me, I get it, he's the reason she's here."

"So, he takes her, hides her away, making me believe she's dead, knowing what losing her would do to me and because he's finally got a conscience now, I'm just supposed to overlook it and be all warm and fuzzy?"

"No, that's not what I'm saying. I would kill to have a moment like this with a mom that actually gave a shit about me. I'm pretty damn jealous of you. You've got what I can only dream of having. So instead of focusing on what he did then, I think you need to focus on what he's doing for you now."

Before I can formulate a response, knowing full well what he's trying to say, yet still having a hard time jumping on board with it, I see another shadow enter the room. If I'd been ready to accept Ryan's words, the second I catch sight of the newest edition to the room, it's all thrown out the window.

Lucifer's here.

Lucifer

I'm aware of the deal I made with Ryan before we made our way here, but as I experience the struggle that Graham faces, coming across his mother again, I cannot see it through. I will not remain hidden the way that we agreed. I need to make things right with the man before me now, even if it is the last thing he wants.

It is the only way to fulfill what Father believes my true destiny to be.

"You son of a bitch. You've got a lot of nerve showing up here right now!"

"Lucifer, what the hell are you doing?"

Both men are turned and facing me now, neither one pleased to see me, which given the way I am handling things in the moment, I expect to happen. Unfortunately I cannot turn back. I have to see this through.

"I am doing what should have been done a long time ago. I am making things right."

"It's a little late for that isn't it?"

"What is the saying that you humans rely on so heavily? 'Better late than never'? I am merely rectifying that which should never have happened in the first place."

"I don't wanna hear it."

"Graham, I know how upset you are, but I think you need to hear the man out."

I am unsure of what took place between the woman and Michael during their time together, but for her to be stepping forward now and giving me this chance, it is a move I never expected to receive, nor one I believe I am deserving of.

"You have no idea what he's done, Mom. There's so much that I need to tell you."

"I've been made aware of everything that he did, Graham. After spending the last twenty-four hours with the angel known as Michael, I've had a whole lot of time to become acquainted with what's been happening in my absence."

"So you know that he possessed me, used me as a pawn to get to Serenity and rip apart multiple people's lives for his own selfish gain? You know that I had to go into Hell to save my best friend because instead of doing the right thing, he dragged her down there with him? You know he tortured me so badly, I'm so haunted that I've been torturing myself?"

"Yes and I believe it's time you stop doing that. Hear the man out, Graham. You do not have to like what he has to say, or even believe that he's changed, but please, for me, hear him out."

He goes silent and I see it as my opportunity to finally set the record straight. It is just as his mother has said. I do not expect him to believe anything that I have to say, but I do want him to listen because it is time that I stand before him and begin to make things right. He is the only one that I truly feel remorse for and he is the only one that until now has been unwilling to hear me out.

"Say whatever you're here to say and then get the hell out of here." He spits out and I feel the hurt and pain laced around the words.

I can join with him, heal him and take away the darkness that I left behind during my time with him but I am unable to take away the hurt that all of it caused. That has to come from him. I only hope that what I have to say next sets a path for him to do it.

"There are so many instances in the time since I have fallen that I regret. Experiences I wish I could go back in time and fix, even though it is impossible to do so. None of those compare to the things I have put you through. You, Graham Hudson, are my biggest regret and the time period I most want to eradicate entirely in an effort to make it right."

"The things I put you and your mother through are unforgiveable. I am not here to ask for your forgiveness. I would never even dream of asking for such a thing, but I do believe the time has come for me to do the right thing by you. It is the reason I came when Emma called on me. I am the reason you experienced the darkness in the manner that you did and it was up to me, and only me, to make that right."

"Yeah, thanks for that. Thanks for being the one to break me and then make yourself feel better by fixing what you broke."

"I deserve that. In fact, I do believe I deserve even more for everything I put you through. It is my hope though that in bringing your mother back to you, the way she should have been all along, that you can see, I am attempting to do the right thing. That even though I didn't have your best interests at heart before, I do now."

His laughter pains me. It is sarcastic in nature, still disbelieving of the changes that are taking place around him and even more so in the changes I have been putting into motion since Serenity gave me the chance to make things right.

"This has nothing to do with my best interests, let's be honest. You're doing all of this because in the end it will get you what you want. It's always about you."

"It has nothing to do with me."

"It has everything to do with you. You healing me, bringing my mom back, making everyone around us believe you're different and you want to do the right thing, it's all selfish and typical Lucifer. Even Ryan knows it, which is why he hasn't said a word since you showed up. He doesn't trust you either. You always have an ulterior motive."

"That may have been the case before, I will not deny that, but it is most definitely not the case now. I am sure you believe I am doing all of this so that I can gain entrance to Heaven again, but you would be wrong in your belief."

"That's doubtful."

"What you do not seem to realize is that I have resigned myself to remaining with Gregory Richards for my remaining time on the planet. I am not looking to go home anymore. As desperately as I want to do that, it is not what pushes me forward any longer."

"You might be able to sell that horseshit to Serenity, and hell, even Emma, considering what you managed to get her to agree too, but I'll never believe that."

"I do not expect you to. I only want you to hear me out. You are not like Ryan and Serenity in that you cannot sense my deception or truth, but I assure you, I speak nothing but the truth to you now. Keeping you away from your mother, stripping you down, breaking you as you have said, it was wrong. It never should have happened and I will spend the remaining time I have here making it right, in whatever capacity I can."

I have said all that I can say to the boy. I have spoken openly and honestly with him, for the first time in our time together and while I am positive nothing is getting through, I can only hope that over time, he will see the truth that I know Ryan can see in my words and come to accept that I am trying to do right by him.

Where Graham Hudson is concerned, my road is paved with only the purest purpose and I will gladly go to my own true death again in an effort to prove it to him. He may believe I am doing this in order to go home again, which would make me selfish, but he has no idea the real reason for all of this.

Graham and I are not so different after all. We both want to be what we are meant to, even when we believe ourselves unworthy. The lesson he needs to learn and the one that I am currently learning is, everyone is worthy of redemption.

It may have taken the loss of my brother to get me here, but I see it now, no matter how deep seeded my belief is that a being such as me cannot be redeemed. It is now his time to learn what I have, to walk the same road, one that will take him where he has always been meant to go.

He only needs two things to get him there and standing here in this room now, I can already see the most important one, even though I'm witnessing it through pain filled eyes.

Graham Hudson will be saved, but not because of what I have given him back today. He will be saved by love.

All he has to do is believe.

Chapter Twenty-Five

Graham

"You believe him don't you?" I ask when I'm sure that both the fallen angel and Ryan are completely out of earshot, leaving me completely alone with the woman that until an hour ago, I believed dead.

"I do. I know what he put this family through, what he's done to your friends, even to his own family, but there was something in his eyes Graham. I can't explain it or expect you to understand but that man, that angel, he feels remorse."

I want to argue with her, it's there on the tip of my tongue, but no matter how hard I try to get the words out, they won't come because she's got a point. I hate admitting it, but what she saw in him, I did too and I really wish I didn't because it makes everything harder to deal with.

"He did too much, Mom."

"This stopped being about him a long time ago."

"What's that supposed to mean?"

"How can you not see it? I've only been back for a few minutes and in just that small window of time I can see it clear as day."

"All that time you spent with Michael, turned you just as cryptic as him."

"This is not about Lucifer and the way you feel about the things he's done, Graham. I've been watching you the entire time he stood here saying his piece. You don't have a problem with him, you have one with yourself."

"No, trust me, it's him."

"The only one you're fooling with that is yourself. You seem to forget, I raised you. I know you, the real you. It stopped being about him a long time ago. Everything you're experiencing now, it's all you."

There are so many things I imagined saying and doing when I got to see my mother again. I always assumed it would happen when I died, so it all seemed like a faraway dream, but having it happening for real, right now, nothing is going the way I imagined it. I can't deny that what she's saying, there's truth in it.

This is about me. I can sit here and blame the darkness, the time I spent hopeless and without purpose, on the fallen angel because he'd been the person to start it when he possessed me, but that was over a long time ago. What's happening now, it isn't on him despite my claims otherwise. It's on me.

"Do you want to know what I think?"

"Considering I never thought I'd hear you speak again, much less tell me what you thought about everything I've been going through, you should already know the answer to that."

"You're punishing yourself. "

"How do you figure that?"

"Michael spoke to me at great length about what happened during your time with Lucifer. I know what you went through. The things you experienced, the people you hurt or affected in ways you never would have had you been under your own control at the time. It changed you. He is at fault for doing that, but everything after, that's on you."

"So all of this is my fault?"

"That is not what I'm saying. When Serenity saved you, you put the blame on yourself for it. That's what drove you to go into Hell in an effort to save her. You needed to do right by that girl because in your mind, you believe you're the reason she ended up there. You took it all on yourself and the more time that passed, it just grew until you couldn't control it anymore."

"You don't know the whole story."

"I don't need to. I know as much as I need to in order to see what's really going on here. You can't forgive Lucifer because you can't forgive yourself."

There's no argument that I can come up with to go against what she's saying so the room just goes silent. I don't want there to be truth in her words, but I can't deny that there is. She's right, about all of it. It's why everything has been so hard for me, because everything she's telling me now is everything I've spent the last six months trying to run from and being driven under by.

This isn't about Lucifer and the time he spent riding around in my skin. It's about how I reacted to it after the fact. The only reason things became so bleak is because I allowed them to. I let the guilt I felt over all the wrong turns I made break me down, turning me into the version of myself I thought I deserved to be.

Serenity sacrificing herself, being possessed by Lucifer in an effort to make sure I survived what was happening to me, I do blame myself for. It wouldn't have happened if I'd never taken the steps to try and save her that first time. Lying to her when we finally did have her back, making her believe things that were selfish and completely untrue, it was another step in the wrong direction for me and one that even now, I have a hard time stomaching. I caused her to lose faith in me, even if it was short lived, blaming Lucifer and what happened between us the entire time.

Lucifer has always been the excuse, but I've always been the cause.

"You're seeing the truth now aren't you?"

"Yeah, I guess I am. I just don't know what to do with it."

"I think I have the answer to that."

"Care to share?"

"Take that truth, the one you can see and use it to change the path you've put yourself on. Stop blaming yourself for things that you have no control over and take a chance with the one thing you can control. Your future."

There are those words again. The same words my best friend told me less than a week ago, now being repeated by the only other person in the world I would trust them from. There's a meaning in them, a message that I need to pay attention to, but there is something else she's said that has my attention and until I talk to her about it, I can't focus on anything else.

"I can't control everything in the future."

"What do you mean?"

"You. I'm still going to lose you."

Admitting that I'm thinking about losing her all over again, especially after she just came back to me, it's hard, but where I expect her to be affected in some way by my statement, she's smiling and it makes no sense. I don't see how losing her could ever be something to smile about.

"All of this time and you still haven't learned anything."

She's laughing now and it's throwing me completely off balance. What is she getting at and better yet, what does she know that I don't?

"We will never be without each other, Graham. Not really. I'm always going to be with you, and after what Michael put in motion, it's going to be a lot longer than I ever thought possible."

What Michael put in motion? What did the angel do and what does it have to do with my mom and her illness?

"What did he do?"

"He broke the rules."

"You think you can give me a little more than that?"

"He's giving me my life back, Graham."

"Are you saying he healed you?"

She nods and I feel what remains of the anger, the betrayal and the pain fade completely away. Without saying a word, only a small motion of her head, she's given me something back that I never thought I'd ever feel again.

Faith.

Michael

If you asked me three years ago where I would have imagined myself in the future, the answer would have been easy. I could see it so clearly that there was no doubt about its validity.

The picture I saw then and the one I am living now are not even remotely similar to one another. Where I imagined myself standing by Father's side as we fought against the evil Lucifer unleashed on the world, my brothers by my side, I am now facing quite the opposite.

I'm standing not by Father's side but across from him and the look on his face is anything but one of pleasure. If I didn't believe so strongly in the decision I made, his look now might concern me, but as it stands, fear is the last thing I feel. It does not matter what he says to me, or even what he plans on doing about the supposed mess he believes I have created, I stand by it and I will not back down.

In going against all that I have been taught to believe, in an effort to give life back to a woman more than deserving of it. I have done the unthinkable, but I will never see it as wrong. No matter what Father wants to throw at me, I will go on from here believing that not only have I done the right thing by the humans in my charge, but by the brother that loved them so effortlessly.

"I never thought the day would come where I would be having this conversation with you, Michael."

"You are not alone in that. I never believed I would find myself here either."

"If you never imagined yourself standing where you are now, then why have you done it?"

"It is what needed to be done."

"You altered the course of existence, doing that which you have done."

"I'm aware of what I have done. I am also aware that there must be consequences for it. I have one request before you level your punishment."

"What is that?"

"There are some things that I need to say that I believe it is long past time for you to hear."

"Are you going to attempt to defend your actions?"

"No."

"Well I am thankful that you at least know you cannot do that."

"That is where you are wrong. I can defend my actions, I am just choosing not to. What I have to say, it's less about what I have done and more about saying to you what should have been said a long time ago."

"Say what you feel you must."

"Since our very creation, you have spoken of nothing but adhering to what has been foretold. You wish to keep to the natural order of things, yet you spend no real time with the very people whose lives you hold in the palm of your hand to learn what the natural order is. Father, it is time you realize that sometimes, the right thing has nothing to do with the course that is already mapped out, but one that has yet to be written."

"You truly believe that."

"Yes, I do and I am not the only one. Gabriel himself knew that Heaven was in need of an overhaul, long before his demise and instead of listening to him, I chose to follow along blindly because it is what I have been taught to do. I cannot do that any longer. It's time that we change the way things have been. The step I took with Graham's mother is the first step in that change, whether you are ready to accept it or not."

"I believe I have heard enough."

"I accept whatever punishment you wish to give me Father, but I will not apologize for what I have done, nor will I allow you to change what I have put in motion."

"For some time now, I have known that the way things have been is not acceptable. It was first made apparent to me through Gabriel and then through your own reaction to a decision I made. During my time with Lucifer, it has again presented itself and now, as I stand before you, it can no longer be denied. You speak the truth Michael."

This is not what I expected to hear. It was a risk, admitting to him the way I felt about not only him, but Heaven as a whole and the last thing I expected to hear was that he agreed with me. No one challenges the Creator. It is something well known after what Lucifer experienced the one time he decided to do it. It appears that there are more facets to my Father then even I am aware of. He still has the ability to shock me to my very core.

"With all of that said, I still believe there needs to be a punishment levied in regards to the rules you broke."

"Of course. I expected as much."

"Your punishment is simply this. Resume your place beside me, Michael. Help me create the change that not only you want so badly, but that which Gabriel went to his death in an attempt to achieve."

"You wish for me to help you? That is my punishment?"

"Precisely. What is above must be below, that has always been my method of thinking has it not?"

"Yes, but what does that have to do with what you are asking of me?"

"We have created a level of peace on the planet that is previously unknown. I do believe it's time that we do the same here. I have spent long enough in the dark ages, it is time that not only do I bring the Hudson boy into the light, but myself as well. It is time for you to come home, Michael."

For as long as I have existed, I have never heard Father speak the way he is now. I am unsure if it is his intent or not, but with the way he is wording things, it appears as though he's admitting something that no being in existence would expect of him.

He's not perfect.

Epilogue

Graham

I'm not sure how it happened, but when I woke up this morning, things were different. At first I thought it might have had something to do with the fact that my mom was back, but after coming to terms with that the night before, spending more than a few hours talking through everything with her, I knew it wasn't that.

It was such a powerful sensation that after spending over an hour pacing back and forth in my room, trying to come up with a reason for it, I finally gave up and decided to drive it out of my system. I had no destination in mind, just me, my thoughts and the open road.

It's only when I end up back in Green Haven that things start to make sense. Whatever felt different today, it had something to do with everything that has taken place in this town and more specifically, what happened in this exact location. I hadn't just driven out of Stephenville and back to my hometown. I'd driven to the very place where it all began.

The church.

So much of my life is wrapped up in this place and it seems that no matter how far away I move, I'll never really leave it behind.

Looking at it now, it looks like any other run down place in town. The windows are boarded up, tags from gangs and even a few from me, the only real signs of color that surround it. To an outsider, it would appear to be just another building forgotten by the city and its residents, but to me it would always mean so much more.

There are only a select few that know the real horrors that this place contains within its walls and it's my hope that as time continues to move on, that it stays that way. I'm not even sure anyone would believe me if they did learn the truth, the events so unbelievable that even I'm having a hard time coming to terms with the reality of them taking place.

This church is where Serenity married Ryan for the first time. It's the place where Ryan gave his life in order to save her, loving her beyond rational comprehension even then. It's the one place in the world where the forces of good and evil came together in multiple bids to end each other. This church, it's about more than all of that though.

It's the place where Gabriel made the ultimate sacrifice, the one thing that no matter how hard we try, none of us can erase, take back or get over.

That's what is different about today. I woke up, I felt my heart beating strong as ever, each breath coming in quick succession, feeling more alive than I ever have, but still missing something.

My mom is right. I can't continue living the way I have been. I can't blame myself for things that I have no control over. I've got to stop living in the past and blaming Lucifer for the things that go wrong in my life. He may have been the catalyst, but I'm the one that chose to let the agony I felt overwhelm me, turning me into something I was never meant to be.

I know why I'm here now. Why of all places in the world that I could be standing, it's here in front of this church. It's because of Gabriel. It's time I accept the things that have happened in the past and use it to create the future that he always believed I was meant to have. I have to do what he wanted me to do from the very beginning.

It's time for me to trust and believe.

When he came to me that first day, he said it was because he needed my help in order to save Serenity. He had done the same thing I'd done when she moved in across the street from me. He'd fallen in love with an angel, his angel and he would have gone to the ends of the Earth to protect her from everything he knew she would end up having to face. What he didn't realize at the time, but I do now, is that she wasn't the only one that needed saving.

I did too.

"I don't have the first clue what I'm doing and I'm pretty sure talking out loud to nothing is enough to have me locked away, but it's time for me to say the things that I never got to say before you decided it was your time to go."

The wind blows around me, stronger in comparison to a few seconds before and it's all the answer I need. He's here with me now. The rest of the world might believe that when he died, he ceased to exist, but I know differently. He was only one being before, but now he's a part of everything. From the bright light of the sun, to the breeze blowing around me, he's here and he's more alive than ever.

"You came here with one clear goal in mind, but what you don't realize is that you accomplished so much more than that. You saved my life and I don't even think you're aware of it. I'm a better person for knowing you and I want you to know, what you saw in me so long ago, I see it now and I don't plan on ever taking it for granted. Thank you Gabe, for everything."

I'm not sure if it's my mind playing tricks on me, but as I turn to go, having said everything that needs to be said, I swear I hear his voice, clear as day around me. As if sensing my own doubt, I hear it again and as I do, the sun breaks through the clouds, opening the sky wide open so that I'm bathed in nothing but the brightest light.

It's only one word, but the impact of that word knows no bounds.

"**Believe.**"

Emma

When I graduated high school and made the first initial plans to go to school here in Stephenville, after receiving my acceptance letter, I had a clear goal in mind. The way I acted before, blowing off classes, screwing around at the mall and all of the other ways I managed to blow off doing any actual work, I wasn't going to repeat. I was going to come here, buckle down and focus on my classes and I would eventually graduate with a degree of my choosing.

That's not what happened at all.

The goal quickly turned and it became just like high school all over again. Parties replaced my study nights, movie nights with Serenity way more entertaining than any textbook could ever possibly be. When she went missing, something inside of me snapped back into place and I realized what my slacking off was really doing.

I thought going away to college would give me what I'd been craving for years back home. This would be the place where I could be myself and not the party going, fun time girl I'd created in order to survive everything I faced then. The problem was, I perfected that girl, until I knew that version of me better than the one that lived deep inside. Serenity going missing brought that girl back to the surface and even though I've still managed to keep up some of the façade, for the most part I've gotten back to being who I was meant to be.

Myself.

At least that's what I thought until I realized when I woke up this morning that I've fallen back into old routines again. Where I would have gotten up and gone to class, despite the way I was feeling; now I'm just laying in bed, hiding away from the world. The exact thing I've been doing since I came here three years ago.

When I hear the knock on the door, I can't help but think that my past has caught up to me. The threat that more than one of my teachers had leveled me with is finally coming back around. I've been found out. It's not until I open the door, and find only a white envelope on the ground in front of me that I'm able to breathe a true sigh of relief.

As much as I want to change and be the person I vowed to be when I graduated high school, I'm glad it's not starting right now, because quite frankly, I'm not ready for it after everything I've been through.

It's only when I'm back in the room and the safety of my bed that I rip the side of the envelope open and pull out the notebook paper inside. I don't recognize the writing, but my heart does leap at the words on the page. Where I'd resigned myself to spending the entirety of the day in bed, it looked like that wouldn't the case at all. Whoever had written the letter, was giving me something I didn't even realize I needed.

They were giving me an escape.

Emma,

Get dressed and meet me outside. You're going back to where it all started.

It wasn't signed of course, so it could have been from just about anyone, especially with the sheer amount of people I know on campus. There's something different about this though. The way it's worded, it doesn't sound like it could be from some random person I hung out with at a party. No, this is definitely from someone I know.

Graham.

I don't want to get my hopes up but I can't help it. I want it to be from him, because the last couple of days not seeing him in class, not catching even a glimpse of him as he makes his way across the campus, has been torture.

235 | P a g e

After everything Serenity told me, giving me her blessing and telling me what she really believes is true about us, the only thing I've wanted is to see him again. I can't take back the things I did and I wouldn't want to even if I could, but it doesn't stop me from caring about him and wanting to be sure that he's okay. It's gotten so bad that I've actually had to stop myself more than a few times from showing up at his room again.

He might be able to walk away and not look back, because he had every right to, but it would never be that easy for me.

If this note is from Graham, how am I going to handle it? He made it pretty clear when he walked out on me a few days ago that he never wanted to see me again, that there was nothing left to say between us. So how would I deal with coming face to face with him again knowing all of that? Could I really trust anything that happened from this point or was it all just doomed to blow up in my face again?

As I do what the note says, getting off my bed and making my way over to the closet, I decide in that moment not to think about who wrote the letter and why. This is my chance to get out of my room and in a way that wouldn't end with me being drunk and needing to be driven home by my very sober best friend. I might not know what it means, but it has to be something better in comparison to everything I've been doing.

Content that my outfit is good enough for whatever waits for me outside the dorm doors, I grab my keys and my phone and make my way as quickly as possible to whoever is waiting for me outside the doors.

It's only when I make my way outside and see Serenity standing by what I remember to be Ryan's car that the disappointment sets in. As much as I didn't want to focus on it, I'd had my heart set on it being Graham standing out here waiting for me and even though it was still someone I cared about, it wasn't the right someone and I feel let down.

"Don't look so happy to see me, Ems. You'll explode all over campus."

"Well, we wouldn't want that. The groundskeepers already have a hard enough time keeping up as it is, obviously." I laugh motioning to the mess all over the grass around me. It's no secret that with the amount of parties thrown around here, that instead of maintaining it, they gave up.

"Get in the car. I've got a class in an hour that I need to be back for."

"If you've got a class in an hour why did you send me the note to spring me from my room?"

"I didn't send you a note. I'm just helping out."

"So, you're kidnapping me for the day. I always knew there was something off about you, but I didn't think it had anything to do with breaking the law."

She laughs as she motions again for me to get into the car and as I follow her orders, I begin to wonder just where she's taking me and what if anything this has to do with the boy we both love. It's only when we're both seated comfortably in the car that I take the chance and ask her, hoping she won't try and keep it from me. The time for secrets between the two of us is long over.

"Stop looking at me like that Ems."

"Like what?"

"You're looking at me like there's something that you're dying to ask but afraid to. You've never been afraid to speak your mind before, so just spit it out."

"Where are we going?"

"Green Haven." She answers easily, easing my mind and making it easier to ask the other question that's paramount in my mind.

"Who sent the note?"

"Graham wrote it, I delivered it."

Having answers should have settled me, but all it did was bring even more to the surface. As happy as I want to be that Graham's reaching out to me, I still can't help feeling like in taking this drive with Serenity, I'm walking straight into a trap and this time, it's going to be something even harder to come back from.

"Why are you taking me to Green Haven?"

"Ems, I know how I want to answer that, but I don't know if it's the same for him so I can't say for sure."

"The note said I was going back to where it all started."

"Really? Maybe we think the same way after all."

"What does that mean?"

"For Graham, just like me, Green Haven is the start of everything. It's the place I was born, though I didn't know about that until recently. It's the place where Graham and I first met and well you know everything else that happened there. It's the beginning and the end of everything."

"So, Graham wants you to take me to the place where he met you?"

"It's not that cut and dry Emma, and honestly, it's got nothing to do with me anymore. If it wasn't Graham asking, I wouldn't want to go back there at all."

For the first couple of years I had no idea what my friend had gone through during her time here and I definitely didn't know the significance of Green Haven in all of it. Since Ryan had filled me in on everything, right around the time Serenity came back to us, I've come to learn a whole hell of a lot about what the place means and it makes sense to me, her not wanting to go back there.

Whatever Graham was asking of her, I had no doubt it was taking everything in her to do it. It just goes to show just how much he means to her. How much he would always mean.

"Stop that. Graham doing this, it means he's starting to see the light again. It's got nothing to do with me, our bond or what we may have shared between us at one time. This is all about you."

"How do you figure that?"

"I know you're blonde and all, but you're not stupid."

"Blonde jokes, really?"

"Think about it and I don't mean, think about what happened to me there, but think about the place itself and why Graham might want to bring you there after everything you've been through."

"I don't think I'm supposed to get it."

"You will, at least you will if I can ever get this car to go any faster."

"How can you be so calm about this?"

She doesn't answer right away and I start to wonder if she's actually as calm as she appears. It's only after driving in the silence for a few minutes, watching her as she remains completely focused on the road ahead of her that she clears her throat and speaks, putting all of my worry and fear into perspective with just the few words she says.

"Because I've seen the way it all plays out."

Graham

I've got her. She's in the car and she's asking a whole lot of questions. You owe me Graham Cracker.

When I decided after saying my goodbye to Gabriel to put all of this in motion, I had no idea how it would all play out, or even if it was going to work at all. I just knew that I had to do what Serenity, my mom and Gabriel told me to do. I couldn't waste any more time taking the wrong steps. It was time for me to take the right ones.

The first thing I needed to do was believe, not only in myself and what I could offer this beautiful woman I'd fallen so completely for, but also believe in her to stand by me, despite it all. From there, I had to do as the other two women in my life had said and take a chance.

So that's what brings me here now, standing in front of the church that I both love and hate, with a shovel in my hands, a very large hole wide open in front of me and a small tree to my left, waiting for Serenity to pull up with her so that I can finally do exactly that.

I'm taking a chance and again I'm doing it in a way that's not exactly normal. It came to me after talking to Gabriel and I only hope when she gets here and I explain to her the point behind it, that she sees how important it is.

I hear the car and the minute I catch sight of it as it's pulling up in front of me, I swear I feel my heart skip a beat. It's time now. This is where I put everything on the line; one more time in an effort to do what I know deep inside is the right move for me. This is where I write my ending, the one that I've always been deserving of, but never knew I could achieve until now.

My eyes never leave the car as I wait, my breath catching in my throat with each passing second, for her to finally open the door and make her way over here. I know what being here means for Serenity, so her not making a move to get out of the car doesn't surprise me. What happens now, she doesn't need to be here for. This is just for us, though if she doesn't get out of the car soon, I'm not against going over there and dragging her out myself.

The door finally opens and I see one leg escape over the side, followed in quick succession by the other one and I know it's only a matter of seconds now before we come face to face again. I'm both excited and scared at the prospect.

The last time I'd spoken to her, I said things I'm not sure I can take back doing all that I am now, but I'm determined to try. All I need is one small glimpse of the girl that showed up every day at my door and I know I can get through whatever comes next.

My eyes never left the car but somehow, when I distance myself from my thoughts and put my focus back where it belongs, I can see that she's no longer in the car but walking toward me, her eyes locked solely on mine, never once leaving as she makes the short trek to where I'm standing, frozen in place, in absolute awe of her.

She doesn't miss a beat as the minute she finds herself standing directly in front of me; the questions begin to fly one after the other until I'm lost trying to keep up.

"Why did you want me to come here? What did you mean by the place where it all began? Why did it take you three days to talk to me? Are you bringing me here so you can say goodbye all over again? Do you get off on torturing me?"

"Emma, slow down."

Serenity honks the horn as she starts to pull away and without breaking eye contact, I wave. Without even having to tell her, she knows what I need and I couldn't be more thankful for it.

"What exactly is this?" Emma speaks again, despite asking her to slow down and when I look to where she's pointing, I see she's finally caught sight of my little project. I'd been hoping to have a bit more time before getting into exactly what the tree and the hole are all about, but it seems she's not going to give me that after all.

"I'm planting a tree. Well, I was sort of hoping we could plant a tree."

I can see by the look on her face that she's lost, which is exactly why I wanted to talk to her about everything else first. It's the only way any of what I planned on doing would make any sense.

"You want me to plant a tree?"

"Yes, but Emma, can we start over? There's some stuff I need to say before we get to the whole tree planting thing."

She nods her head and again that same skipping feeling in my chest happens again. She's giving me the chance to say everything I should have said from the start. I just hope I don't screw it up. I'm pretty sure this is the last shot I've got at this and I've got to do everything in my power to make sure it's right.

"The things I said to you the last time we were together, they were wrong. I was wrong and I'm sorry. I never should have said them and you were right all along. I didn't mean any of it. I was just upset."

"Graham," she whispers but before she can say more, I cut her off at the pass. I want to hear whatever she's got to say, but not yet. I'm not done yet.

"The day I took you to watch the boats come in, I told you that I didn't want you to be anyone other than you and a day later I turned around and yelled at you for doing exactly that. What you did, going to Lucifer, it wasn't wrong. You did the right thing; I'm just sorry I didn't realize it sooner."

I'm not entirely sure it's coming out the way I want it to in my head but there's no stopping me now that I've started. She's standing here and even though she still looks uncomfortable, she isn't turning away, which means she's still willing to listen.

She's doing exactly what I want her to do—being herself.

"You and me, we're not so different. You've been running, changing, becoming something you felt the rest of the world wanted since the day you walked in on your dad, holding onto his secret and I've been doing the exact same thing. I've been running too, but not from anyone in particular. I've been running from myself. It's only in spending time with you, real time the way we've been doing between classes and in the morning that I realized it. Emma, I meant what I said that day at the zoo. You are a butterfly and more than that, you're my butterfly because you stopped me from running."

"You gave me my life back, but not the old one I was running from. A new one. You showed me how to live again and not just live, but live the right way. I wanted to hate you for what you did, not because of what he meant to me, but because I was jealous. You did the one thing that I didn't have the strength to do. Emma, you stood face to face with the man that put it all in motion and you asked him to do the one thing I couldn't. You asked him to heal me because you couldn't live with the alternative. You brought me back to life."

"I'm standing here now because you couldn't do the one thing that I did easily. You couldn't give up on me."

The entire time I'm speaking, I'm not paying attention to how she's reacting. All I focus on is making sure that I say everything that needs to be said and resigning myself to dealing with the fallout once it's done. Looking at her now, I'm seeing her reaction to my words clear as the sky above me and it breaks my heart.

Tears are making their way down her face and she keeps wiping at them in an attempt to banish them from her face, like they don't belong there, or she's attempting to play a part again, something I definitely don't want. I don't want her to try and be the strong one right now. She's already proven to me that she's the stronger one of the two of us. Right now all I need is for her to be herself, not the person she thinks she needs to be.

"Why do you keep wiping the tears away?"

"I don't want to cry. I've done that enough lately and I hate it."

"Why are you crying?"

"What you said—it's a lot."

"Tell me what you mean by that."

"It's true. Everything you said is true. It's just a lot to take in. I have been running, but I swear now, I have no idea what I'm even running from anymore. At first, it was running from that secret, the one I held on to so tightly so my family wouldn't be destroyed. Then it became me running from myself, the person I became in an effort to appear normal to everyone else. It's been going on for so long, I don't know if I'll ever be able to stop."

"Do you want to run now?"

"No, but I'm afraid."

"Afraid of what?"

"Not being good enough, failing in some way and letting everyone down. It's those things, those fears that make it easy for me to become someone else. As long as I was the Emma that didn't have a care in the world, the boy crazy girl that's always on the lookout for a good time, then everything else couldn't get to me."

"It is getting to you though, don't you see that?"

"I'm not sure what you mean."

"You may appear good enough, and you might not be failing anyone around you or letting them down, but you are letting someone down. Pretending to be someone else, you're letting yourself down."

The last thing I want to do saying all of this to her is hurt her feelings, but as the tears start falling again, this time, her hands not coming up to meet them in an effort to wipe them away, that's exactly what I've done. I'm just not sure what I can do to fix it.

"You're right."

"We both need to stop running."

"Yeah, we do, but how?"

"We do it together, Emma."

This is the reason I wanted her here today. I spent so long believing that what I was going through, I had to handle on my own; that there wasn't a person alive that would be handle the gravity of everything I brought on myself. The thing is, I was wrong. There was always someone strong enough to stand and fight everything that was thrown my way and she was standing in front of me the whole time. It just took until now for me to see it. It's time for me to admit that I can't do everything on my own, no one can, and that sometimes, it's okay to ask for help.

Emma taught me that. In going to Lucifer and asking for help, she'd proven it. She wasn't going to let me go through anything alone and now it's my time to do the same for her. It's time for the running to stop and the real living to begin.

"What are you saying, Graham?"

"I'm saying what I should have said a long time ago. For the first time in a really long time, I'm ready to live again, but this time, I don't want to do it alone. I can't do it alone. I need my butterfly. I need you."

"Okay."

As happy as I am to hear her say anything in the moment, there's the sting of disappointment that it's not at all what I'd be hoping for when I went through all of this in my head hours before. I know I haven't earned it, but I couldn't help hoping that in admitting everything I have, that there would be a little bit more excitement. That maybe she felt the exact same way.

"What do you want?" I ask, my voice cracking just slightly under the weight of what really lies behind the question. It's as if we're right back where we were a few days ago and I need to hear her say she wants me as badly as I do her.

"I want to know why you want to plant a tree here."

Again, not what I was expecting, but now something I'm more than ready to explain to her. With my heart already on the line, I've got nothing left to lose. It's time to go all in.

"This church, it's significant. It's been both the beginning and end of things and the reason I want to plant a tree here, is because this place, it reminds me of us."

"How so?"

"It's been abandoned, left alone and forgotten about. It's just been a piece in the background for so long now that its worth is no longer something that's determined. It's just like us, Ems. We've spent so long running from ourselves that we forgot what it's really like to live, what we're really worth."

"So, you want to plant a tree here, with me, so that we can know our worth?"

"No. I want to plant a tree here because of the meaning behind what planting a tree means."

"What does it mean?"

"The tree, just like the church, is us Emma. Planting it here of all places, there couldn't be a more perfect place. When we place the tree into the ground here, giving it water and everything else it needs to survive, we're creating new life. This tree, for me at least, is my way of starting over new, creating a better life than the one I've been living and just like I said a few minutes ago, there is no one else in the world that I can start this new life with, but you."

"Graham…"

"Emma, I love you. I'm afraid of what admitting that means, but not so afraid that I'm willing to run from it. This time, I'm ready to face it, all of it, no matter what it means. I can't start this new life without the butterfly that made it all possible."

"Graham," she sighs, her eyes which had been focused solely on the tree seconds before, now trained on me. "I love you too."

"Then tell me Emma Daniels. Will you create a new life with me or am I too late?"

"You could never be too late. In fact, you're right on time."

The End

A Light In The Dark Playlist

M.I.N.E (End This Way) by Five Finger Death Punch
This Is War by 30 Seconds To Mars
Wrong Side Of Heaven by Five Finger Death Punch
Alibi by 30 Seconds To Mars
Trying Not To Love You by Nickelback
Hurricane by Parachute
Simple Man by Lynyrd Skynyrd
Far From Home by Hinder
Alone Together by Fall Out Boy
Cat and Mouse by The Red Jumpsuit Apparatus
Lullaby by Nickelback
Butterflies by Stereos
Hurricane by 30 Seconds To Mars
Save Me by Hinder
It's Over When It's Over by Falling In Reverse
Dead and Gone (ft. Justin Timberlake) by T.I.
The Mighty Fall by Fall Out Boy
Should Have Known Better by Hinder
Meant To Be by Parachute
Heaven's Gonna Wait by Hedley
Heart by Heart by Demi Lovato

Acknowledgements

I've managed to thank Joey in every single book that I've written, but it's this one where the acknowledgement really means the most. You knew that when I finished book four, it wasn't the end and you wouldn't let it quit until I wrote this story. For that, and so many other things, I thank you. It really is because of you that this book happened at all. I am eternally grateful to you. As always, I love you!

The ladies with me in the HMC, it wouldn't be a Love United story without all of you. Thank you all from the bottom of my heart for your continued support and love and even more than that, for sharing the love of men with me each and every day. It helps more than you know! So Jennifer Kendrick, Jennifer Hicks, Jill Fritz, Faith Walsh, Michelle Smith, Jenn Lierman, Erin Narr, Portia Lowery, Savanna Decker Linda Rabinowitz, this goes to all of you.

I wouldn't be me without my children and it wouldn't be a book of mine without them getting the acknowledgement they deserve for being exactly who they are. Thank you for being my real life angels and for making me blessed everyday to be surrounded by your light. You're the greatest gift I've been given and I will forever love and treasure you with everything I have and everything I am.

To my fellow authors Ryan Ringbloom, Jennifer Weiser, Theresa Troutman and Kristen Mazzola: Not only have I found enjoyment from your stories, but I have also found some of the most beautiful souls in having the friendships I have with you. Thank you for taking the time to speak with me, both as a reader and a writer and know that with each project that I take on and bring forward into the world, it's your words of encouragement and awesomeness that help make it happen.

You're all such phenomenal women and I am in awe of you each and every day. I'm blessed to call you friends.

To each and every person that takes the time to pick up one of my novels, spending not only their hard earned time, but money as well, thank you from the bottom of my heart. It is readers like you that keep me going and I will forever love and cherish each and every one of you for taking a chance on me. You're the best, never forget it.

About The Author

Melyssa Winchester is a mother of four from Toronto, Ontario, Canada. When she's not knee deep in adolescent awesomeness, she's falling in love, one book boyfriend and girlfriend at a time. She is a lover of all things romance and will forever believe in a real and try happily ever after.

When she's not off being a mom or writing you can find her doing one of two things. Reading or buried under the covers watching Supernatural, Sons of Anarchy or Veronica Mars.

Melyssa is currently working on Before The Light Book #1: Hold Onto Me (Michael's Story) that follows the lives of the characters from the Love United Series before they came together. She is also hard at work on a standalone title Shades of Blue and plotting many more upcoming projects for the future.

You can find her on the web, either at her personal site, Facebook (which she just might have an obsession with) or Twitter (@WinchesterBooks) where she talks incessantly about her kids, her writing and all things book boyfriend related.

www.ingramcontent.com/pod-product-compliance
Lightning Source LLC
Chambersburg PA
CBHW070555130626
46556CB00001B/175